HAVENS
IN THE STORM

by

Stephen B. Pearl

Also by Stephen B. Pearl

By Anhk Shen Publishing
Cats

By Brain Lag Publishing
Tinkers Plague
Tinkers Sea

By Pendelhaven Publishing
Horn of The Kraken

By Damnation Press
War of The Worlds 2030

By Dark Dragon Publishing
Nukekubi
Worlds Apart

By Club Lighthouse Publishing
The Hollow Curse
Slaves of Love

HAVENS in the STORM

ISBN print book: 978-1-7753641-3-9
ISBN e-book: 978-1-7753641-2-2

Cover Art: Kimberly Ann Hornby
Cover design: Stephen B. Pearl and Joy Hughes-Pearl.

For more information on Stephen B. Pearl, go to
www.stephenpearl.com.

Published by
Anhk Shen Publishing
Hamilton, Ontario, Canada

Dedication

I dedicate this book to the millions slaughtered in the name of theological expansionism. To all who fear for their safety and that their children will be stolen from them because they will not bend knee to the god of another.

I dedicate this book to all bound by laws based on the faith of another. Laws that seek to tell people who they can love and how they can express devotion. Be this a Pagan in the modern world or a Christian in a Muslim nation.

I dedicate this book to all those who struggle to bring about a world where the separation of church and state is more than a pretty catchphrase. You are heroes.

I dedicate this book to the gods, no matter what you perceive them to be, for to me, they are the caretakers of our universe.

Ankh Em Ma'at, Blessed Be, may your god(s) go with you.

Acknowledgements

Where to begin. I want to acknowledge my beloved wife, who has put up with me for so long. I love you Joy.

I also want to give a shout out to any batá readers who have helped with the creation of this book.

Then there are organizations like the SCA that gave me real-life experience that factored into the writing.

Also, the hundreds of books on mystical practices that have contributed as well as the WCC who lent perspective and expertise.

In short, thanks to everybody who lent a hand over the years it took this project to come to flourish.

As well, a special thanks to anyone that takes the time to review any of my work. Reviews are the lifeblood of writers. You make the difference between a happy writer producing the fiction you love and a ditch digger with a broken dream.

TABLE OF CONTENTS

Chapter 1
Defeat

Dominel charged a centaur that was a third larger than himself and his horse combined. The beast's pike slid against Dominel's shield as his lance pierced the monster's chest.

"That's for my brother," he snapped. Before he could free his lance, another centaur closed on him. Drawing his sword, Dominel parried the spear thrust.

"Give up, human. Your cavalry's line is broken. Surrender and I will grant you life," threatened the centaur.

Dominel's only answer was to begin circling his foe on the blasted, uneven ground that formed a wedge-shaped slope leading to Duran Pass.

A third centaur and a human appeared on a rise of land behind Dominel's foe. The other human drove his lance-point at the third centaur. The beast stepped back, tripped on one of the tree stumps that littered the ground and stumbled into Dominel's foe.

Dominel charged, knocking his enemy's spear aside then drew his blade across the beast's human-like throat. Blood showered Dominel's plate armour, painting it splotchy red. The third centaur turned to face Dominel, only to have its other foe's lance point blossom from its chest.

"My Prince, look out," cried the man who had wielded the lance.

Too late Dominel noticed the mutties diving beneath his horse. He pulled his feet from the stirrups and fell to the ground, rolling as far from the animal as he could. Two child-sized, dog-faced creatures, clad in leather jerkins were gutting Dominel's mount where it stood. Grunting with the effort, Dominel gained his feet and attacked the mutties, slaying them with two quick blows.

Trumpets sounded the retreat, and he glanced around. The centaurs drove the remains of the cavalry before them, leaving the dismounted humans to face an oncoming tide of monstrous infantry.

"The Storm has us for sure," said a panicked voice.

"To me! To me men of Bani! We'll win through to our lines," bellowed Dominel.

"I'm here, my Prince," spoke a blood-soaked man. "Scrantian?"

"Yes, my Prince. Keep rallying the men. Set them in a wedge formation, wounded in the centre. We'll have to cut our way back to the barricade."

"Standard wedge. If you see a footman's shield on the dead, drop your horseman's kite shield and take it. The dead won't mind!" shouted Dominel.

The unhorsed men hastened to follow the order. In minutes the monster infantry enveloped the humans' formation. Screams filled the air as the wounded and dead fell to the ground. Dominel lost himself in a pattern of thrust and parry, barely aware of his growing weariness.

"My Prince. We've reached the front, and the cavalry is charging," called Scrantian.

Dominel thrust with his sword, spilling the guts of a minotaur, then stepped to the wedge's centre.

"They're coming for us men. Be ready," he yelled.

The horsemen struck the centaurs, who were leading the Storm's charge. Dominel's troops fell upon the monsters advanced force. The monsters, caught with no room to manoeuvre, jostled one another, impeding each other's thrusts and blocks. In minutes the humans had slaughtered the beasts.

Dominel led his men through the log barricade that blocked the pass Guarded by his father's castle. The area behind the barricade was a buzz of activity. Soldiers manned the defence while chirurgeons removed the wounded to the castle, half an hour's march away. Siege engines twanged and thudded as they hurled rocks at the enemy. The stench of fear filled the air.

"The king demands your presence," said a herald, as Dominel watched the last of his men pass behind the barricade and its huge gate swing shut.

"I will be with the king as soon as I have seen to my men," replied Dominel.

"He said immediately."

"I may be the youngest son, but I have things other than being disowned to worry about right now. I will join him when my men are seen to."

"As you will, Prince Dominel," breathed the herald.

"Was that wise? The heralds like you little enough as it is, and your father is king," said Scrantian. He had removed the left arm of his armour and was inspecting a small wound.

"Are you fit to command in my absence?" asked Dominel.

"It's just a scratch, Your Highness."

"Good. See that the wounded are taken to the chirurgeons' tent. I want any man who can't fight to surrender his horse to one who can. We have more men than horses, so let's use what we have. All the horses should be watered. Send a herald to fetch down a salt lick. Those loud-mouthed parasites should be good for something.

"Get some lanterns as well. Those accursed clouds that follow the Storm are crowding out the sun. If this keeps up, we won't be able to tell friend from foe. Make sure the men drink something. No wine! We need them alert."

"Yes, my Prince. Might I also suggest we send those with leg wounds to join the archers on the keep's battlements? That will free a few more able bodies to join us here."

"Use your own judgment. You know I trust you." Dominel strode away.

Arriving at the flap to his father's tent, Dominel was stopped by the guard and stood listening to the conversation within.

"By the ancient gods, you slime crawling, demon lover. If it weren't for your kind, the Storm wouldn't be here at all! You'll go where I tell you and fight when I tell you," bellowed the King.

"But, Your Most Gracious Majesty. I simply thought that my order could do more good in the keep's temple, praying for our deliverance. The Covetous God can be most gracious to his children," whined the chief prelate's voice.

Dominel's lip curled in distaste.

"Gods and demons! Your god was the one who caused all this. If your order hadn't slaughtered the magic users, they'd still be guarding the gates to our world, and none of these thrice accursed monsters would be here."

"But the sorcerers were evil," pleaded the priest.

"So say you. It seems to me, they couldn't have been so bad if they guarded us from the Storm. Be honest. Your order feared their power. You disgust me, you snivelling worm!

"I have spoken. Your order will head the infantry defence. There's no risk of you stabbing someone in the back that way. The only reason I haven't finished off the lot of you is that I need sword fodder. Now go."

Dominel pulled down the visor of his helmet to hide his smile. The pasty-faced priest left the tent, his leather armour flapping about his scrawny frame in his haste.

Sticking his head through the flap, the guard announced Dominel then gestured for him to enter. Pushing up the visor of his helmet, Dominel stepped into the tent.

"The Herald tells me you felt my summons was unimportant," opened the king, his grey-bearded face pulled into a grim expression and his blue eyes flashing.

"I told them I would come as soon as I had seen to my men. The Third Cavalry is my responsibility, given by you, and I do not take it lightly, Your Majesty."

A smile broke across Dominel's father's stern features. He motioned his son to sit at the table that filled the tent's centre. A map of the surrounding terrain covered the tabletop.

"You have your mother's spirit; I'll grant you that, boy. I called you here to give you some bad news." The smile left his face.

Dominel looked at the man and for the first time realised how old he was. *It's not just the grey hair and wrinkles, and his armour hides his paunch, it's how he moves. He's lost hope.*

"Son, you are my youngest, and you are now captain of the First Cavalry."

"Falik and Dalose? How?" Dominel swallowed hard as memories of his brothers flashed through his mind.

"In the charge. Your companies sent out spotters and found the stake traps. Falik and Dalose didn't. Demon spit, I told them to be careful. They lost half their horses in the charge. The rest were surrounded, only a handful escaped. I am placing all remaining cavalry under your command."

"Scrantian suggested sending out the scouts."

"And you listened to him. You keep listening to people who know. I've only you and Falkner left. Seventeen years isn't enough to learn everything, so you keep listening to people who know and maybe I won't lose any more sons."

"I… Father. We won't win, will we?"

"No, but we can see to it that they never forget the price of Duran Pass. The countries to the west are counting on us to slow the Storm while they pray for a miracle. What I wouldn't give for one wizard.

"That peasant girl of yours. Amber was it? She's stayed with the chirurgeons. I was wrong about her. She will make you a fine consort when you marry the Duchess Karmilla."

Dominel smiled at his father.

"Now commander, you should prepare your troops. The Storm are massing. I need your cavalry to spearhead our counter."

The two men rose. For a moment they stood unsure of the emotional ground between them then they embraced, their armour making a thunking sound. Dominel left the tent. As he walked towards his troops, he scanned the battlement. Veterans, dressed in battered armour, stood ready for the final conflict in the kingdom of Bani. The wounded had been removed to the keep, and a hush had fallen over the camp. Reaching the cavalry, he scanned his men. Hopelessness hung on them like a shroud. Only grim determination held them in their places.

"What is the word?" asked Scrantian.

"We ride to the defence. And there is another thing." Raising his voice, Dominel called, "Standard barrier."

A lad, too young to shave, mounted on a dapple gelding moved to Dominel's side. He dipped the standard so that the muddy, blood-spattered flag of the Bani cavalry hung before his prince.

Drawing a dagger, Dominel cut away the trim that showed it as the flag of the Third Cavalry. All looked on as the unadorned, white horse on a green-field standard of the First Cavalry was raised. Where the trim had been, the flag's colours were bright and clean.

"Dominel, your brothers?" asked Scrantian.

"I am the second son of the house of Otinerus, King of Bani, Captain of the Bani First Cavalry," Dominel proclaimed.

"I'm sor--." began Scrantian.

Dominel held up his hand. "Later. Soon we will live or die. Either way, the time for tears is not yet come."

Scrantian nodded once then spoke. "I suggest a three-point attack, allowing the infantry to guard our back. That should draw off the largest beasts and give our light companies a chance to deal with the small ones."

"Yes. I want every man equipped with caltrops. When we have to retreat, I want to see crippled monsters all across the line," said Dominel.

"That will make any further charges impossible!"

"We have fewer than one hundred horse left. If any of us make it back to the barricade, we won't be attacking again. We'll be running to warn the other kingdoms the Storm is at their doors."

Scrantian dipped his head. "As you command, my Prince."

The First Cavalry waited behind the barricade's gate, with each second seeming like an hour. Guttural howls announced the Storm's advance. Moments later trumpets signalled the attack. The gate swung open, and Dominel and his troops galloped into the fray.

Lances splintered, and swords broke, shields rent and strong men died, but nothing stopped the Storm.

Dominel and Scrantian galloped into the midst of a company of ogres. The beasts looked like hairless gorillas with pig snouts. Dominel's sword rose and fell as blood sprayed in all directions. A pikestaff hooked his shield, dragging him from his horse. Dazed he fought to rise against the weight of his armour. Scrantian reared his horse, allowing the beast's hooves to pummel the ogre that bent to dispatch his prince. Dominel fought to his feet in time to see a spear pierce his friend's helm.

"You murdering bastards," screamed Dominel. Forgetting his fatigue, he snatched up his sword and charged the ogre that had killed Scrantian, driving the blade deep into the beast's belly. There was a blur at the edge of his vision then everything went black.

Chapter 2
Perils on the Road

Dominel awoke, in the mud, his head throbbing. Through an effort of will, he slowed his heart and brought his pain under control. After a time he opened his eyes then rose to his knees. The bodies of monsters and men were on all sides. A dead ogre lay beside him, with his sword protruding from its belly. He looked towards the barricade that blocked Duran Pass, it was breached. Allowing his eyes to follow the pass he saw smoke rising from where he knew his father's castle stood.

I must have been out a long time, he thought.

Struggling to his feet, he stumbled to the ogre and pulled his sword from its flesh. Blade in hand, he staggered across the battlefield. At first, he paused to check the fallen humans he saw. Finding none alive he soon put all his efforts towards leaving the field of his defeat.

No use in going to the castle. He shook his head and felt metal scrape against his scalp. Pulling off his helm, he stared at a hole in it the size of his palm.

"Gods!"

Dominel continued his trek, collapsing in the tall grass by the side of the road when his legs crumpled beneath him. After drinking from a ditch, he fell into a haunted sleep.

When he awoke, he ached all over.

What am I going to do? Yesterday I merely wanted to get away from the battlefield. Now what? he pondered as he lay in the grass.

'You are the last of our line. You must regain the throne,' his father's voice admonished him.

Against the monsters, there is no hope!

'You must survive,' stated Scrantian's voice.

I'm hearing things, thought Dominel.

'Live, my lord. The Border Mountains will be safe for a time,' spoke the voice of his betrothed.

"That's silly. They were overrun months ago," Dominel muttered.

'The wizards made their last stand there. That magic still lives. It will keep the monsters at bay, my love,' whispered Amber's voice.

"It's a goal at least," he agreed.

By rocking back and forth, he turned face down on the grass then pushing up with his arms, gained his feet.

"Damnable plate! At least you can move in chainmail. I feel like a turtle when I lie down," he grumbled and started towards the distant mountain range.

Hours later he stopped at the ruin of a village. Hunger gnawed at him, so he decided to search the landowner's house. Shuffling through the smashed-in doorway, he saw bodies and the splintered remains of furniture.

"Another abattoir. The Storm is consistent."

The second room he looked in was in the same condition as the first. Heat-brittled bone crunched under his feet when he stepped through the doorway. A blackened section of floor marked where a fire had burnt.

Lucky for me the front has moved west. The beasts that made camp here have probably followed the fighting.

He crossed the room to another doorway that led to what had been a kitchen.

This does not look hopeful.

'Search, and ye will find,' echoed Scrantian's voice.

"I'm losing my mind. Scrantian, you're dead! Why do you keep pestering me? I couldn't save you. Gods, I wish I could have. What does it matter? I'll search, old ghost, maybe the monsters missed something."

'Down, my sweet Prince,' whispered a voice on the edge of perception.

"Amber?" Dominel spun around looking for the peasant girl who had been his real love. "Still hearing things! Amber's as dead as the rest."

'Feel, love. The time to feel again has come,' urged Amber's voice.

With this his pain surfaced. He fell to his knees sobbing. Later he looked at where his legs had disturbed the dust and saw a seam in the floor.

What? he thought.

Kneeling, he swept the dirt away until he found an iron ring. Grasping it, he pulled. A trap door opened, revealing a stairway leading into a room that was a man's height square and full of shelves.

Dominel's stomach growled as he descended the stairs, closing the trapdoor behind him.

Something jumped from the shadows. A knife clanged against his armour. Leaping from the stairs, he grasped the wrist of his attacker and slammed it against the wall. The knife fell to the floor.

Dominel stared at his foe in the dim light from the pantry's small window. She was human, a girl of maybe thirteen summers, with brown hair, which hung in greasy strands obscuring her grit-covered face. She wore rags that might have once been a gown. Her breasts barely dented the fabric, and her dirt and blood-covered legs showed below the tattered hem.

"I won't hurt you," said Dominel.

She swung her free hand at his face. He caught her arm and held it.

"Please stop. I won't hurt you," he repeated.

A shudder ran through her, and she collapsed against him.

"What have you been through?" he murmured. Sitting her on the floor, he investigated the room.

The shelves were stocked with cheeses, salted meats, dried fruits and herbs. To Dominel's delight, a barrel of ale sat on the floor. Noticing that the girl's eyes were open, he spoke to her.

"Are you hungry?"

She stared at the ceiling and didn't move.

"I won't hurt you."

She remained motionless.

Dominel moved to her side and took her hand. "Please, speak to me," he said then released his grip. The hand stayed suspended as if he still held it.

"Odd?" he whispered and lifted the girl's leg. Releasing the limb, he watched the girl hold it in position.

"Strange!" He muttered and posed her in what looked like a comfortable position.

After eating he removed his armour and fell asleep.

Guttural voices arguing in a strange tongue woke him. The girl, on the other side of the room, sat still and silent. He drew his sword and waited by the stairs.

If they want me, they'll have to pay for me, he thought. After a time the voices grew dim as the intruders carried their argument away from the ruined house.

Moving to the girl's side, he whispered, "Are you all right?"

She stared straight ahead, as if he wasn't there.

"I'm Dominel, Prince of Bani. Who are you?"

The girl made no response. Dominel backed away and stared at her.

"Hungry?" he asked.

Still no response.

"Well, I am." He took a bite from a cheese. Returning to the girl, he pressed a piece of cheese into her hand.

"You have to eat!"

She remained silent.

Dominel forced some cheese against her lips. She opened her mouth and accepted it without losing her blank expression. After she swallowed, he guided the cheese in her hand to her mouth, and she began to feed herself.

"That's better."

Later that day Dominel finished searching the landowner's house. He found little of value, although in one room there was an iron mirror leaning against the wall. He stared at his reflection. His armour was caked with mud, while his blond hair fell about his shoulders in greasy strands. One side of his head was covered with dried blood and scabs. His angular face was filth-streaked and bore several half-healed scratches, while his pale-blue eyes looked haunted.. He mentally shook himself and returned to the safety of the cellar.

"They've fouled the well," he told his silent companion.

The next day he searched the peasant huts, finding a pair of scissors. That evening he and the girl lost all but the scantiest caps of hair.

"That will keep it out of our eyes."

The girl stared straight ahead and didn't reply.

A week passed with little change. Dominel sharpened his sword, cared for them both and waited until the dwindling food supplies convinced him to move on. Fashioning packs from sacks that had held dried herbs, he stuffed them with the remaining food. After donning his armour, he strapped a pack to the girl's back and shouldered his own. Taking the girl's hand, he led her up the stairs. She followed but showed no sign of life beyond that. After listening at the door, he pushed it open.

Once outside they followed the road towards the mountains until they could walk no further then took refuge in the remains of a barn. Dominel found a well of good water and saw to it they both drank their fill before they settled in a heap of straw for the night. Despite his exhaustion, sleep evaded him, so he was awake to hear the girl, who lay beside him, crying out. "No! No! Please no!"

He rose onto his elbow and stared at her.

"No!" she whispered then sobs shook her. "Father," she cried then "No! No! No, please!"

Grasping her shoulders, Dominel shook her. She snapped awake.

"It was a dream. We have to be quiet," he said.

She didn't move.

The next day they walked for hours before coming to a place where a stream split the road. The sound of the water as it splashed and gurgled over the rocks added a spark of life to the dead land that seemed to follow the Storm.

"We'll stop here to eat," said Dominel.

He was refilling the packs when harsh voices split the air.

"Gods!" he swore, glancing around in search of a hiding place. The grass by the stream was trampled, and there were no trees or large rocks nearby. Muttering a curse, he reached for his sword.

Two mutties appeared on the road and seeing the humans leapt down the slope, swords clasped in their childlike hands. Dominel pushed the girl towards the stream. She took two steps and stopped with the water lapping about her ankles.

"Demon spit," he cursed.

The monsters separated, flanking him.

"Come on, you filthy mutts, stand together," Dominel turned to face first one enemy then the other.

Yipping, the creatures circled him, like dogs worrying a bear. Dominel lunged towards one of the beasts. The other jumped him, clutching his neck while trying to thrust its sword into the gap in his armour where gorget met breastplate. Dominel slammed the pommel of his sword into the small beast's arm and was gratified to hear bone crunch. The monster howled in pain before dropping to the ground.

The second beast lunged. Dominel thrust his blade through its throat. Grunting with the effort, he dragged the impaled carcass around and threw it onto its companion. The mutties fell, in a tangle of arms and legs, and before they could recover Dominel finished his bloody work.

"Pity it's not always so easy," he mumbled, wiping his blade. "Sometimes it seems as if for every one you kill ten arrive."

The days passed, and the food dwindled, but little else seemed to change. A week after leaving the cellar they drew near the mouth of one of the lesser passes into the Border Mountains.

"Something is wrong. I can feel it." Dominel pulled the girl to a halt and examined the road.

"I should have seen it before. Those ruts, heavy carts have passed this way. Had to be monsters." He turned to the girl. "What do you think? Not much. That's just what I expected." Hiding the girl behind a bramble, he crept to the top of a rise that overlooked the road ahead.

His heart quailed at the sight of a company of monsters camped in the entrance to the mountain pass.

The mountains must be safe. Otherwise, why place them under siege. I'll--. A rough hand closed about the back of Dominel's neck, and his body was jerked into the air. He experienced a moment of blind terror before he was turned to face the horrid visage of a hill troll. Stinking, carnal breath issued from the troll's maw, which was full of razor-sharp teeth. The beast's nose resembled a pig's snout, and above it were two blood-red eyes. Its skin was the colour of a rotting corpse.

"Yum yum!" exclaimed the troll.

Dominel's mind filled with panic. All the troll had to do was close its hand, and his neck would be crushed, despite his gorget.

"You be Grim, yum yum, lunch, yes, yum yum," remarked the troll.

Can't get my sword out in time, but maybe? thought Dominel.

"Maybe yes, maybe no," he said.

"Huh?" asked the troll, a puzzled expression falling over its face.

"You Grim's, yum yum, lunch," it added after some thought.

"Grim want, yum yum, lunch?"

The troll thought hard, obviously taken aback.

"Yes, Grim want lunch."

"Grim want gold?"

Grim stared at Dominel before replying.

"Grim want gold, Grim have, yum yum!" The troll smiled as if he had succeeded in some incredible mental task. "Grim, eat now, yum yum," stated the troll. It grabbed Dominel's arm with its free hand and prepared to pull it off.

"WAIT!"

The troll stared at him in a quandary.

Do it right, Dominel thought. "You can have gold and, yum yum, lunch."

"Grim like gold."

"Well you see, once you've eaten me, I won't need the gold I have hidden in the mountains. So I want to give it to you as a gift."

"Gift? Why you give Grim gift?"

"Because you're such a handsome fellow and since you're going to marry my sister, you must have a dowry."

"Marry sister?" the troll's face was a mask of confusion.

"Of course. She's waiting for you below the hill. We can go get her now."

"Sister not gold," said the troll, now utterly slack-jawed.

"First we must get my sister, so she can help carry the gold to you. Since you can't go into the mountains."

"Sister bring gold. Me bring sister!"

"Good! Good! She's just over there," said Dominel, pointing to where the girl was hidden.

Grim was there in a few strides and picked up the girl in his free hand.

"How come she no move?"

"Well... umm... You see my dear fellow, it's, well... Um... It's because she's overcome with joy to meet you. We had better hurry. The sooner you get the gold, the sooner you can eat me."

"Yum yum," replied Grim.

"Oh, dear me. How are we going to get by your friends in front of the pass? I guess you'll have to share your gold and lunch with them."

"No share lunch. Me, Grim, smart. Me get you through." Grim strode away, a human dangling from each hand. "Me, Grim, have bag, use carry things. You fit good Grim's bag. You gold fit good Grim's bag," explained the troll.

Dominel soon found himself set roughly onto his feet, with the girl beside him. Grim stared at them with a puzzled expression.

"You sure you bring, Grim, gold, yum yum?"

"Of course I will, Grim. You'll need the gold to care for my sister, now won't you?"

"Grim think gold in mountains. Grim like, yum yum. When Grim eat, yum yum, Grim start with head so, yum yum, don't hurt." Grim pulled a large, canvas sack out from under a bramble and held it open. "Grim say get in sack."

"Thank you, Grim, you're very kind." Dominel led the girl into the sack. Grim's large hand closed the top of the bag, and Dominel felt himself hoisted onto the troll's shoulder.

I can't see anything and the stench! I mustn't vomit, thought Dominel as he was jostled by the troll's swaying gait. The sound of harsh voices speaking in strange tongues surrounded him. At one point he felt pawing hands examine the sack as it swayed on Grim's back. Half-panicked, he elbowed Grim through the fabric. He felt the troll turn and heard a growl. There was an answering phrase then Grim turned and continued walking.

When Dominel thought he could stand it no longer, the top of the sack opened. Grim looked in.

"Me, Grim, smart! Me bring you other side of camp. Now you get gold, yum yum."

"Of course," replied Dominel. Rising, he filled his lungs with clean air. Grasping the girl's hand, he dragged her to her feet.

"It's only a little way up the trail, would you like to come?"

"No! No. Grim go no farther. Magic strong, make Grim old."

"Oh well. We'll be back soon," said Dominel. Taking the girl's hand, he led her into the mountains. Grim watched them climb the pass.

"Thank you, Nanny Franks, for telling me all those fairy stories. The nightmares were worth it! And thank the gods that trolls are dumb!" said Dominel, once they were well away from the troll.

"Yum yum, come back. Me no want gold," called Grim, just before he fell out of sight behind a bend in the trail.

"You wait there. I'll be back when I have your gold," yelled Dominel. Then he added to himself, "and pigs fly over a blue moon!"

Chapter 3
Friends Along the Way

Dominel followed the pass into the mountains until he came upon a cabin. The stable beside it suggested that it had been a relay post for the king's horsemen. He led the girl to the cabin's door and knocked. After a long wait, he opened the door and found himself staring at the dangerous end of a crossbow.

"Yur won't be takin' me or mine, yur filthy beasty," threatened the old man holding the weapon. He was a wild figure with grey hair and a beard sprouting off in all directions. His body was clothed in old, loosely-fitting, leather armour, and a sword hung from his side.

"Believe me, sir, I have no intention of harming anyone," said Dominel.

"Huh, well now. Yur don't look like one of 'em beasties. Though yur smell bad a' one. What be yur name?"

"I am Dominel, Prince of Bani, last of the line of Otinerus."

"I was thinkin' all yur people be slain."

"Not all. They left me for dead after I was knocked unconscious. I've been making my way to the mountains ever since."

"I be thinkin' yur be tellin' the truth, but how can I be sure?"

"I don't know. How I can convince you I am who I say I am? Please put the crossbow down. I'll lay my sword aside, and we can talk. My companion needs rest," said Dominel with a gesture towards the girl.

"Humm... well now? Yur be about settin' yur sword aside, and yur can be comin' in."

Dominel leaned his sword against the cottage's wall then watched as the old man set his crossbow on the table behind him. Holding his palms open and in plain view, Dominel stepped into the cottage then reached back and pulled the girl in.

"Emma, get yurself out here," called the old man.

A door opposite the entryway opened, and an old woman with grey hair neatly combed into a bun scurried into the room.

"Now who be this stranger yur havin' in with all them beasties down the way?" she demanded.

The old man made to reply but was cut off by the woman.

"What's this now? A wee lass." She shuffled towards the girl, her plump body jiggling as she walked.

"Now yur comin' in. 'T'aint proper to leave a lass standin' in the door."

"She doesn't talk," said Dominel.

"Aw that be sad, but little wonder. With all the horror this poor lass must 'a' seen travellin' through lands held by them beasties."

The woman took the girl's hand and closed her eyes for a moment. Her brow wrinkled in concentration then she spoke again. "It's a wonder she be alive at all it is, with all the pain in the wee thing."

She led the girl to a seat at the room's large, central table.

"I made sure she ate," said Dominel.

"And a good thing yur did, or she'd a' starved. She's given up on the world she has."

"Come on, lad. If Emma says yur all right, yur be all right. Pick up yur sword; we'll go fer a walk. We be above the Storm's murk here and should be enjoying the sun while we have it," said the old man.

Dominel nodded and allowed himself to be led from the cottage.

"I be Jason. I be the livery master here before them beasties came. Since then me and me Emma have been getting by doin' as we could. Lucky for us the mountains still be safe, but Emma says that won't be lasting."

"Excuse me, your wife seemed to see into the girl. As if she could sense what the girl had been through, is she some kind of sorceress?"

"No, lad, she 't aint. Leastways, not the type yur be praying for. She'd just started her learning when the final battle was fought, nigh on forty years ago. I hid her, and she escaped. She don't know how to keep them beasties back. It be sad it be. She can see the wall the old masters built getting weaker, but she don't be knowin' how it were built. She can't be a helping yur."

"Oh."

"I know how yur feel. Seems all the great wizards be slain and 't aint nothing we can do. Emma tells me the walls won't be breakin' tomorrow. We has some time."

"Time for what?"

"To live, lad. Yur should know, where there be life, there be hope. Elsewise yur never have gotten this far, now would yur?"

"I guess not."

"Good! Now let's be headin' back to the cottage so's we can be havin' a look at yur lady friend. She be yur sister?"

"No. I met her along the way. She needed help, so I helped."

"It be good to know that. That be why we'll win this. We's cares, and the gods be likin' that."

By now they were back at the cottage door. Jason opened it and stepped inside. Dominel followed.

"How be she?" asked Jason.

The girl lay motionless on the floor, at the far side of the room by a hearth.

"Her body be all right. Her mind, it be a different matter," answered Emma.

Emma motioned for Dominel to take a seat opposite her at the heavy wooden table that occupied the room's centre.

"That girl has been through sommet that forced her away from our world. She be living in a world of her own now. It be a guess if she ever comes out of it," Emma explained.

"What did she live through? Do you know?" asked Dominel.

"I don't be knowing. If I could be sharin' it with her, I could be makin' it easier fer her. I could help her, but she be too far down fer me to reach."

"Isn't there anything we can do?"

"We's can be a prayin', lad. We's can be a prayin'. Fer now the best thing fer her is rest. Yur both been pushed harder than a body should. Yur safe here, so yur should be about restin'."

"I'd appreciate that," said Dominel, feeling like there was a heavy hand pushing him towards the floor.

"That be good. Now we should be about cleanin' and dressin' yur in some new clothes. Yur scent's enough to knock a goblin dead," remarked Jason.

Minutes later Dominel stood dripping wet and shivering beside the glacial stream behind the cottage. He soaped himself then, with a grimace, leapt back into the icy flow. His muscles cramping, he scrambled out onto the bank.

"Here, lad, be wrappin' yurself in this," said Jason, holding out a towel. "I see you gave your cloths a scrub. I'll be about a hangin' them up. I'll fetch yur armour in as well. Yur be gettin' to the cottage, Emma's orders, and I shan't be crossin' Emma. She's a nasty one when she be roused."

Dominel dried himself then, with a glance at the blue sky and the pine forest on the valley's slopes, walked to the cottage. No sooner had he entered the little building then Emma pushed a mug of broth into his hand and led the girl towards the stream.

"Me Emma don't be wastin' a minute," remarked Jason, as he stepped through the door. "Yur look a sight better than yur did."

"I feel better."

"I'd be wagerin' on that. Why don't I get Emma's scissors, and we can be fixin' yur hair. Must 'ave been chopped by a ghoul to be so ragged and yur beard could stand a trim."

Dominel soon found himself in a chair with Jason clipping and fiddling about him.

"Now that be an improvement."

Dominel looked at himself in a small mirror comparing the face he now saw with the one he had seen in the mirror at the ruined house. This new reflection sported a pointed beard that seemed to lengthen his face, while the hair, though short, was well sculpted. What truly caught his attention were his eyes. The shades of his brothers no longer stared through them. The haunted quality was replaced by a strangeness, vaguely threatening in its aspect. He stared at his reflection then jerked his gaze away.

"Thank you, I look more myself now. How are my clothes?"

"They be drying." Before Jason could finish his sentence, the door opened. Emma walked in, leading the girl who was wrapped in a blanket. The cleaning had done wonders for her. With the cover of dirt and dried blood gone, her skin was an olive shade. Her face was pretty, made of rounded curves, with a slightly pug nose, her brown hair shone in the light coming from the doorway.

"Are yur gonna be sittin' there and a starin', or be helpin' the wee one to a chair?" demanded Emma.

Dominel stood and helped the girl to a seat. She was still oblivious to her surroundings.

Several uneventful days passed at the cottage. Dominel started doing the heavy work around the place that posed a problem for the old couple. By the second week, he felt at home and was pleased that Jason and Emma seemed to welcome his presence. It was thirteen days after his arrival before anything changed. Dominel was stepping out of the cottage's door when Emma called to him.

"Be comin' back in the house."

"Very well," he agreed and took a seat at the table.

"Dominel, I've been watchin' yur. Now I've a question for yur." Emma took a deep breath before continuing. "Would yur be willing to learn the bit of the art I've to teach?"

Dominel's eyes glistened as elation ran through his soul. "Yes, yes." Forcing his voice to calm he added, "I would be honoured to become your student."

Emma began to chuckle then laughed loud and hard before speaking again. "Yur and yur flowery talk. I've not much to teach, but what I have be yurs. We'll be startin' tonight."

That night Emma led Dominel to a plateau on the mountainside overlooking the cottage and began his instruction.

"Before anythin' else, yur must be a learnin' how to relax," she began.

"I am relaxed," he objected.

"Nay, yur aren't. Yur no be relaxed before yur can be feelin' every muscle in yur body and knowin' where it be."

"You mean like a warrior before going into battle, where you're totally aware of your body but detached from it?"

"Lad, if yur can be doing that yur near a year ahead of startin'. Show me what yur can be doin'."

Dominel took a stance with his feet shoulder width apart and tilted his pelvis forward for balance. Then taking the three deep, slow breaths his sword master had taught him, he allowed all thought to drain from his mind. He was filled with the euphoric floating sensation of the warrior state, while at the same time he was totally aware of his body. Muscles, nerves, tendons were all within his sensory field, ready to be commanded by his will. He rested in the warrior mind for a few moments before returning to the everyday world.

"Well, lad, that be impressive fer sure. Now, can yur be using it to heal yurself?"

"Heal myself?"

"Aye, yur can be stoppin' bleedin' or makin' yurself stronger in meditation."

"My swordmaster told me that some can make themselves stronger, or faster. He never mentioned anything about healing."

"Well then, lad, I know where I'll be a startin' yur lessons. Now yur be listenin' to Emma. To be stoppin' the flow of the blood is easy, all yur got to do is..."

#

Weeks passed. Each night Emma took Dominel to the plateau to perform some mystical exercise. Many of the exercises struck him as inane. Who cared how hot or cold his hands were? He kept studying though, snapping up the bits of useful knowledge amongst the seemingly useless dross. Until one day Emma stopped him as he was stepping out of the cottage's door.

"After tonight yur must be leavin'," she stated.

"What!"

"After tonight, yur must be leavin'. I've taught yur all I know. Now yur must find yurself another teacher."

"But there are no other teachers. All the masters have perished!"

"Aye, all the masters be gone, but yur meant fer summit more than waitin' fer the shields to fall. Yur must be movin' on!"

"Where?"

"That be what we be about seein' tonight. Now we'd best be goin', the night be gettin' on."

As they walked towards the plateau, Dominel observed his surroundings. He could plainly see the blue sparkles of energy that filled the world. Looking skyward, he saw the wall of energy that shielded the mountains. It curved over him like a giant, glass bubble. As he watched the shield flickered ominously then stood firm once more.

"How long will the shield last?"

"I reckon another two or three months where it be now, but I could be wrong."

"What will happen when it crumbles?"

"It won't be crumblin'. It be made so it shrinks when it be too weak to keep its size. It gets smaller and smaller, till it be too small to be guardin' a mouse. It will be years before it shrinks past me cottage, so there be nothin' to worry about. The old masters, they were strong they were. Now shush."

By this time they were at the plateau. Emma instructed Dominel to kindle a fire in the centre of the flat area and to sit staring into the flames.

"Watch the fire as yur were taught, don't be thinkin'. Let yur mind see in the flames. Remember yur want to be knowin' where yur to go."

Dominel sat staring into the fire. Slowly his mind cleared of thoughts. The flames danced before him, gradually coalescing to form a cave's mouth at the end of a fiery trail. The fire crackled and sputtered, he felt his eyes drawn to the smoke. It moved to the east, towards the centre of the mountain range, despite the still air. He fell back, his head throbbing.

"What were yur seein'?"

"I saw a cave at the end of a trail and the smoke. I must go east!" Dominel paused then repeated himself with firmness. "Yes, I must go east."

The next morning he donned his battered armour.

"I made yur sommet for yur trip," said Emma who indicated a pair of packs on the table beside her.

Dominel opened one of the packs and saw it was full of food. "You shouldn't have, you've little enough for yourselves."

"Now don't yur be being foolish we've enough. Sides, these be traveller's rations. Dried meat and spice rolls," countered Jason.

Inhaling deeply, Dominel could smell cinnamon and nutmeg coming off the rolls. "They smell delicious."

"Aye, they be tasty, but the spice be keeping 'em fresh. They'll last a moon afore they go off so's you'd notice," remarked Emma.

Dominel started securing one of the packs and a water skin to the girl.

"Shouldn't yur be leaving the lass?" asked Jason.

"Be lettin' the boy alone. We're too old to be taking on a wee one who can't be doing for herself. Besides, it be sure the lass won't be findin' healin' here. Goodbye, me lad, be carin' fer yurself," said Emma. She helped Dominel don his pack and embraced him in front of the doorway.

"Don't worry about the girl, Jason. I can't explain it, but I feel she belongs with me. Both of you take care, and thank you for everything."

Dominel stepped out the door with the girl in tow.

Chapter 4
High Country

Dominel and the girl followed a track that paralleled the stream behind the cottage. Cliffs, with occasional pines clinging to them, rose on either side of the narrow road as it wound its way deeper into the mountains.

"Tomorrow we should reach the main pass. If I remember the maps properly. I bet there are lots of people there," he said to the girl.

She stared blankly ahead.

"At least you don't talk too much. Ah! I know it's not your fault," he muttered. "I should set up camp, night's closing in."

Later, he stared into their campfire letting the flames cast images into his mind. They flickered and danced then slowly took form. He saw an army standing on a shore staring at a fleet of retreating ships. He saw his face in the flames, his lips forming words he did not know. The fire flared, and the image was lost. Sighing, he lay down to sleep.

#

The next day they started along the trail, but Dominel paused at a spot where a deep gorge branched off to one side. A stream flowed from the gorge's mouth joining the stream beside the road.

"Can you feel it? Not that you'd answer if you could. It's as if someone were pulling at my guts," he said.

Clearing his mind, he allowed his inner sense to guide his eyes. His gaze came to rest on a series of stepping-stones in the stream bed. They formed a trail up the gorge, deeper into the mountains.

"This is insane, but Emma told me to trust my instincts."

Dominel led the girl onto the first of the stepping-stones. After thirteen stones a rising path opened up beside the stream. Dominel followed the path until evening was closing in.

He examined his surroundings, seeing nothing but rocks, craggy cliff faces, a few scrub pines and brambles.

"Gods, it's cold! I'd better make camp," he said.

Leaving the girl in a rock fissure, that blocked the wind on three sides, he gathered bracken for fuel and kindled a fire at the open end of the groove. The girl shivered but was otherwise still.

Night closed around them making their small fire a puddle of warmth and light in an otherwise dark and threatening world. A blood-curdling howl rent the air and Dominel drew his sword. He scanned the darkness beyond the fissure's open end. A shadow moved in the darkness beyond the fire's glow. The deeper darkness took on form as it drew nearer the flame, revealing itself as a wolf. The beast had wiry grey hair and was impossibly large. The strangest thing about it was that its eyes shone with red light, like sunlight passing through a vial of blood.

"A werewolf! But how could it penetrate the shield?" gasped Dominel.

The beast snarled and leapt to the far side of the fire.

"Stay back," commanded Dominel, brandishing his sword.

Squatting, the creature glared at him, the flames flickering between them. They stood thus until the fire began to burn low and the werewolf inched forward. Fumbling behind him, Dominel found a piece of wood and tossed it onto the flames. The werewolf stepped back growling.

Marvellous! What happens when the fire burns out? Only silver works on werewolves. Of course, if I can hold out until morning, it will turn back into a human, thought Dominel. The pile of bracken he'd collected now seemed woefully inadequate.

"How to make it last," he muttered. He remembered one of his sessions with Emma. She had had him make a candle burn higher and lower at her command.

If the wood burns lower, it will last longer. But I've never affected a campfire before, and I don't know how high the fire has to burn to keep that thing back. It's my only chance!

Dominel stared into the flames willing them to shrink. The werewolf crept closer until it stood only an arm's length from the fire. As the fuel was consumed the beast moved nearer, forcing Dominel to add more wood. The fire flared, driving the werewolf back. Dominel joined his will to the flames and forced them down to a slow burn.

The night wore on, and the werewolf stayed. Dominel strained to control the fire, but his strength was ebbing. His head throbbed, and his body shook in a cold sweat.

Why don't I give up? A quick death followed by a long sleep, he thought. Then out loud, "NO!"

He added the last piece of wood to the blaze. It kindled and flared. He tried to slow the quick burn, but his power was spent. Rising he slumped against the chasm's wall, sword in hand. Before long, the fire was little more than hot coals, and the werewolf stood less than a hand's breadth from it. The beast's mouth dripped saliva.

The monster howled, pawing the air in frustration then it ran off.

"What?" Dominel looked up to see the last corner of the full moon disappearing behind the mountains. "Gods of my fathers, thank you." He collapsed into an exhausted sleep.

He awoke to someone shaking him. Opening his eyes, he stared into a face covered with a grey-streaked, black beard. Brown eyes met his gaze, and he noted a high forehead ending in a tangle of black hair.

"If you were going to kill me, you already would have. Can I assume you're a friend?"

"That you can, lad. I was out hunting when I saw you and your lady friend. I'd like to offer you my hospitality. I think you should accept. There's a werewolf about," answered the stranger.

"I had a standoff with it last night," said Dominel, as he stood to better inspect the man.

"Did it hurt anyone?"

"No."

"I am Solin, son of Gumfrey, Count of Fretin." The stranger extended his hand.

"Dominel, Prince of Bani, for all that means now, and my companion has, to the best of my knowledge, no name."

Solin shook his head sadly. "The Storm must have done evil things to her."

Dominel sighed. "Evil enough. I've not heard her speak a word since we met."

"Sad. But I forget my manners. My cabin is only a short way along the trail. We will be more comfortable there."

Dominel gestured for Solin to lead, and taking the girl's hand brought her to her feet.

Soon they came to a shelter made from a large fissure in the rock over which Solin had built a roof, and sealed the open end with a wall of split logs. He pulled back a corner of the bearskin that served as a door.

"Please enter," he offered.

Dominel had to stoop to fit through the crude doorway and could barely stand erect in the chamber beyond. The inside of the shelter was wedge-shaped with its widest section at the door. The narrow end of the wedge contained a stone hearth with a smoke hole above it. Against the wall to his left was a cot. The centre of the room was dominated by a table made of piled stones, surmounted by rough-hewn boards. A chair, hacked from a log, sat at the table. To his right was the only item in the shelter that showed any refinement of craftsmanship, a deacon's bench covered in ornate carvings.

"Welcome to my humble abode, Prince Dominel. I apologise that it is not as grand as my palace but as it is at present, in, shall we say, unfriendly hands, this will have to serve."

"Thank you, this is much better than the ground."

"Yes. If you will excuse me, I'll go to the storage shed and get us some food. You must be famished after last night."

"Thank you."

A few minutes passed before Solin returned bearing oats, a bag of herbs and a waterskin.

"I'm afraid I've no wine. Grapes don't survive this high up the mountain."

"Why do you live up here?"

Solin knelt in front of the hearth and started piling coal onto the glowing embers.

"I have my reasons. For one thing, there's a pit of coal not far off that supplies me with fuel."

Solin placed a pot over his small fire and began to prepare a stew.

"You could use wood further down the slope."

Solin paused and growled, "I like it here. There aren't people around asking dumb questions."

"Why doesn't the werewolf bother you?"

"I put wolfsbane and silver on the door and smoke hole. It keeps him back. This shelter is quite safe from lycanthropes."

"Do you know the werewolf in its human form?"

Dominel's hand inched towards his sword.

"I know him, a good person. Lycanthropy is a curse, not a choice! That is why he moved to these mountains, so others would be safe from him. It is too far for the monster within to run to the nearest human settlement. Though now, with fugitives flooding the mountains, that may change. Where can he run? The porridge is ready."

Dominel took a seat at the table behind a wooden bowl of porridge. He was soon finishing his third helping.

"I'm sorry to eat like this."

"Quite all right. You've already more than paid for your keep with your company. Human companionship is a rare gift here."

"That I can imagine. I respect your decision to stay here for the safety of others."

Solin paused where he squatted tending the fire. "You guessed."

"It wasn't difficult. Deception doesn't come well to you. How did you get through the mountain's shields?"

"I walked. I'm only a monster when the moon is full."

"Hmm, yes. Is there anything you can do to free yourself?"

"Short of killing myself, I don't think so." Solin took a seat in the rough chair.

"There must be something." Dominel looked speculative.

"It's said the wizards had a way, but I certainly don't know it, and there aren't any left to ask."

"True, much to all our sorrows."

Dominel and Solin talked through most of the day. As evening drew in Solin ushered Dominel into the cot and settled the girl on a sheepskin by the hearth.

Dominel dreamt he was wandering the halls of his father's castle. He was searching for something he had lost, but he didn't know what. As he searched, he became aware of something following him. He knew he had to find what he sought before the creature caught him.

He burst into room after room, but what he wanted never appeared. Sweat soaked his clothing as his breath came in ragged gasps. Throwing open a door, he found a tall man with a grey beard in the room beyond.

"Can't find it, can you?" snapped the stranger.

"No," replied Dominel as he heard the creature following him draw nearer.

"You won't if you keep lolling about. You've wasted enough time already!"

"Certainly," agreed Dominel, as he made to run out the door.

"Oh yes, before you go. I think you should know you're dreaming. Whatever it is, just turn it into a toad."

"Dreaming?" muttered Dominel. A rat, the size of a panther, leapt into the room.

I hope I'm dreaming.

He reached for his sword and said aloud, "You're a toad!"

The image around him blurred. He found himself by a pond with a man-sized toad crouched in front of him. The wind whispered through the trees, and the toad croaked a near-deafening sound.

"I am dreaming!"

He felt very detached from the person standing in front of the giant toad. The creature leapt at him, Dominel stepped aside and said, "You're a normal sized frog." The toad disappeared and in its place appeared a small, green frog.

'Interesting.

Dominel enjoyed himself by turning the frog into a garden snake, a sparrow and finally a kitten.

This is fun! Now for something worthwhile, he thought.

He focussed his attention on a nearby tree. A moment passed then the tree began to change. Soon a stunningly beautiful maiden stood in its place. Her brown hair fell just below her shoulders, while her slender body, with its large bosom, was covered by the flimsiest of lace, leaving her shapely hips and legs clear to view. Desire sparkled in her brown eyes. Dominel walked towards her and took her in his arms. His experimenting for that night had only just begun.

The next morning he awoke and moving cautiously, so as not to disturb the girl, he stepped outside.

"Hoy there. How was your night?" Solin strode down the trail.

"Better than you could imagine. But I have to move on." Dominel scanned the sky, hoping the weather would give him an excuse to stay.

"I felt as much. Something told me you wouldn't be staying. Where will you go?"

"Farther along that trail I was on. Do you know where it leads?"

"Hmm, as far as I've taken it, it leads higher into the mountains. I've never reached the end of it. I came up from the south. Why do you want to follow it?"

"I don't know. All I can say is I feel drawn to it. If that makes any sense."

"It doesn't! Then again, in our world what does? Before you go, fill your bags with food from my stores, I've plenty to spare, and take some extra furs. It gets cold in the mountains."

"Thank you." Dominel turned towards the cabin.

Solin caught Dominel's arm and stopped him. "If you should find a way to break my curse, no matter how dangerous, promise me you'll return."

Dominel stared at the older man. "I promise."

An hour later Dominel was leading the girl higher into the mountains. They walked all that day and deep into the night. He was uneasy despite Solin's assurances that a were-creature could only be forced to change on the three nights of the full moon.

The next day dawned cloudy and cold. Dominel had to force his stiffened joints to move. Soon he and the girl were ascending the trail. They had walked for an hour when the sleet started. They trudged on in search of shelter while the storm about them grew. The sleet gave way to snow and wind drove against them making the furs they wore flap like flags. The girl shivered silently; Dominel felt the cold cutting him like a knife. After what seemed an eternity, they came to a spot where the cliff jutted out at an angle to the wind, creating a small, protected area.

Fighting his way through the snow, he dragged the girl to this crude shelter and huddled close to her. Without the wind to drive it, the snow fell gently about them forming a soft blanket. Dominel felt warmth tingle through him. It started with his frozen hands and feet and spread. He felt drowsy and began to nod. The wind howled like the moan of a lonely spirit. He lay in the snow. His limbs were heavy, and all he wanted to do was sleep. Slowly the notes of the wind resolved into new sounds.

"Get up, you stupid fool!" commanded the voice of Dominel's father.

Dominel opened his eyes and looked up. Towering over him was the form of his sire, the snow clearly visible behind it.

"Get up!" it ordered.

"Sleepy," mumbled Dominel.

"Get up now, or you're going to die of the cold."

"Cold? It's warm."

"That's what it's like, you fool. You are the last of our line, and I won't have you dying in some snow bank like a miserable bear cub! Do you understand me?"

"But it's over. Everyone's dead. No one to fight for. Nothing to fight with."

"You're never beaten until you think you're beaten! Demon spit! If I can come back to the world of men from the land of our ancestors to talk to you, the least you could do is wake up to listen."

"I'll try."

"Good! Now, remember how I raised you and don't give up the fight. Follow me!"

Dominel tried to rise and couldn't. He tried again, this time struggling to his feet. He reached down and grabbed the girl. She groaned and lay still.

"What's keeping you?" demanded the spirit, as snow blew through the blue of its floor length robe.

Dominel stared into the grey-bearded face and up at the blue eyes. "Ggggirl."

"Oh yes, you have taken up with some trollop. Should have expected it, knowing you. You'll just have to drag her or leave her. Now get going!"

Gripping the furs the girl wore, Dominel pulled. Slowly she began to move then, as he overcame her inertia, she jerked clear of the snow.

He could never say how long he followed the grey head of the ghost through the swirling storm. All he knew was that by the time he stopped at the mouth of a cave his strength was spent. He collapsed on the ground.

He found the numbness had left his arms and legs, replaced by painful throbbing, but now he could think clearly.

"Well, don't be an idiot, get in the cave and out of this wind," snapped the ghost.

"Ba--ba--ba--Bears?"

The ghost rolled its eyes in disgust. "Would I feed my own flesh and blood to bears? Get in that cave!"

Grabbing the girl, Dominel dragged her into the cave. Shortly beyond its mouth, the snow gave way to a dry, stone floor. He looked up to see beams spanning the ceiling.

"What?"

"The wizards used to mine coal here. It was also their secret escape route. Unfortunately, they never had the chance to use it. Build a fire, there are dry ties from the mine cart tracks and coal on the walls."

"Y... y... you're real!" breathed Dominel.

"Of course I'm real. We're all real."

"I th--th--thought I w--was g--going m--m--mad. H--h--hearing th--th--things."

"You're no madder than you ever were. 'Though that's not saying much." The spirit vanished.

Forcing his aching legs to move, Dominel made his way along the passage, which sloped steeply up. After stumbling six strides, he came to the end of an old mining track. With numb fingers, he grasped the hatchet Jason had given him and chopped kindling from the nearest tie. Using flint and steel, he struck a spark, then another, until the tinder caught. Nursing the fire, he piled larger pieces of wood onto the blaze. He crawled back to the girl and dragged her to the fire before collapsing beside it.

As the fire warmed the air about him, Dominel felt his strength return. At first, he only fed the flame, building it with wood until it burnt high and bright. Then he knocked coal from the walls to add to the flames. Much later, he laid his soaking clothes out to dry then turned his attention to the girl. She lay by the fire like death. Her lips were blue. Kneeling beside her he felt for her breath, sensing a faint pressure against the back of his hand.

Sighing, in weariness and relief, he removed her soaked garments and examined her body. Her hands and feet were white and tipped with frostbite. The rest of her skin was icy to the touch.

"Gods!" he exclaimed. Completing his examination, he pushed her closer to the fire. This done, he slumped against the cavern's wall and allowed his exhaustion to overtake him. His last waking thought was that his father had saved him. He had really been there!

"Dark, darker, darkest. Light, lighter, lightest. High, higher, highest. This is magic," explained the voice.

"Who are you?" asked Dominel, not sure whether he slept or woke.

"You."

"Me? I must be dreaming."

"Does it matter?"

"I can't see."

"You don't have to. Just listen. The student is almost ready, and the teacher awaits."

"What?"

"Don't be dense! Why did I have to be reborn in the form of a pigeon brain?"

"What?!"

"Shut up. You are not sensitive enough to hear me for long. Thus I will only say this once. Follow the tunnel and go ever down, until you see a lake flanked by trees. Then ever up you must go, or else you pay your life as toll."

Dominel awoke shivering. The fire had burnt down to glowing embers that he built up. This done he turned to the girl. Her hands and feet were red, but her breathing was strong. He pushed her hair back from her brow. Her eyes snapped open, and she pulled away from him. She glanced at her nakedness then at his. Screaming, she attacked him, scratching and biting. Dominel caught her wrists.

"Stop it, stop it. I'm your friend, remember? I saved you from the house and the blizzard."

The girl lashed out a knee, striking him squarely in the groin. Gasping with pain, he released her wrists. Like a wild thing, she ran towards the tunnel's opening. Several moments later he felt sufficiently recovered to pull on his clothes and follow her. She stood at the tunnel's mouth, staring out over a landscape of cliffs and drifted snow.

"Please. I saved you from that," he explained.

The girl turned and looked at him, a numb expression on her face. He held out his hand. She shied away. He didn't move.

"You must be cold. Come back to the fire. I won't hurt you."

She stared at him then tentatively took his hand and returned to the warmth.

"What's your name?"

The girl stared at him numbly as she dressed.

"I'm Dominel. Do you know where you are?"

She continued to stare at him in silence.

"Can't you speak?"

She continued to stare.

"Hmm. Maybe you don't speak Colinan. I'll try Merchantese."

"You... umm... name?" he asked.

The girl stared at him.

Dominel shook his head. While trying to plan his next move his dream intruded upon his consciousness. *Through the tunnel? What was it my father said? An escape route for the wizards. There must be a wizard's stronghold at its other end. I haven't anything to lose.*

His course decided, he tried to remember when he had last eaten. Deciding it had been too long, he and the girl settled for a meal. As they ate, he spoke to her.

"We're going to follow this tunnel. We'll need light, any suggestions? None. That's too bad because I don't have materials for torches. What to do?

"My armour, it won't burn! Yes, it should do nicely. What do you think?"

The girl stared at him blankly.

"I'm glad you agree."

Rising to his feet, he reached for his battered armour.

"Let's see, there may be fighting yet, I don't want to damage it too badly. A knee cup should do."

Using one of his daggers as a pry, he pulled the left knee free from the rest of his armour. Cutting two long strips from one of the hides Solin had given him, he attached them to the kneecup so that they crossed over its centre. Taking a piece of wood from an old mining cart trestle, that was as long as his arm and less rotten than most, he pushed it through where the leather crossed.

The girl watched curiously.

Finally, Dominel filled the knee cup with bits of coal and slivers of wood. Using both of his daggers, he levered a flaming piece of coal into its centre. The wood caught and sent out a dim wavering light. He smiled at his makeshift brazier. The girl, seeing that he was happy, giggled.

Donning the remainder of his armour and shouldering his pack, he led the way along the passage. The corridor sloped up for fifteen strides from their resting place then divided into two. One passage led up. From this came a draft of cool, fresh air. The other led down a flight of rock stairs. This had a musty smell.

Dominel, mindful of his dream, started down the descending way.

Chapter 5
Deep Dark Places

Dominel counted the stairs, coming to a downward sloping tunnel after the fiftieth step. This passage was typical of the mine. It was about two strides wide and three high, with rough-hewn walls, over which the brazier's dim light sent dancing shadows. As he led the girl forward, they became a puddle of light in a sea of black.

They walked for hours with infrequent stops to pry coal from the walls and eat. Occasionally passages branched to the sides, but they held to the main course, which led ever down. The stillness of the cavern made the sound of their footsteps a thundering intrusion.

When Dominel called a halt, his eyes felt grainy, and weariness gripped his body.

"We should sleep here," he said.

Prying coal from a deposit in the wall, he built a fire in the centre of the passage.

The girl stared at him as he nodded then fell asleep.

#

Dominel opened his eyes and looked at the bedchamber. The large canopy bed at its centre was draped in gauze curtains. A fire raged in the ornate hearth that filled the wall to his right, making it uncomfortably warm and stuffy. Tapestries covered the remaining three walls. A stifling, smoky perfume filled the air.

"Come to me, my lord." A seductive alto-voice beckoned from the bed.

"Karmilla?"

"Betrothed," spoke the voice. The bed curtains parted. The Duchess rose and sashayed towards Dominel.

Her body was draped in gauzy silk, which did little to hide its well-proportioned curves. In the fire's golden glow the wrinkles by her eyes vanished, making her look younger than her thirty-five years.

"I thought you preferred the company of your chambermaids?" observed Dominel.

"You will need a legitimate heir, and there is no reason it should be a chore for either of us." She played with a long strand of her ebony hair.

"What of Amber?"

"She is a consort. She knows the line must be secured. Once I have borne you a son that lives past five summers, she can have you to herself."

"You know I have fought against our marriage."

"There is no reason you should feel suffocated by it. We are both civilised nobles. We can be friends. We both know the duty that our station places upon us. Our union will strengthen both Bani and my Duchy."

Dominel felt his temperature rise and his breath quicken. Moving to the woman he traced the line of her back.

"Yes, good. You are much better than that dotard my father chose." Karmilla caressed her young betrothed firm flesh.

Dominel pulled away. The heat from the fire was overwhelming. With Karmilla's help he stripped off his tunic, but it made the room no cooler. His breathing was like a bellows.

"Yes, my Prince, yes. To the bed."

Without knowing how, Dominel found himself upon the bed, Karmilla towering above him. He tried to kiss her, but his need to breathe made it impossible.

"I am ready for you, my young Prince. I will take you now!" hissed Karmilla. Dominel felt Karmilla's hands stroking his chest. The weight of her crushed his lungs and his breathing became harder still. Then her hands were locked about his throat.

"What?" he gasped before sound was choked from him.

"Yes. Join me. Yes," screamed Karmilla. Dominel struggled to pull the hands from his throat. Dots swam before his eyes. The hands became talons, choking the life from him. His vision blurred.

"No, my love," spoke a soft voice. The talons eased their grip. Dominel gasped in the burning hot air and looked to see Amber standing beside the bed. Her honey-blonde hair fell over her shoulders, and her emerald eyes seemed to glow in her lovely youthful-face.

"Amber. What?" gasped Dominel.

"Leave us, peasant!" snapped Karmilla.

"Why do you do this? He is hope for our kind," challenged Amber.

"The Covetous God is my hope. He has promised me new life as a ruling species if I do this thing for him." Karmilla raised her hand as if to strike Amber.

"Dominel, choose. Love or lust. Life or death," pleaded Amber. A tear trickled over her cheek, standing out against the golden hue the fire cast upon her skin.

Without thinking Dominel reached to wipe the tear away.

"No! I can please you. I can please you," screamed Karmilla, but she vanished as soon as Dominel touched Amber's cheek.

"Amber, I am sor...."

"Hush, my love. It is the way of our time. She used that to trick you. Had she lived and the two of you married, your succession would have had to be secured in noble blood. I accepted that I would never be more than consort when I accepted your love. With your love that would have been enough, had I lived. Know you dream of a danger you truly face. You must wake now or join me in death and in doing so betray our species last hope."

"I don't want to. I want to stay with you."

"I am but a ghost in a dream. Soon I must depart to the land of our ancestors. I could not have tarried this long save the gates to the realm of the dead are overburdened by the war. All are forced to wait their turn. You must live, my love. You must save our world. You are hope. Live and find a living love to share that life. Promise me?"

"I promise."

Smiling, Amber vanished.

Dominel awoke with a cough that shook his body. Forcing himself to move he rolled over and looked at the fire. The flames burnt low despite the unused fuel amongst them.

The fire's eaten the prana from the air! I have to get away before I choke to death! thought Dominel.

He forced himself to his knees then collapsed.

"Have to get away!" he whispered, as blackness enveloped him.

#

The girl awoke to the sound of coughing. She had moved away from the fire when she had grown too hot. She felt dizzy and sluggish, and she could smell smoke. Sitting up she watched Dominel collapse. A soft voice she couldn't understand prompted her to action. She didn't move. The voice grew louder then her body jerked awkwardly to its feet. Holding her breath, she rushed to Dominel and dragged his prostrate form away from the fire. She stopped when it was a red dot in the distance and collapsed against the wall. She paused and tenderly stroked the cheek of the unconscious form before her.

#

Dominel's head swam, and he had no strength to move. He became vaguely aware of someone touching his cheek. He forced his eyes open and looked into the girl's face.

"Farewell, my love. My turn has come," she whispered in Amber's voice then she slumped against the wall like a marionette with its strings cut.

Dominel slipped into unconsciousness. He awoke coughing. His head swam, and he felt nauseous. Trying to rise, he fell retching. He gulped air, filling his tortured lungs. Slowly his head cleared and he noticed the darkness about him.

Did the fire go out? He thought. Groaning he moved and bumped against something soft. Reaching out he felt fur-clad legs. *The girl.*

Forcing himself to sit, he looked up the passage to where the fire was barely visible. He tried to speak, but a coughing fit stopped him. A cool hand pressed against his brow. When his coughing fit ended he gasped out, "You saved my life, thank you."

The girl shifted where she sat beside him then was still.

"Must get light," he croaked, his throat releasing a bolt of pain as he did so. The girl didn't move. Rising he leaned against the cavern's wall and stared at the fire where it smouldered and smoked.

"How to reach our gear? I'm in no shape to hold my breath! If only there were a draft, but it's as still as death down here. Spirits of air, what I wouldn't give for a breeze?" he pondered aloud.

The air about him moved, whispering into his ears, "What would you give for a breeze, child of men?"

"What?"

"What would you give for a breeze?" whispered the air.

Dominel shook his head and asked, "What would you like?"

"Sweet spices and wine."

"I've none."

"Sweet spices. We smell them. Give us half of what you carry. The fire will bring it to us."

"Sweet spices? Emma's journey rolls! Agreed!"

The air began to shift until a breeze wafted up the passage. The fire brightened, and Dominel scrambled towards it. Collecting their gear, he filled his brazier with burning coals and made to leave.

"Our bargain, child of man! Be not false with the sylphs, we children of air remember insults!" hissed the wind.

Dominel opened his pack and pulled out their store of rolls, dropping half of them onto the fire before hurrying down the passage.

In minutes he and the girl were once more following the descending slope.

That was strange. Of course, this was a stronghold of wizards. There's no telling what of their magic remains. Was it really Amber, or just a dream? Dominel pondered the events as they walked.

Monotonous hours later the passage changed. The air grew damp and water condensed and trickled down the walls. The floor became slippery and dotted with puddles and, to Dominel's dismay, the deposits of coal grew less frequent. After almost having his brazier burn out he filled one of their packs with coal.

Long after their pause to gather fuel, they came to a pair of large wooden doors blocking the passage. These were covered with ornate carvings and across their top was a script Dominel didn't recognise.

"At least it's different," he commented and grabbed the large, brass ring that hung from the door nearer him. Despite its obvious weight and age, the door opened easily. Cautiously, he stepped through the doorway, and what lay beyond dazzled him. He stood in a chamber forty strides across, with crystal-studded walls. The crystals took the dim, red glow of his tiny brazier and reflected it until it filled the room. A path of what looked like gold ran from the door to the edge of an oval lake. The lake was about twenty strides across, bisecting the chamber. On each side of the path stood trees carved from marble bearing fruits of pure crystal.

Dominel moved into the room, the girl at his heels. He didn't notice the door closing behind them. They followed the golden path to the water's edge where a short pier projected into the lake. An ornate, bronze brazier stood at the pier's end. Moving to the brazier, he filled it with coal from his pack and dumped the contents of his small brazier on top. The fuel burnt with a clear, white light, unlike any he had ever seen coal produce. The crystals sparkled brightly as cascades of colour filled the room while the lake's surface became a mirror of glittering lights. His eyes were dazzled by the display, and his soul was called to take flight into the beauty around it.

He only slowly came to realise that he had to cross the lake to reach the doors at the far side of the cavern. Studying the chamber, he placed everything's location in his mind. Scanning the far bank, he noticed a boat moored at the pier opposite the one on which he stood. Studying the walls, he could see they were perfectly smooth, offering no hand or foot holds.

"Why does everything have to be the hard way?" he grumbled, as he began to strip.

The girl glanced at him where he stood half naked on the pier. She screamed, ran towards the door and struggled in vain to pull it open. Dominel ran to her. She turned on him kicking and biting. Remembering the last time she attacked him, he covered his groin and backed away.

"I'm going to swim the lake," he explained, in an attempt to soothe her. She stood, back to the door, glaring at him.

He shrugged, removed his trousers then, placing one of his daggers between his teeth, lowered himself into the water. The lake at the pier's end only reached his chest, but it swiftly grew deeper. The water was cool but his body adjusted to it by the time he was a quarter of the way across.

Something bumped against his side. He knocked at it instinctively. Something else bumped against him, and he felt a cutting pain. Glancing at the source of the pain, he found an eel clinging to his flesh.

The creature was translucent, but already beginning to redden as it sucked blood into itself. Treading water, he grabbed the eel below its head and pulled it from his side, ripping his skin as he did so. Bringing it forward he glanced at the beast's circular mouth of razor-sharp teeth. Using his dagger, he cut the creature in half and tossed the parts away.

A moment later he felt another bump, then another. The water was alive with eels. They were attaching themselves to his body faster than he could pull them away. In terror, he sprinted towards his destination until he saw the lake bottom rise beneath him. Standing, he strode towards the pier pulling eels from his upper body. Dizzy and weak from loss of blood, he hauled himself onto the dock and pulled the creatures from his legs before falling unconscious.

He awoke to screams and darkness. The fuel had burnt out in the brazier, and no light graced the chamber. The screams continued. He identified the girl as their source.

"Must be the dark. I hope it's the dark! Gods, it's cold. Best not to think about it. Now how am I going to cross the lake without light?" he muttered.

As he pondered this, he noticed a dim bluish haze radiating from him. Ignoring his nausea and pain, he rose to one elbow. Across the lake, he could see a haze of violently convulsing reds and oranges.

What in the name of the ancient gods? he wondered. Then something Emma had said echoed in his mind. "All things that be livin' be about makin' power, and somes can see it flowin' about um."

With an effort, he rose to his knees. "I think I'm going to retch. Demons of the pit. If there is a part of me that doesn't hurt, its dead. I wish the room would stop spinning." Groaning, he forced himself to look around. The bluish haze allowed him to 'see', if 'see' you could call it. It was more a matter of sensing where the haze was interrupted. He crawled along the pier towards the boat. The girl screamed again as he pulled himself into the small craft. Fumbling in the dark, he found a pair of oars and managed to get them in the oarlocks. By this time only the sound of whimpering came from the far shore.

Shivering he crawled to the bowline, cast off and rowed to the opposite shore. When the boat grated against the lake's bank, he grasped the bowline and leapt onto the ground. He caught his balance before the boat driving back yanked the rope taut and sent him sprawling back first. Air blasted from his lungs, leaving him winded, but he kept his grip on the line.

He forced air into his lungs then, shaky and sore, crawled to a rock and tied up the boat. He struggled to his feet and made his way towards the girl.

"It's all right. I'm back," he said and was gratified that she stopped whimpering. "I'm going to get us some light."

He walked towards where he guessed their packs were. Working by feel, Dominel filled the large brazier with coal and kindling. Fumbling with flint and steel, he struck sparks until the fuel lit. At first, it was a dim glow, but the light increased until the cavern was restored to its full radiant glory. As the light returned, the girl grew calm.

Dominel looked at himself. His body was covered with circular welts, and his skin was as pale as death. He hurriedly dressed against the cold then devoured half of their food supply.

As he ate the girl approached him and placed a hand on his shoulder.

Her pain, her longing, I feel it. She has such need. She's so empty, and she wants...It's gone, he thought, as her hand slipped away. *How could I feel that? Emma said she could feel others' emotions, but I never did before. Time to worry about it when we're safely out of this cave.*

"I'll pull the boat to the pier, and then I can row us to the other shore," he explained to the girl, who stood watching him. "We'll fill our water skins before we leave." She cocked her head to one side and smiled.

Minutes later they left the chamber passing through wooden doors identical to the ones they'd used to enter. It took a while, after the door closed, for Dominel's eyes to adjust to the dim light of his brazier. As soon as he could see they continued along the passage.

The tunnel sloped gradually upwards, and smaller tunnels branched off the main way. Over an hour later Dominel found a coal deposit to restore his supply. With a sigh of relief, he slumped against the wall.

"We'll rest here. Gods, I feel drained. Of course, given that those eels drink blood, I guess I have been." He grinned at his own wit.

The girl stared at him as he settled himself for sleep.

"You've got this far," remarked a voice.

"What?" Dominel tried to orient himself.

"I didn't think you'd make it. You're lucky the Gods gave you the body of an ox to match your wit."

"Who are you?"

"I'm your brother."

"You're not one of my brothers! None of them ever sounded like you."

"Don't be an idiot! I was your brother in your last life, remember?"

Dominel had a fleeting sense of recognition, as if he faced a familiar foe.

"We didn't get along, did we?"

"I see you begin to remember. That is for the best. Now you inept serf, though we were foes, I must play my part in awakening you. Pity though that is."

"You mean I'm dreaming?"

"Dunce! You have been dreaming all your life. Now you're in a dream of a dream, and you're closer to waking than you have ever been! Listen!"

"From darkest night, from brightest day,
From each of these they fell one day.
A crystal fragment it was shorn
To open door, cross on the morn."

"I hope you remember that, my moronic sibling!" The voice fell silent.

Dominel awoke feeling like someone had stretched every muscle in his body then let it go with a snap. He found his pack by feel before he noticed it wasn't completely dark. A light, as bright as his brazier, reached them from further up the passage. Rising, he woke the girl and gathered their packs before leading her to the light's source. The air grew cold as they approached a small side passage. It was walled in white marble and curved gently so its far end couldn't be seen. A single, downward step led into it.

"No!" whispered a voice in the back of Dominel's mind.

Ignoring the voice, he shouted, "We're through," pulling the girl into the side passage beside him he ran its length. The tunnel ended at a stone balcony overlooking a rocky canyon.

"Fresh air. I never thought it could be so sweet. Gods that wind's cold. I don't see any way down, do you?" asked Dominel not expecting a reply.

A grating sound echoed dully from the passage behind him. He turned to look the way he had just come.

"Gods! No, a trap," he screamed.

A slab of rock was slowly moving out from the wall to block the passage.

"No way down!" Dominel threw himself between the passage's wall and the moving stone trying to hold it in place. The girl joined him, but their efforts accomplished nothing.

"Get through!" he commanded.

The girl stared at him.

Demon spit! he thought, as his elbow bumped against his sword hilt. *It might work.*

Drawing his sword, he braced it between the wall and the stone. Grabbing the girl he sprinted into the main cavern. The stone pushed against the sword, which held a moment then bowed and snapped. The stone slammed home, and darkness engulfed them.

Dominel stood panting and trembling for a long time. When his hands steadied, he fumbled in his pack, finding his flint and steel and a lump of coal. Using rag, torn from his clothing, as tinder, he lit his brazier. The coal caught and the darkness was driven back by a wavering, red glow.

"That was too close!"

They journeyed for several hours. A change became apparent in the tunnel. Rarely at first, but more frequently as time went by, they smelt drafts of fresh air and saw beams of light coming from side passages.

Soon the light was constant enough for Dominel to extinguish his brazier. They walked until the daylight grew dim then kindled a fire and made camp.

#

A jester clad in the traditional red and yellow of his profession danced and cantered before Dominel, singing a taunting song.

"Lost your way
I would say.

Lost a precious thing.
Gone for sure.
It is no more.
Sword snapped like a bowstring."

"Hold it. Who are you to taunt me, how was I to know it was a trap?" demanded Dominel.

"Then ever up you must go, or else you pay your life in toll," teased the jester who skipped away.

#

Dominel awoke in the dim light that filtered into the cavern. He yawned, stretched, and woke the girl to continue their journey. They followed the passage, which now ran level, until Dominel felt a tingling along his spine. He jerked to his right and seemingly pushed his hand through the wall. Grabbing something cold and hard, he pulled back his hand and examined its contents. It was a crystal that shone with a white radiance. He stood transfixed by its beauty, his being filled with peace and love for all things.

"Master," said a melodious voice.

"What?" asked Dominel.

"Think of love, the satisfaction of helping others, the joy of children as they laugh and play about you. You desire a partner in this life, someone sharing your trials and triumphs, a person who completes you and puts loneliness to flight."

"Who are you?"

"The essence within you. The crystal of light. A catalyst. Feel the love of true friends and the gratitude of others. I offer so much. Choose my path. You have tried to live well until now, continue as you have begun."

The voice grew silent in Dominel's mind. A force jerked him to the left. He reached out, his hand passing through another illusionary wall. Grabbing another hard, cool object, he brought it into view. This time it was a malformed black crystal.

"You hunger. All you survey can be yours. You can be king, your every whim law."

"I'm not like that," countered Dominel.

"Of course you are. You hunger for women to cater to your lusts, living to give you pleasure. Think of the mastery you have of those who fear you. If the fear is great enough, others will suffer any degradation to fulfil your desires. Choose me and this power is yours. You can order the world as you will."

"No. I don't want a world of slaves."

"Don't be hasty. Think of it. If a woman denies you, you can have her brought to you in chains for your satisfaction."

Dominel's loins stirred at the thought of a willing woman, chained and helpless, ready to grant his every whim.

"That intrigues you. Any woman, willing or no, can be yours in this manner."

"Willing or no?" repeated Dominel. The import of the words struck him. Screeching in horror and disgust, he pulled away from the crystal, shaken by the knowledge that it had only offered to fulfil his own base desires. He made to throw the dark crystal away, but the words from his dream echoed in his ears.

"From darkest night,
From brightest day,
From each of these they fell one day.
A crystal fragment it was shorn,
To open door, cross on the morn."

Dominel placed the dark crystal in an empty food bag and holding the shining crystal continued along the passage.

Soon they reached a place where the cavern's walls were carved into reliefs of dragons, mermaids and other strange beasts. The floors were covered with mosaics, depicting scenes from legend.

They walked past ever more ornate artworks until an iron door blocked their way. The door was engraved with a pentagram, with one point above the other four and several words in a strange script. Dominel reached for the door handle and pulled, but nothing happened.

"We're stuck. All that journey wasted," he said and sank to the floor with his back against the wall.

The girl frowned and joined him on the floor.

"All we've been through for nothing! Unless?" He stared at the crystal in his hand.

"To open door, cross on the morn. All right. I've no choice, so I'll wait."

Hours later Dominel awoke to a chattering sound. The cavern was dark. He reached towards the water skins and was rewarded with a nip on his hand.

"Rats! We are close to the surface," he pulled away the cover he'd thrown over the crystal of light. The crystal shone, and Dominel picked it up. With a frightened squeal, several furry bodies ran away from the food bag.

Dominel sat up and stared at the door. He noticed that the cavern was growing slowly brighter. Looking up, he could see a shaft cut into its roof. A beam of light pushed through the shaft and struck the centre of the pentacle on the door. Snatching the dark crystal from his pack, he rushed forward. The light revealed two slots, in the centre of the pentacle. Fumbling in his excitement, he pushed the crystals into the depressions. A hum filled the air as the door opened.

Dominel shook the girl awake and collected their gear, before racing through the door. He ran up a short flight of stairs, emerging into the light of a new day.

Chapter 6
When the Student is Ready

Dominel stopped at the top of the stairs. He was standing on a balcony carved into the mountain about two strides across. A stair descended from the platform's right side, linking a series of balconies ending at a valley floor.

The valley was stunning, with mountains towering on all sides and a narrow, glacial river wandering its length. Trees covered the lower slopes, while snow-clad peaks stood out in bleak contrast to the vibrant life below. The valley's far end was defined by a sheer cliff, over which the river fell with a roar.

Dominel heard a cry and glanced up to see eagles circling.

"It's beautiful!" he exclaimed.

The girl walked up beside him on the shelf of rock and stared over the idyllic woodland.

After strapping on his armour and pack, he led the girl down the stairs into the valley. Dominel counted thirteen more balconies branching off the stairway. Each of these had a door set into the mountainside. He tried and failed to open each door. When they reached the base of the stair, they settled onto the soft soil.

Minutes passed before Dominel rose, stretched and walked into the forest. The girl leapt to her feet and followed him.

The woods were full of overgrown trails that wound their way between deciduous trees, just coming into leaf, and tall evergreens. Birds sang, and deer grazed placidly in the valley's meadows.

"This has to be the most beautiful forest in the world," he said, as he inspected a clearing filled with spring flowers.

"Bbb bbootful" echoed a soft voice behind him.

"What?" he exclaimed, spinning around to stare at the girl.

"Bbbbootful," repeated the girl, smiling.

"You can speak! Why haven't you said anything before?"

The girl stared at him, smiled and said, "Bootful."

Dominel smiled back at her.

"No. You can't speak, can you? But you can learn. So be it. I agree this place is beautiful."

"Bootful."

Dominel grinned and led her down the path. Wild grapes and a staggering variety of fruit trees grew along the trails' edges. They came upon a clearing full of dandelions and made a meal of the leaves.

When the sun descended behind the mountain peaks, Dominel found a place where pine trees grew thick and close, creating a hollow where their lower branches had died. They spent the night under their shelter.

The next day he constructed a lean-to and fire pit. Taking one of his daggers and lashing it to a branch he made a crude spear.

"I have to go hunting."

"Bootful," replied the girl rising to her feet.

"You stay here."

The girl looked at him quizzically and stepped forward.

"No, stay!"

The girl looked at him obviously puzzled.

Dominel took a step, but she followed.

"Demon spit."

"Demon spit," repeated the girl brightly.

Dominel looked at her in astonishment.

"I'm going to have to watch every word I say, aren't I?"

She smiled at him.

He looked around the meadow then had an idea. Taking a bit of wood left from making the lean-to, he split its base into two and pulled it apart. He cut two more slits farther along its length, one on either side of the branch.

Finally, he whittled the top into a rounded oblong and cut a few quick slots to form a face. Taking a tattered fur he cut a hole for the head, and one for each arm then pulled it onto the stick man.

"This is for you to play with," he offered, passing the crude figurine to the girl.

She took the figurine, looked at it then stood it on the ground. It fell over. She snatched it up, cradling it.

"You remember dolls. That's good, you play with dolly, and I'll go hunting."

Hefting his spear Dominel walked from the clearing. This time she let him go.

Late that evening a scratched and bloody Dominel returned to the clearing with a deer carcass over his shoulders.

"If I'd known it was going to be that hard, I wouldn't have started," he griped, as the girl moved to meet him.

She stared at him with a quizzical expression on her face.

"I know what you're thinking. I'm a prince. I should know how to hunt. Well, I do. I got the accursed thing, didn't I? It's just when I hunted with the royal court we had dogs and woodsmen to flush the game, and I was on a horse."

The girl smiled at him and said, "Bootful."

"Thank you for the vote of confidence. This spear isn't exactly made for throwing either. I'm lucky I caught anything!

"I better dress the meat. It won't take long."

The girl skipped off to play.

Half an hour later the deer's heart and liver sizzled on spits over the fire, while Dominel hung the rest of the carcass in a tree.

"This is going to be good," he said, returning to the fireside.

"Good," mimicked the girl, who sat across from him staring at the roasting meat.

"And this valley is a beautiful place," he added, looking into the ink black, silver-flecked sky.

"Bootful."

"Yes beautiful. I'll have to teach you more words, won't I?"

"Bootful."

Grinning Dominel reached for the roasting meat.

Over the next few nights, the moon grew smaller, until it was dark. Then it rose again, a silver crescent.

Dominel lay in his lean-to trying to sleep. Every time he began to drift off chanting echoed in his mind, but when he fully awoke it was gone.

"One: I'm going mad. Two: this was a stronghold of wizards. Take your pick, Dominel. Either way, you're not getting any sleep until the voices shut up," he grumbled and crawled from the lean-to.

Closing his eyes, he entered the relaxed state his master at arms had taught him and Emma had refined. The chanting returned. Opening his eyes, he followed the sound through the woods until a white radiance appeared before him. His trance deepened as he walked towards the luminance. Without realising what was happening, he strode into the centre of the light, which seemed to both surround and pervade him.

"What's happening?" he asked. No words came, only an echo of thought that moved through the light as ripples on a pond.

"Welcome, Ackdominel, Welcome home," replied the light. A feeling of warmth and love pervaded him.

Dominel floated in a warm place as he heard himself reply. "Thank you Franlor. Are you to be my first teacher in this life?"

Dominel wondered at what he said, yet it felt so natural. A strange sensation filled him. He felt as if he was staring down a long corridor of time, populated with beings he knew were himself, but yet were not. Being after being, all different, all the same. His consciousness reeled, and his sanity rebelled.

"Yes, Ackdominel. As we discussed you will be prepared to carry the power emblems to the island of Haven. You must go to the lowest lodge tonight. There I will teach this consciousness. Now you had best go, this consciousness is already unbalanced from having the door flung open."

"As you say." Dominel/Ackdominel opened his eyes not having realised that they were closed.

"What was that?" Dominel felt an irresistible desire to open the lowest door off the stair. "It's locked," he told himself, as his feet carried him towards the doors in the cliff face.

"Knock, and thou shalt enter," muttered a voice in the back of his mind.

He walked towards the lowest of the doors. Upon arriving he grabbed its handle and pulled, but nothing happened! Releasing the handle, he knocked on the stone. The door creaked open. He stared into a room that seemed to glow with a light similar to that cast by a half moon. The light came from everywhere and nowhere in the chamber. He stepped through the doorway into a square alcove about the length of his body across. It was hewn from the rock of the mountain. There was a door on each of the chamber's walls, which were ringed with cloak hooks, and a bench sat by the entrance.

Intrigued he walked to the door on his right and opened it. This led to a round room nearly four strides across. A silver circle dominated its floor. At the circle's centre was a cloth draped altar with an object sitting atop it. He moved to the circle's edge and stared at the object. With a swirl of dust, it leapt into the air. Dominel now saw that the object was a human skull.

"Gods and demons!" he spat as he backed towards the door.

"I mean you no harm, Ackdominel," spoke a man's voice. It was deep and resonant. Its very tone seemed to still the terrified race of Dominel's heart.

Dominel paused, staring at the skull that regarded him with empty sockets. "Wh… What are you?"

"I am your old friend, Franlor. It is my task to teach you the first lessons of the high art in this life."

"I am not Ackdominel."

"Of course you are! Ackdominel was your name in your last life. Ackdominel is your name among the keepers of the secret way. Ackdominel is your wizard name."

"The what?"

"You will learn that in time."

"Very well. What are you?"

"I have already told you."

"No, you told me who you were, not what."

"Really, Ackdominel, you were born into a bit of a dunce, weren't you?"

Dominel felt a chill run up his spine at the displeasure in the skull's voice, even as the macabre way the jaw moved with each word fascinated him.

"Oh, very well. I am a shade of a wizard," continued the skull. "When the life force of my last incarnation ebbed, I gave myself up as a sacrifice to see that my order would not fail. Oh sit down, and I will tell you the whole story. Then maybe we can get on with something important."

Ackdominel stared at the shade then sat on the floor.

"It started many mortal years ago when the exponents of the Covetous God gained ascendancy amongst the rulers of the lands. They declared that all those who thought differently from themselves must be converted or slain. Thus, the persecution began. They hunted down the followers of nature and the hunt, as well as any others who dared to think for themselves. The numbers of the practitioners of the high art dwindled. The followers of the Covetous God killed the mightiest wizards in our sleep. Our lesser brethren were dragged before the courts and false confessions tortured from them.

"We foresaw our downfall and knowing what would happen to the world with no wizards to protect it, took action.

"Are you sure you comprehend this? Perhaps I should speak slower?"

Ackdominel looked at the skull, which was drifting back and forth across the circle as if pacing. "Go on."

"Several of us, whose time on the mortal plane was soon to end, poured our remaining life essences into magic vials. We sacrificed what worldly life remained to us and went to the borders of the spirit world. Those that remained placed the vials in magic seals, along with those parts of the body that could endure the wait."

"Bones."

"Maybe you're not as dense as I guessed. To continue.

"The greatest of our order sacrificed all that remained of his life and took to wandering the earth as a homeless ghost. He was held to the world by the life force that he had sacrificed. Able to see and hear, but unable to touch or affect anything. This allowed him to select the time and place of his rebirth. Once he was once more incarnate he would, with the help of our brothers and sisters in the spirit world, come to us. Thus, we might use the life energies we left behind to enter this world and teach him. In this way, our order would not die."

"Why wouldn't this wizard already know everything?"

"He would and he would not. When one enters a new body, the memories of the old are hidden. They become little more than vague feelings and natural aptitudes. Thus you must be taught to reach your memories. This is a natural thing. Because Ackdominel did not journey to the spirit world like most souls, your knowledge is closer to the surface. We hope to accomplish the work of decades in a few short years. But we have no time to waste!"

"What must I do?"

Franlor looked at Ackdominel, and the barren skull seemed to radiate joy.

"You must be Ackdominel, the reincarnation of the master of my order, and my student."

Ackdominel sat silently. Visions of the monstrous hordes running before him, lightning wreaking havoc in their ranks, filled his mind. "What is my first lesson?"

Franlor began.

Time passed like a breeze, as Dominel sat listening to all Franlor had to say. His mind was enthralled by the words and their content. After a long while, the shade paused.

"It grows light. We must finish for today. You must return for further instruction at moonrise."

"Why can't we continue now?"

"The sun is too mighty. Its raw, unfiltered power is capable of disrupting delicate enchantments. Besides, you must rest." The skull settled on the altar.

Dominel sat collecting himself then rose and left the chamber, closing the door behind him.

He inspected the two remaining doors of the lodge. One of these led to a small room occupied by a serviceable rope bed and dresser. The other led into a kitchen. The kitchen consisted of a hearth cut into the wall, a central table and walls lined with cupboards. Looking closer, he found that the cupboards were full of jars of non-perishable food.

He ran from the shelter with a whoop of jubilation and didn't stop until he came to his lean-to in the clearing. He found the girl in the process of dressing her stick doll. She looked at him and smiled.

He gasped out, "I've found us a new home."

"Home?" mimicked the girl.

"Yes, a new home. I've opened the first door into the mountain."

"Door?"

"You really don't understand, do you? Come with me. I'll show you." He grabbed her hand and ran towards the rooms carved into the mountainside.

After showing the girl the chambers, his enthusiasm began to fail, and weariness overtook him. So shortly after the sun was full up, he lay asleep on the rope bed.

When he awoke, he rose to find that the lodge had been dusted and swept. Going into the kitchen, he found the girl staring at a pot of water sitting over a cold, empty hearth. He looked at her inquiringly. The girl stared back and said, "Eat. Eat."

Dominel smiled at his own foolishness.

"It needs fire to get hot," he explained, as he moved to the coal bin.

"Fi-re."

"Yes, fire. You did well cleaning. I'm proud of you."

The girl beamed.

Dominel began to prepare the hearth, as he did so he thought of the girl cleaning the lodge. The whole lodge!

He bolted towards the ceremony room's door, grabbed its handle and nearly wrenched his shoulder from its socket trying to open it.

The girl, who had followed him into the central chamber, watched him quizzically. He released the door handle and looked at her, "It won't open!"

Smiling she went back into the kitchen.

Dominel spent the rest of that day examining the cupboards' contents and separating out the spoiled portion. Finally, though it felt like it never would, evening came. He waited on the balcony for moonrise. Slowly a sliver of silver became apparent over the mountain peaks. With haste, he moved to the ceremony room's door and pulled it open. Taking a deep breath, he stepped in. The skull hovered above the altar.

"I was afraid," began Dominel.

"That the door would not open," finished Franlor. "Fear not, it will always open when the moon is in the sky. Now let us begin."

The skull talked through the night, cramming Ackdominel's mind with information. When Dominel left the ceremony room, he went straight to bed and collapsed into a troubled sleep.

He dreamt of ancient fires and a complex web of gold. Each golden thread touched all the others. Suddenly several of the threads unravelled and the web fell apart, like rags blown upon a stormy wind. One lone thread strove to hold the pieces together. He heard himself scream and awoke with sweat on his hands.

He lay on the bed collecting himself then pulled on his tattered surcoat and went outside. The sun was only slightly past the noon, but he knew he wouldn't get back to sleep, so he searched for the girl. After nearly an hour he found her in a clearing, waving a stick about as if it were a sword. She duelled back and forth with her imaginary opponent, a determined look on her face. It took a long time for her to notice him.

"Hello," he said.

"H, h, hello," she replied then smiled triumphantly.

"You're learning quickly."

She smiled then her attention slipped. She playfully brandished her stick sword, challenging him to a duel.

He stood still as stone. Painful memories of battles lost flooded his mind.

She challenged him again. He brushed off his melancholy.

Who knows, maybe it will help restore her memories, he thought, as he chose a suitable stick and moved to answer her challenge.

The two duelled with Dominel easily blocking the girl's sweeping blows. She grew bored of the game and left to play with some pebbles she had gathered earlier.

That night found Dominel in the ceremony room with Franlor.

"Did you dream well?" demanded the skull.

"I slept horribly! I had nightmares."

"I did not ask how you slept! I asked how you dreamt!"

Dominel quickly described his dream of the previous night.

"Good, Good! You have seen the pattern as it was and as it is."

"This pattern, what is it?"

"Everything! All things affect all others. The pattern is the way they relate. Eternity is like a great cloth, and each thing in creation is a single thread."

"So when the wizards were murdered, threads were ripped from the pattern and it began to fall apart!"

"Yes, you are beginning to understand. The thread you saw holding the remains together represents the students of the last wizards."

"Students?" demanded Dominel, hope leaping in his heart.

"Yes, students. Did you believe you were the only one? Many orders prepared for the downfall. You are not alone, Ackdominel. You are, however, one of a precious few."

"Can I reach the others? Maybe together we could--."

"Once you are trained, my student, once you are trained. For now, let us discuss the basic premises behind the manipulation of astral matter into semi-permanent forms."

Time passed quickly for Dominel. His nights were filled with instruction. His days with practising the arts taught him and playing with the girl. To amuse himself, he began to teach her the art of the blade. She learned quickly, and he was soon forced to don his armour when they played swords to avoid receiving a painful collection of bruises.

One evening when he entered the ceremony room Franlor's skull rose laboriously into the air.

"Are you well?" asked Ackdominel.

"That is a stupid question. I am dead! My energy is almost spent! My time as your teacher is through."

"But I've so much more to learn."

"Learn it you shall. On the first day of the new moon, you must go to the next lodge up the mountain. There another teacher awaits you. Before you leave this chamber, show honour to my bones. Within this altar is a cavity. Take what it contains and place my remains there.

"Fare thee well. Remember the new moon. That is the time for beginnings."

Having finished speaking the skull drifted to the altar top and lay still.

Dominel numbly moved to the altar, wrapped the skull in the silken coverlet it sat upon and lifted it. This revealed a hatch with a brass ring set at one end. The hatch opened to reveal a chamber containing a long, pale-blue robe and a golden key. He took the objects and put Franlor's bones in their place. Closing the hatch, he left the room.

The girl was waiting for him when he stepped through the ceremony room's door.

"Wrong, Dominel?" she asked.

"He's gone."

"Dead man go?"

"Yes."

She grasped his hand, smiled and said, "Eat."

Dominel led the way to the kitchen.

Chapter 7
Monsters in and out

The new moon was riding up the eastern horizon. Dominel stood before the door of the second lodge, holding the gold key taken from Franlor's altar. When the dim moonlight touched the door, a keyhole appeared. Dominel eased the key into the lock and turned it. The door swung inwards, revealing an entry hall identical to the one in the lodge below, save that a comfortable looking chair sat opposite the door. Moving to the door on the chamber's right he pushed it inwards. Entering the room he saw a padded throne in a circle of silver set into the floor. A skeleton sat upon the throne.

From the size, Ackdominel guessed the skeleton must have been a woman.

He cleared his throat and called out, "I am Ackdominel. I have come as Franlor instructed."

"So you have," returned a soft feminine voice, which issued from the skeleton.

Ackdominel shuddered at the way the jawbone moved, and the empty eye sockets stared through him.

"I have come to learn what you would teach."

"Good, let us begin. I am Shanal and our time is short. Listen well!"

The night passed quickly. Ackdominel discovered that learning from Shanal was a pleasure. Listening to her voice sparked warm feelings. When he closed his eyes, he saw not a skeleton but a handsome, older woman with long grey-streaked black hair, tan skin and dark eyes. She was dressed in a dark blue gown that accentuated the curves of a well-proportioned body.

By morning his mind spun with information, and a soft voice echoed in his ears. It was reluctantly that he left the ceremony room. He made his way to the kitchen where he found some meal that hadn't spoiled and prepared breakfast. Soon after this, the girl joined him. She now wore a tattered assortment of his old clothing, as well as her own. Dominel was dressed in the pale blue robe of a novice of the Keepers of the Secret Way.

"One of these days I'll have to find you something nice to wear. You're far too pretty to be in rags," he commented, watching her across the table.

The girl looked at the floor, blushed, and said, "Me pretty?"

"Very." Dominel stroked her cheek and moved to embrace her in a brotherly way.

She stiffened then, screaming, drove her fist into his gut.

The blow caught him by surprise, and he buckled over while she sprinted into the other room.

After catching his breath Dominel felt like yelling, but his compassion halted him. "You must have been through something horrible. I am sorry."

The girl glared at him through the doorway then her features softened into a smile.

"I wish there was some way I could reach you. Help you to deal with whatever those horrors did to you. Maybe someday?"

The following night Ackdominel sat in the ceremony chamber listing to Shanal.

"When channelling forces beyond your own power, it is important to keep your personal energy systems clear of all obstructions. As well, you must constantly hold in your mind what you wish to accomplish in its entirety. As an example, when the wizards created the shield over the mountains, each of us had to keep the thought of the area the shield was to cover in the front of our minds. As we did this, we also had to focus on the shield's purpose and specifications. Increasing the shields charge after it was erected was easier. We simply channelled energy into the shield. The pattern carried the energy to where it was needed."

"Wait. Are you saying it is possible to increase the shield's power with this technique?"

"Yes. In truth, this section is being taught out of sequence. You must practice channelling energies, and I feel your practice should be to some purpose. Your efforts will not prevent the shield's collapse, but they will delay it."

"Then it is a skill truly worth knowing."

"Any skill is worth knowing! Now to continue…"

#

It was evening of the following day that Dominel made his way to a wooded meadow near the centre of the valley and sat cross-legged on the grass.

I have to relax if this is going to work, he thought. Closing his eyes, he forced his breathing to become deep and regular. His senses opened up to the world around him. He felt his body expand, becoming one with the land around him. Rivers of energy flowed through the valley, converging and splitting then stretching out over the surface of his world. He felt them as tracks of hot and cold across his skin and saw them as ribbons of sparkling light against his closed eyelids. Reaching with his will, he drew their force to his physical form. The power built within him until he felt ready to burst. Shifting his focus he sent a beam of sparkling light, visible only to those trained in the ways of magic, straight up to where the shield arched above the mountains. Minutes passed, sweat soaked his clothes then he groaned and fell back to lie on the ground.

"Shanal said it would become easier with practice. I hope she's right!" he muttered, as he fought to still the pounding in his head.

#

Dominel moved through the various lodges, receiving a gift from each once his studies at that level were complete. By the end of his first year, he had reached the fifth lodge and had an excellent view from his balcony. The girl had continued to broaden her vocabulary at an alarming rate, often seeming more like she was remembering something forgotten than learning the words anew. She also excelled in learning the arts of battle. They were, however, no closer to unlocking her past than they had been upon coming to the valley.

Dominel sat upon his balcony, arrayed in the gifts his teachers had given him. He was still clad in the robe Franlor had left him, but now he also wore a dark-blue cloak. About his neck hung an amethyst pendant, and his waist was girthed by an ornate belt holding a ceremonial dagger. He was lost in thought, his mind filled with a technique he had just learned and its implications. Sensing a presence behind him, he looked over his shoulder to see the girl emerging from the lodge.

"You unhappy?" she asked, seeing his expression.

"Me? No, not really. Just thinking. I've learned how to do something that could help you remember."

"Remember?"

"Yes, the time before you met me. Before we came here."

"Oh," said the girl, sounding hopeful, sceptical, and scared at the same time.

"Would you like to remember?"

"I don't know. I'm happy now. Would remember change that?"

"It might. It also might explain why you won't let me touch you, or why you're afraid of being naked. If we knew, maybe we could fix it."

The girl stared at the valley below for a time then asked, "If I remember, I be smart like Dominel? Know how to make fire and other things?"

"You would know everything you knew before, but you have to be the one to decide."

She fell silent for a time before saying, "I, I, want to remember."

"Good. We'll do it this evening after I've slept." Grasping her hand, he added. "I'll do everything I can for you, little one."

"I know."

That evening Dominel went in search of the girl, finding her in a clearing close to the stair's base. He led her back to the stair where they sat on the ground facing each other.

"It's not too late. You don't have to do this."

The girl looked at him and in a small voice said, "Do it."

Dominel took her hands and reached deep into his mind. Deeper and deeper he descended, into the core of his being. Ackdominel saw himself as a mote of energy then his thoughts turned to the girl.

Merge, his mind commanded. His consciousness drifted towards hers. He saw her, a shining light before him. They drew closer then touched and joined into a single light.

What is this? Who am I? Where am I? demanded the part that was the girl.

We are Ackdominel. I am with you.

We are one, returned the girl, now at peace.

Yes, one.

Ackdominel examined their joint consciousness soon finding what he sought. In their thoughts a wall loomed, blocking the way to a section of their mind. The Ackdominel part of their mind drew closer to the wall, even as the part that was the girl backed away in terror. Ackdominel focussed his will and moved to the wall's base. The girl fought against him, and it was all he could do to keep the joint consciousness there.

He almost turned away, but he could feel a desire almost as great as the fear. It radiated from the girl's side of their mind, a desire to open the wall, to know! Placing his will against the wall, he called, "Be gone!"

Gradually the wall dissolved. Their consciousness was caught in a flood of memories.

They knew themselves; she was Melanie, a pretty, fourteen-year-old daughter of Sir Calidids. It was a beautiful day as she was relaxing in her father's fields, picking wildflowers. The world was wonderful. A handsome count's son would soon be arriving to pay court to her, and there was nothing sweeter than living. She saw a stranger, in rent and dented armour, gallop up the lane to her father's house. Melanie ran towards the newcomer as he dismounted and started talking frantically with her father. She reached them as her father was leading the other man into the house.

"Father, what is happening?" she asked.

Her father turned to look at her. He was an older man, with steel-grey hair and moustache, upon a handsome oval face. He smiled at her, revealing a tracery of laugh wrinkles about his deep, blue eyes.

"I have to go, my pretty. The border is under attack, and I am summoned to my knightly duty of defence."

"Father, let the younger men go."

"No!" he snapped then his voice softened. "I've still strength to wield a blade in defence of our land. It is my duty, but come here."

Melanie approached. Her father hugged her before he entered the house to arm himself.

The next few days were spent in hectic activity. Melanie helped her mother order the local peasants into companies, in case the Storm should break through their first line of defence. Then it began. It was heralded by ragged men on spent horses riding towards the royal palace; the ragtag survivors of a fierce battle against impossible odds. They followed! They filled her memories. She wanted to lock them out but couldn't. Line upon line of monsters marched forward sweeping the peasants, armed with their axes and hoes, away like leaves upon a hurricane.

The beasts marched on, finally reaching the house.

Mother stood before a window, releasing arrow after arrow at the invaders. A javelin pierced her skull, and she fell, blood spurting from her wound. Melanie picked up the bow and began to let fly, cursing herself for not paying more attention when her father had taught her how to shoot. Soon the arrows were spent, and the Storm moved forward without fear. An ape-like ogre, with large yellow fangs, beat upon the door, splintering the oaken beam that held it. Kalin, an old, lame peasant her father hired as a gardener, thrust at the monster with a spear, driving it deep into the creature's breast. The beast lashed out with a huge, iron club, crushing Kalin's skull. The ogre scuttled into the room, blood pouring from its wound. Melanie hacked at it with the kitchen knife she was carrying, but it clutched her wrist and twisted it until the knife fell clattering to the floor.

Now the nightmare began in earnest. The horrible ogre dragged her to a bed and forced her down. Its stinking breath fell upon her face as it ripped at her clothes. Pain laced up from between her thighs as she felt rough hands pawing her body. After the ogre, there was another horror, a creature with two heads.

She felt defiled. Sickness and gore rose up from the depths of her existence. She pleaded for death, but the only response was more pain. They lashed her to the bed, and still more pain followed. Her body was bruised. She felt sick and ashamed. During a brief respite, she looked out the door through tear-filled eyes. A fire burned in the main room. On a spit over the flames hung the limp form of her mother. As she watched, an ogre ripped off an arm and began to gnaw on it. She screamed, but this only brought more pain in the form of a small goblin with yellow skin and blood-red eyes. The beast struck her and snarled, "Shut up!"

Agony became her world, with night and day lost in a blur of tears. Occasionally a horror would enter the room to molest her or force water down her unwilling throat. After an eternity she heard a horse on the cobblestones outside and the sounds of steel against steel. Her father burst into the room, his armour in ruins, the visor from his helmet torn completely away. She could see a deep graze across his forehead. He cut her bonds and grabbing her headed for the door. The sound of huge, flat feet running reached her ears.

Cursing, he dragged her to the pantry's trap door and wrenched it open. He lowered her into the darkness as a large creature with a bear-like body, a wide fur-covered face and shark-like mouth, burst into the room. The trap door slammed shut above her. The sound of combat drifted down to her. Other sounds soon joined in, as more monsters crowded into the room. One thing then another thudded against the floor above. Something crashed with the sound of falling metal, and everything became silent and dark.

Grief assailed him/her, loathing, self-loathing. They felt defiled. Dominel felt pain where no man could. He felt a shame rarely known to men. The girl wept. Dominel wept as he drew out her pain, taking it onto himself, accepting the horror of her memories, making them his own, lightening the girl's burden. When he could stand no more, he broke the contact.

Time passed. They sat on the grass weeping. Dominel wanted to bathe to relieve the unclean feeling that filled him, but he knew it wouldn't help. His loins throbbed with a remembered pain not his own and gore rose in his throat.

#

The girl sat, loathing the touch of her own skin, the skin the horrors had touched. She felt herself slipping towards the oblivion she had used to wall back the pain.

No! I can't! I won't. This is my chance to live again, I will have my revenge! This thought fired anger within her, and she fought against the remembered pain. *It won't conquer me this time! I'll make them pay for my parents and what they did to me,* she added as she wept, oblivious to all save her seething emotions.

#

It was deep in the night before they stirred. Dominel was the first to rise stiffly to his feet, feeling horrid.

Hate for the monsters flared in him to heights before unimagined. He stumbled towards the river where he washed and washed, hoping to remove the taint of the shared memories and abducted emotions. When he could stand the cold no longer, he dragged himself from the freezing waters and collapsed on the grassy bank.

When morning came, he returned to the lodges, where he found the girl sitting at the stair's base, with her head in her hands.

"Melanie?" he asked softly.

The girl looked up angrily.

"Are you all right?"

"Yes," she answered, her features softening. "I remember."

"I know, so do I."

"It was horrid!"

"Yes."

She glared at him and was preparing to snap out, how could you know? when she realized what he had done. "You took it on yourself. Didn't you?"

"As much as I could. It was too much for one person to deal with. Almost too much for two."

"Thank you."

Both fell silent for a long while.

The next night Ackdominel resumed his studies, but memories interfered so that by morning he had gained little ground. He left the ceremonial chamber feeling tired and stupid. Making his way to the lodge's kitchen, he found the girl preparing a meal.

"Hello," he said and collapsed into the chair.

"Hello," she replied, and after a pause continued. "It's funny. I used to think you were so smart to make fire and do all the things I'd forgotten how to."

"You used to get excited over little things too. I remember how you giggled and danced when we blew dandelion seeds into the wind."

"Yes." She dished their meal into a pair of the porcelain bowls they had found in this lodge. Pulling a jug of syrup from a shelf, she brought it to the table.

"How long has it been?" she asked, taking a seat opposite Dominel.

"Well over a year."

"The first thing I remember is that cottage near the mountain's base."

"That's where Emma began to work on you. She didn't have the knowledge or power to touch your memories. Which is good. They would have destroyed her."

As Dominel spoke he glanced about the kitchen, which was more ornate than the ones in the other lodges but still basically the same. *Will the girl be the same?* he wondered.

"I just remembered the way you and I played swords. That must have been boring for a warrior such as yourself," said Melanie.

"It kept me in practice. I taught you the basics," replied Dominel, a thin smile coming to his lips.

"You did? Good!" Melanie's voice took on a menacing tone.

"Why?" Dominel could feel the woman's desire for vengeance fill the room like a cold fire, burning and freezing in the same moment.

"Because I am going to destroy those monsters. They'll pay for what they did to me." Melanie's hands clenched into white-knuckled fists.

Dominel stared at her in silence then asked, "When?"

She paused, and her fists relaxed.

"When?" she repeated, sounding shocked. "Why as soon as I can get out of this valley!"

"Well. If you want to commit suicide, it certainly is your business, but excuse me if I don't join you."

"What?!"

"At best you're only half trained as a warrior. Besides, it won't be blades that win the final victory against the Storm."

"Then I'll take as many of them as I can before I fall." Melanie stared at Dominel haughtily.

"There will be a time for that. The battle will be a long, hard one. Give yourself time. Right now your death would be to no purpose. Wait a while then maybe you can fight for a reason. We'll drive these beasts from our world, but not today."

"I will wait, but only so long."

"I ask no more." Dominel turned his attention to his porridge.

The river of time flowed on, and the agony of remembrance began to fade from Dominel and Melanie's minds and hearts. Dominel continued to train Melanie in the use of sword and dagger and added a bow to her arsenal. The bow was a crude affair, made from gut and a bent branch, with arrows formed of sharpened sticks and fallen bird feathers, but it served to refine the skills her father had taught her.

As Dominel taught Melanie, he also concentrated on his own studies. He was now in the sixth lodge and had gained a dark blue, initiate's robe upon leaving the fifth.

With each passing night, he gained a deeper perception of the universe around him and the magic within it.

The year continued. Dominel passed into the seventh lodge then the eighth. It was while he was in the eighth lodge that he awoke to a feeling of great disquiet. Rising he hurried to the balcony to find the world a chaos of conflicting energies. Power surged and fluxed on all sides.

"Gods!" he exclaimed. He reached out with his mind and checked the mountains' shield. It fluxed and flowed as if a great force pounded against it seeking to push its way past.

Ackdominel sat on the balcony and forced his breathing to become deep and regular. He felt his inner being loosen and sensed himself slipping free of his mortal shell. Like a sword from its scabbard, Ackdominel's spirit rose into the air. After checking the strength of the golden cord that connecting his thought body to his physical one, he willed himself to the source of the attack.

Arriving instantly, he hovered inside the shield inspecting what lay beyond. An encampment of monsters filled the opening of the largest mountain pass connecting Bani to the western kingdoms. The sky beyond the shield was a sea of black clouds. Just outside the shield's area of effect stood a creature with a head resembling a squid and a body similar to a man's. It was clad in a black robe and waves of force emanated from it, crashing against the shield. Ackdominel watched, not understanding what he saw, but knowing it had to be stopped.

Whispering a prayer for strength, he began his attack. Reaching out with his will he focussed it against the inside of the shield and began to pour energy into the barrier. Immediately he felt a foreign will resisting his efforts. The shield strobed with light only a mystic could see, as the fabric of its creation bent against the onslaught of two powerful but opposed wills.

This isn't going to work. I'm only holding it at bay, thought Ackdominel as he pulled his power back from the shield.

The squid-headed creature also paused. The tentacles about its mouth writhed and a hissing sound issued from its beak.

What now? thought Ackdominel.

A bolt of malevolent force leapt from the squid creature, forcing a passage through the mountains' shield, and striking Ackdominel.

"Gods of my fathers!" He swore, as his personal defences shuddered. Glancing up he saw the mountains' shield close around the hole the blast had ripped, leaving a weak spot. *I can't let it damage the shield. I have to take the battle into its mind. Keep the power contained around it.*

Ackdominel's spirit body dove at the creature, disappearing into its physical form, grappling for control of the alien mind.

"Get out! Get out! This is my mind, my body. Get Out!" screeched the creature's thoughts.

"I will not leave!" countered Ackdominel, as wave after wave of thought energy buffeted him. He pictured himself clinging to a rock as a hurricane swept around him. The mind-scape altered to match his mental image. The wind roared as he dragged himself to a place where a rock outcrop provided shelter. The outcrop represented a section of his foe's mind the beast couldn't consciously access.

"Where are you?" bellowed the squid creature. In the mind-scape, it stood three times the height of a man. It rampaged over the mental terrain, searching for Ackdominel.

Ackdominel slowly removed his concentration from the conceptional landscape. The terrain around him remained, drawing its energy from his foe's expectations as if the beast was dreaming.

Good. One less thing to drain me. Now to find a weakness. Ackdominel began following the creature's alien thought patterns until he touched its memories.

"Good," he whispered then noticed that the conceptional world around him was beginning to fade. *"Not fast enough, squid face."*

Savagely he dragged forth the beast's memories. The mind-scape altered, becoming a stage where the past was played out. The memories encompassed the squid beast making it experience them exactly as it had originally. It was a time when as a child it had been mentally beaten by older, stronger children of its species. Next Ackdominel made the monster relive the savagery of its teacher's attacks during the training that allowed it to master its abilities.

Ackdominel watched as a brutal life spread before him. His compassion caused him to pause, but then he became aware of other memories, people pulled before the beast and how it devoured their minds; the pleasure the creature drew from inflicting pain. The abused had become the abuser. Glancing up he saw that in his pause the beast had seized control of the mindscape.

"Human! I know where you are," it screamed. The mental image of it reached for Ackdominel. He felt mental claws scrabble against his will. His grip on the beast's mind began to loosen.

Images of hideous death filled Ackdominel's mind. The mental terrain altered. He saw his brothers as shambling corpses coming to drag him into death. His father, sunken-eyed, maggot-riddled and rotting, laughed ghoulishly at his plight.

"Illusion. Only illusion! My father's spirit is free! It came to me!" He nearly laughed as the twisted images dissolved into nothingness.

Seizing the moment it took for the squid beast to choose a new attack, Ackdominel dove into his foe's psyche, pulling up another agony. It was a mental duel with a hatchling from the same nest pool when the beast had been young. There was too little food in the pool. They were the only two left. As close as its kind could come to love, they shared the feeling, but only one could live. In victory, the creature had lost itself.

Ackdominel released the full force of that long-buried grief. In the material world, the squid beast fell to its knees sobbing. Mentally, emotion stole its ability to focus its thoughts.

Ackdominel shifted his target from his enemy's mind to its body. Mentally clutching the alien heart, he squeezed. The heart fluttered, stopped and as the beast teetered on the abyss of death, Ackdominel's spirit raced back behind the mountains' shield.

He watched as the squid beast fell to the ground.

"Too close. Its mind was so twisted," breathed Ackdominel. An inner sense of danger niggled at the edge of his mind, and he increased the strength of his personal shields. Before he was finished a savage attack struck him.

Gods! I thought I'd killed it. That blast was even stronger than its last attack. Strengthening the shield that surrounded his thought body, he examined the area for his foe. The squid creature's corpse lay where it had fallen.

"What the?" he began, then he spotted it standing by a rock only paces from the mountain shield boundary. A creature identical to the one he had just vanquished, except its hips flared out like a woman's.

The female squid creature stared at him then its tentacles writhed. Fiery red tendrils of energy lashed towards Ackdominel. Gesturing towards the earth, he summoned its power. Waves of brown energy intercepted the red and drew it into the ground.

A female voice spoke in Ackdominel's mind. *"You killed the student. Can you defeat his mistress, manling?"*

I don't dare enter this thing's thoughts. I barely survived the other one. I have to battle it in the physical world and just hope the shield can take it, thought Ackdominel. Then he spoke aloud, *"You come as invaders. Leave or die."*

The female squid creature hissed as another bolt of energy flew at Ackdominel, ripping a hole in the mountains' shield as it passed through. Ackdominel shaped his own energies into a mirror, reflecting the energy back along its course. It streaked toward his foe, who, with a wave of her hand, dissipated the energy.

"You will have to do better than that, manling."

Shifting to the offensive, Ackdominel pictured a small, blue arrow in his mind. He saw it, knew it, felt it then directing it, using knowledge gained from his earlier duel, let it fly at his foe. The arrow struck the creature's shields, piercing them like a needle through cloth. It then entered the beast, burrowing deep into its alien brain.

Ackdominel sensed amusement welling up in his enemy.

"Manling, you are a fool. The weakest child of my kind could cast a bolt with more force than your paltry attack. Now you die."

The creature prepared another assault and without warning fell dead. Ackdominel sighed and grinned at his own cleverness.

"Cunning, intellect, imagination. These are the marks of a true duellist. Brute strength against brute strength is nothing but the makings of a barroom thug." Scrantian's voice echoed in Ackdominel's mind. He smiled at the memory.

The seemingly useless arrow of energy had done its task. After entering the squid creature's brain, the bolt had lain quietly until the beast had attempted its next spell. Then the arrow had drawn the spell's energy into the beast's brain, killing it instantly.

In other words, old friend, sneaky works!
Ackdominel returned to his physical body.

Chapter 8
Friends from Afar

Dominel opened his physical eyes to the sight of Melanie staring down at him, her face a mask of worry.

"What happened?" she demanded.

"They've wizards among the monsters. A pair of them attacked the shield," answered Dominel as he stood.

"What? We have to get weapons, gather troops, build--."

"The battle has been fought and won."

"By who? How?"

"By me. In my astral body. For a first time, I think I did rather well. I'm still alive and as sane as I ever was." Dominel smiled.

"But, but…. you were just sitting here."

"My body was, not my mind." Dominel massaged his throbbing temples and stumbled to his bed.

When he awoke Melanie cornered him in the dwelling's kitchen and demanded he explain everything in minute detail. Afterwards, she fell silent.

"What is it?" he asked.

"You said you strengthened the shield."

"Yes."

"But the shield is still receding?" She drummed her fingers on the table.

Dominel leaned back in his seat. "The shield over these mountains is too large for one person to maintain. All I did was strengthen a small area of it."

"Oh. Do you think there'll be more of those squid-wizard things?"

"Probably. There can't be many of them, or we would have seen them before."

"You hope." Melanie grinned. "I hear squids don't have bones. I can hardly wait to find out."

Ackdominel told his tale to the mummified form of his latest teacher, Wellorm.

Wellorm, his white linen mummy wrappings showing clearly in the gloom of the ceremony room, sat silently upon his throne within the circle as Ackdominel spoke. Finally, his voice dripping with disgust, he said, "I thought we had destroyed those foul creatures. Beware them, Ackdominel! You did well to vanquish them. They must have lost much of their evil art since my days of life. Do not underestimate them. They are your deadliest foes."

"What are they?"

"They are the mind feeders. Many years ago they entered the earth plane in their never-ending quest for food. It fell to our order to stop them. The battle raged at the gate. We finally pushed into their world. I thought that we destroyed them utterly. A few must have escaped our hands to return and trouble us now."

"But why destroy them if all they sought was food?"

"They are parasites! They subsist on the thoughts of others. They feed on the mental energies others create. They drain their victim's mind of every thought, every glimmer of energy and leave the body to rot."

Ackdominel swallowed hard. "That being the case you had best tell me how to fight them effectively."

The next morning Dominel went to bed, having learned more than he had ever wanted to about the mind feeders.

Later that day, he wandered the woods, enjoying the late afternoon sun. Melanie was in a clearing, practising blows against a tree stump with a stick she used as a training sword.

"Hail," he called.

Melanie paused in her practice. The way the sweat-soaked material of his old, blue robe clung to her lithe form caused him to swallow.

"Hello. Did you sleep well?" she asked.

"Very. Have you been practising long?" He struggled to keep his eyes on her face.

"Most of the day. Our discussion yesterday set me to thinking."

Oh, gods, I'm in for it now, Dominel thought. "About what?"

"I need a sword. Do you know anything about making them?"

"I was a prince! Princes don't work forges."

"Demon spit! I'll need a sword when we leave the valley and a better bow. Daggers are not enough."

"I'm sorry I can't help you. My sword snapped trying to slow a stone slab, remember?"

"Isn't there anything you can do?" She allowed her lashes to half cover her hazel eyes.

Dominel swallowed as she smiled at him seductively.

"All I can do is try. Maybe when we leave, you could pick up a sword before we get out of the mountains."

"The old wizards made magic swords," her voice took on a seductive lilt.

"Yes, they would enchant swords. Some of them were master smiths as well, but I'm not."

"Oh," she said pouting prettily.

Dominel, despite himself, drifted closer to her, smelling the aroma of her sweat and feeling the warmth emanating from her body.

Melanie saw him move closer. Tension gripped her, which for a moment warred with desire. She abruptly stepped away. "I have to finish my practice."

"As you will. I'm going for a swim in the river."

"But it's freezing!"

"I know! Thank the gods for that!"

Melanie's request preyed upon Dominel's mind until, while listing to Wellorm, the answer came to him.

"Once one can control one's personal energy and the flow of energy in their surrounds, one can open gates to other planes. This is important because a great deal of information may be gathered by holding discourse with beings from the other planes."

Ackdominel's ears perked.

"Is it possible for beings from the other worlds to enter ours through wizard opened gates, or do they have to use the natural ones the monsters entered through?" he asked.

"Beings can enter through wizard opened gates, so long as there is enough matter of the appropriate type for their spirits to infuse with life. In fact, some wizards used to have frequent visitors from the other planes," explained the mummy.

"You told me before that there are friendly beings in the other worlds, as well as monsters."

"Yes, there are Ki-rin, the orders of good dragons, elves, dwarves, djinn and many others. Why?"

"Would some of them be willing to aid humans?"

"They have their own problems. I doubt they would send an army!"

"Not an army. Craftsmen. And not for nothing. I would give them the mountains when the humans left. After all, they are part of my kingdom," explained Ackdominel.

"It could work. Why do you want craftsmen?"

"I need swords, bows, armour, and weapons of all kinds. The mountain range is swarming with refugees. I'll have to arm them if we're to reach the safe haven prepared for us."

"Would it not be easier to have a human smith do the work?"

"I'm sure they are. The problem is most smiths are more accustomed to making horseshoes than spearheads."

"Do what you must. I will teach you how to summon beings from the other planes and pray that it brings no grief. To begin with, you must touch the essence of the plane or dimension you wish to reach inside yourself first. For example, if you wish to reach the plane of earth, focus on your sense of stability, your practicality, your material nature. The law of attraction, that like attracts like, will see that you reach your desired goal," began Wellorm.

Ackdominel had to wait before he could put his plan into action. Wellorm would allow him no time from his studies saying that his time on earth was too short to waste. The days turned into weeks then into months. One evening Dominel entered the ceremony room and found Wellorm sitting upon his throne as usual, but his voice was faint and far away. Ackdominel spoke softly.

"Your time is nearly over, is it not?"

"Yes, Ackdominel, it is. Soon you must go to the tenth lodge. You have learned well and will soon be done with this place. Fight well!" The mummy said no more.

Ackdominel approached the mummy and stared down at a sheathed sword that rested across its knees. Reverently he removed the blade from the dead, bandaged flesh and drew it. The blade shone with a light of its own. Symbols, in a script Wellorm had taught him, ran its length. Ackdominel read the symbols aloud.

"To call and command am I."

Returning the sword to its sheath Ackdominel left what had become a tomb.

He walked to the lodge's bedroom, opened the door and looked in. Melanie lay on the bed. Smiling at her he turned and walked to the lodge's entrance. He paused to look at the quarter moon, which shone behind a light veil of clouds.

"Almost a month before I can enter the next lodge. I'll have time to call for help."

He made his way to the eighth lodge where he spent the night.

Dominel awoke shortly after dawn and climbed to the ninth lodge, where he met Melanie in the kitchen.

"You're late leaving the ceremony chamber today," she observed, as he took a seat at the table.

"Wellorm is gone."

"Then you're going to the tenth lodge. Good!"

Melanie placed a bowl of stew in front of him and sat down.

Dominel took a mouthful of the stew and paused. He gave silent thanks that, since the awakening of her memories, Melanie had taken over the cooking chores.

"When will you be starting the next lodge?"

"What? Oh… not until the new moon rises. Before then I have to go away for a while."

"Go away? Where to? The far end of the valley?"

"No, back to the chamber of the lake."

"Why?" Melanie shuddered.

"Because it is the only place where I can do what I must. I want you to stay here though."

"Oh no you don't. Where you go, I go!"

"Melanie, there's no need for you to come along. I won't be gone long."

"I'm going!"

"No, you're not."

"Yes, I am!" She put her hands on her hips and glared at him.

"No, you're not!"

Long after the stew had grown cold, Dominel realised one of the great truths that apply equally to mighty wizard-kings, or humble swineherds. No man is as stubborn as a woman!

Thus it was that he prepared two packs of supplies and set them aside for the following morning.

The day of their departure was cold and rainy, which made the cavern seem less unattractive. After shouldering his pack and donning his magical items, Dominel, who was still grumbling about female obstinacy, led Melanie to the cavern's mouth and descended into the dry darkness of the passage.

The door at the passage's end stood open as they had left it over two years before. He paused.

"What are you waiting for?" demanded Melanie.

"I'm deciding on something." Dominel pulled the crystals from the door, allowing it to close with a bang.

"Why did you do that?"

"Because we'll need light and it will keep unwelcome guests from entering the valley." Dominel placed the dark crystal in his pack.

"Guests! What guests?"

"Who can say? I've still four lodges to pass through. I'm not about to take unnecessary chances. Shall we go?"

They walked down the passage by the light of the crystal, which blazed in Ackdominel's hand illuminating the cavern fifty paces in either direction. They travelled all that day and most of the next before coming to the large, oaken door of the crystal chamber. Here Dominel lit a torch he had brought and passed it to Melanie.

"This is where I want you to wait," he said.

"I'm going in with you!"

"It is too dangerous. I can take care of myself through what I have to do, but I can't take care of you as well."

"I'm going with you." Melanie stamped her foot.

"Melanie, let me explain your options. You can stay here, or I can get the rope from my pack and tie you up. Either way, you're staying here!"

"You wouldn't dare!" She glared at Dominel.

"Enough!" said Ackdominel, in a voice that though low, throbbed throughout the cavern. "Stop being a child. I am a mystic. You are not. I will do this alone!"

Placing his hand against the door, which opened to his touch, he strode into the chamber of the lake allowing the door to close behind him.

Melanie stood silent and sullen then threw herself at the door which remained closed.

"Marvellous, just marvellous," she snarled.

Dominel held the crystal aloft, allowing its light to refract from the walls, giving the room a wondrous lustre. The marble trees seemed to sway, and the lake's surface was transformed into a billion diamond facets.

It is better like this. I don't have to swim with eels or put up with nagging, he thought.

He took several moments to let his body calm from his argument with Melanie. Finding a flat area to one side of the pier, he dropped his pack. Moving to the end of the pier he mounted the crystal of light on several knobs in the brazier's bowl. The crystal fit perfectly. Next, he tied a strip of hide to the dark crystal and lowered it into the lake, securing it to the brazier's stand. An eel bumped into the black crystal and turned to stone.

Nasty, but at least there its magics won't disrupt my ritual, he thought and returned to his preparations.

Soon Ackdominel stood within a circle scribed in chalk on the floor and consecrated to the four elements. A triangle filled with stones was marked to the north of the circle. He reached with his mind probing the rock around him, reaching beyond the rock to the essence of rock, then beyond that essence to the home plane of rock. He sought a mind open to his own. When he was about to give up, he sensed something. Ackdominel opened the way and spoke, "Hello."

"Hello. Who be there? This better no' be a trick, or I'll bury ye bones," replied a gravelly voice.

"It is no trick. I am Ackdominel, child of the Secret Path. I wish to speak to a citizen of the elemental plane of earth."

"Do ye now. Let's have a look at ye."

Ackdominel concentrated on the triangle. He found himself and his circle in a world as different from any he knew, as night is from day. Light glistened all about him. Energy flowed on all sides of his circle. He felt as if he was in an endless corridor with rooms branching off in all directions. A strange figure stood in front of him.

It was shaped like a stocky man with a large nose, bushy, grey-flecked, brown hair and beard. It could have passed for a man, save it stood roughly half a man's height.

"So ye be a human. I was thinking they'd killed all their wizards," said the little figure.

"Almost all. May I ask the name of to whom I speak?"

"Me name! I can't be telling ye me name! If ye be knowing me name, I be in ye power. I won't be placing meself there, I won't."

"I'm sorry. Actually, I meant what others call you."

"Oh, if that be all. Call me Tom, wizard and healer, second grade. Why do you be callin' the plane of earth, I'd like to know?"

"I've a proposition for you. I need tradesmen to supply arms to help me reclaim my world and if it can be arranged, warriors."

"Tradesmen and warriors ye be saying. What be in it for us?"

"The richest gift any can give."

"Gold?" Tom looked vaguely interested.

"That's only a small part of it."

"Gems?" asked Tom, greed obvious in his aspect.

"They are nothing compared to my gift, though they are part of it."

"Magic?" The dwarf now looked ready to burst with acquisition.

"Part, but not all."

"What?" Tom was nearly slavering.

"The mountains from which I cast my thoughts. All that rest two or more man lengths below the surface, I will give you for your aid. It would be yours to rule as a free principally under the sceptre of the king."

"Ye can't be given us that. The land be the king's."

"I am the king! Last of my line. All I ask in return for this is that your people swear fidelity to me, as a principality under my sceptre. I will charge thee with the defence of the mountain realms and call on thee for a tithing of arms."

Tom hummed, obviously deep in thought then he spoke. "A free principality ye be saying?"

"As any other in my realm."

"And who would be prince?"

"Whoever the dwarves that come choose. Think of it. All the stone in these mountains. The vast underground realm you could have and all the hidden riches yours for the finding."

"It be a deal. Imagine Prince, Frack Mik Nak, of...." Tom fell silent and paled. "Ye heard it. Handsome is as handsome does. Don't be using me name agen' me."

"Of course not, good Prince. So long as you and your subjects are loyal unto me, and my descendants, your name need never be mentioned again."

"Ye be a good and gracious king. I'll be needin' time to be gathering me subjects and some essentials."

"When should I reopen the gate?"

"There be no need of that, Ye Majesty. I'll be gone but a few moments. Haven't they taught ye time don't be meaning a thing?"

"I forgot," replied Ackdominel, not wanting to reveal his ignorance to the dwarf.

Tom flashed out of view then returned.

"All right now, be opening the door," called Tom.

Ackdominel closed his eyes and concentrated. Suddenly he was back in the crystal chamber, staring at the pile of stones in the triangle. They stirred and shifted until they formed into the figure of Tom, only now because his body had been born of stone, his skin was grey.

"I've two hundred others that be on their way," said Tom.

Ackdominel grabbed his sword, snatched a pebble left over from Tom's entrance into the world from the triangle, and ran towards the door with Tom in hot pursuit. Throwing open the door Ackdominel rushed by Melanie and jammed the pebble onto the passage's wall. Using his sword point, he traced a large triangle about the pebble and stood back.

The rock within the triangle formed into a diminutive figure, which when it was complete stepped forward and bowed.

"Benwick at your service, Your Majesty," said the second dwarf.

Ackdominel acknowledged Benwick with a smile. Another dwarf was already forming at the back of the short triangular passage left by Benwick's entrance.

"I hope there's enough rock," muttered Dominel.

"There be," said Tom. "So this be me principality. Well, I'll say that room with the crystals be a fine bit of work. We'll be a bit setting things to rights in the rest of the place."

Melanie pushed past Tom to glower at Dominel.

"What in the names of all the gods are you doing?" she demanded.

Dominel smiled at her and said, "Melanie, I would like you to meet our new ally, Prince Tom, of the dwarfen principality of..."

Tom provided, "Crystavan."

Melanie stared at Tom then screamed. "As if we don't have enough problems with trolls! You have to bring dwarves!"

At that moment the fourth dwarf was stepping out of the ever-deepening passage. In a flash, its battle axe was out, and a fury entered its eyes. "Trolls! Where be they? I'll cut 'em down! That's why I be here, haven't had a good fight in a hundred years."

"They're not here yet," explained Dominel.

The dwarf looked disappointed and walked down the passage to join the others. Melanie fell silent.

When the last Dwarf had arrived, Dominel warned Tom about the trapped tunnels, collected his equipment and began his journey to the surface. That first march

Dominel and Melanie only walked far enough to escape the clamour of the incoming dwarves before stopping to eat and sleep.

Dominel busied himself by pulling a blanket from his pack while trying to ignore Melanie's glowering gaze.

"When you said you were calling for help, I thought they'd be humans. Not, not...."

"Dwarves. They're living creatures like you or me. They're our friends."

Melanie snorted. "At least they kill trolls. They can't be all bad."

"Don't concern yourself. Once we leave the mountains, you probably won't live long enough to see them again. They'll keep the mountains free of monsters, and by the time we humans fight our way back to them, we'll both be long dead."

Melanie had never considered the possibility of the war lasting beyond her lifetime. The thought daunted her, and she fell silent.

Chapter 9
Troubles to be Dealt With

The next day Dominel and Melanie walked to the mine's door and placed the crystals in their slots to find they had no effect.

"Demon spit!" muttered Dominel.

"What is it?"

"The door won't open until dawn."

"What? Can't you do anything?"

"No."

Dominel wasn't sure when he fell asleep, but he knew he dreamt. In his dream, he saw his teachers as they had been in life. They sat about him in a ring.

"Hello," opened Ackdominel.

His teachers remained silent.

"Have I done something wrong?"

Franlor spoke.

"It is nothing you have done, Ackdominel. The pattern is decaying faster than we expected. The shields are less durable than we had hoped."

"The shield about the mountains is strong."

"For a time. Many of the other orders' shields are failing, and their students are less ready than you."

"What can I do?"

"Little. Continue your studies and aid the members of the other orders, no matter your personal feelings."

Dominel was shaken into wakefulness by a dwarf with a shaggy, black beard and a round merry face.

"I be begging yur pardon, but I was about finding yur," said the dwarf.

"Oh... Who are you? What do you want?" demanded Dominel. He sat up and with a groan remembering why beds had been invented.

"If it be pleasing, Yur Majesty, they call me Tuck. We've a problem."

"What is it?"

"If Yur Majesty will be allowing my impertinence. Seems yur were making a small oversight when yur were calling us."

"What?" demanded Dominel, as the ceremony he'd used flashed through his mind.

"Well, if yur will be pardoning me saying so. T'ain't no food," answered Tuck.

"Food? Of course! I'm a fool. You need food. I can't do anything until morning when this door opens, but I've a store of provisions. I collected them for when I lead the humans out of the mountains. You're welcome to them."

"Can't open the door 'till morning, yur say? Why be that?"

"It's magically locked."

"Well, I guess we'll be havin' eel for a tother day."

"Eel?" asked Dominel, in vengeful glee.

"Yes. We be catching those beasties since yur left. Travelling be hungry work."

"As soon as morning comes we can bring up the stores."

"No! Pardon, Yur Majesty, if me people be caught in the sun of yur world our spirits be going back where we be from, and our bodies be turning to stone."

"You'll have to get the food the following night then. Tell me something. If you can't go outside, how will you grow food?"

Tuck chuckled before replying. "Yur see, Yur Majesty, we be havin' farms back home, where the sun don't be as strong as yur's, as don't need the light of day. We grows what yur folks be calling mushrooms. Trouble is, it'll be a while afore our plants take."

Dominel spoke with Tuck until the door opened. Waking Melanie, he left the cavern for the surface world. He spent much of that day avoiding Melanie, who was in as foul a mood as he had ever seen her. Finally deciding to face her displeasure he joined her in the meadow where their first lean-to had stood.

"Say it so we can clear the air," he began.

"Say what?" she asked, all innocence.

"Tell me you don't like me bringing dwarves to our world. Tell me that there are already enough nonhumans here. Tell me that no good will come of it."

"Why should I? You just did!"

"You drive me mad! I'm trying to save our world. We're outnumbered. Not a chance of winning, and you complain about me calling allies!"

"When they're not human!"

"Gods and demons, woman! They're our friends! They hate the monsters as much as we do!"

"No one hates the monsters as much as me!"

"Grow up! Do you think you're the only one who has a score to settle? Those beasts killed my parents, my brothers, took my family's kingdom, made me a refugee in my own land. And don't forget I experienced what you did, every bit as much as you. I just refuse to let hate blind me to reality. Why do I bother? Go on. Wallow in your hate and self-pity. I've better things to do!"

Dominel stomped out of the clearing, leaving Melanie weeping.

He strode through the woods, anger rumbling in him like a storm, but as the sun began to wester, he grew calm and found himself feeling tired and alone. He sat by the river staring into its depths, trying to lose himself in its flow.

His perceptions were clouded by his upset, and she moved silently. Thus he was unaware of her presence until she laid a hand upon his shoulder.

Dominel leapt to his feet, turning at the same time.

"It's only me!" gasped Melanie, startled by his reaction.

"Sorry."

"I was wrong! Have been wrong, about so many things." Saying this Melanie pulled Dominel close and kissed him.

At first, the kiss was tentative, only a nervous fluttering of lips, but it soon grew more insistent. They sank to the grass at the river's side. Dominel's hands gently caressed her, testing the waters of each new experience, ready at every moment to fall back. Under his caresses she melted, tension became calm, became passion.

It was nearly dark when Dominel rose from the grass, feeling a placidness he hadn't felt in years.

Melanie looked at him warmly. "I never dreamt it could be like this."

Dominel smiled at her. "We had better get back to the lodge. The sun's almost down."

"I know, but it's so delicious here."

Melanie stood and pulled on her light-blue robe.

Dominel led the way to the lodges and had only topped the stair when he heard dwarfish voices in the passage before him.

"Hail. It's almost sundown," he called.

"Greetings, Yur Majesty," hollered Tuck.

Smiling Dominel entered the passage. Upon reaching the door, he could see a line of dwarves disappearing into the darkness.

"Have you brought the whole kingdom?" gasped Dominel.

Tuck smiled where he stood at the head of the line. "There be only fifty of me people, if it be pleasing, Yur Majesty. The others they be busy turning the mine into our home. By the by, you wouldn't have a map of the place, would yur?"

"I'm afraid I don't, why? Have you run into trouble with the traps?"

"Not a bit. It just be searching the place will be taken awhile. We should have been about bringing the tothers."

"Others?"

"Aye, there's more be wanting to come. We figured it be best to start small. So the first group can be getting things set for them as follows."

"Very wise. It looks like the sun's gone down. Let's get you that food."

The next hour saw a steady procession of dwarves marching to the lowest lodge then carrying pots of foodstuffs nearly as large as themselves to the mine entrance.

Eventually, the job was done. Tuck and Dominel stood before the mineshaft, looking at the containers within.

"Will that be enough to last you? There is a little more in the lodge if you need it," said Dominel.

"Aye, if it be pleasing, Yur Majesty. It should be lasting until we be harvesting our first crop. We don't need as much as humans in the way of vittles."

"I'm glad to hear it."

"Aye, it's our nature. If Yur Majesty would be excusing me, I'd best be moving. Prince Tom be waiting on these vittles."

"Of course, and good journey to you."

In minutes the dwarves were out of sight. Dominel descended to the ninth lodge where Melanie waited for him.

"Is it done?" she asked, an edge in her voice.

"Yes, they've food enough to keep them until they can grow their own." Dominel walked over and kissed her.

"Good! You can relax for the rest of the month."

"No. I still have to summon other aid."

"What! You're not summoning more unhuman creatures are you?"

"Yes, I am! I am going to call the Sylvan plane of the elves. I intend to ask if they would aid us for the area above ground in the mountains. Legend has it that they're incredible archers."

"Elves! Bad enough you give our world to dwarves! At least they stay underground, but to give the surface to elves. Where will humans live? Should we sprout wings and fly!"

"Humans will live where they always have. Millions have died in the war. We couldn't hold all the kingdoms if we tried. There's more than enough room for our allies. Furthermore, I didn't give all the kingdom away, only the area of the mountains!"

Melanie glared at him. Dominel rose and walked to the door.

"Where do you think you're going?" she demanded.

"To the eighth lodge, where I can get some peace."

"Don't you dare leave this lodge! Not unless you want the first time to be the last!"

Dominel paused at the door. The very nature of the threat enraged him. "Melanie, loving is a gift two people give each other, not a reward for submission to another's will. If you don't see it that way, then earlier was a mistake!" He stomped out of the lodge.

They didn't speak for several days, nurturing their respective grudges. Finally, the night of the full moon arrived, and Ackdominel moved to the clearing he had chosen for his ritual.

Using his sword, he traced triangles about two trees. He then cast a circle about himself. Facing a different compass point for each, he called the elements of creation, earth, air, fire and water, to guard his circle and aid him in his rites. Standing in the completed circle, he began chanting softly, feeling the energies as they flowed about him. Raising the wand he had been given in the fifth lodge, he called aloud.

"Wood and stream, on moonbeam.

"Breeze that blows, oh masters of bows.

"Power and stealth, I call the elf."

A hush fell over the woods. Not a breath of air stirred. Slowly a light formed in one of the triangles. The light grew and solidified into a figure, almost human in appearance, save that its skin shone with the radiance of a star and its ears formed delicate points, which protruded from under its long, silver hair. The being was tall and slender, clad in a robe of leaf green that matched the colour of its eyes. It personified beauty and majesty.

"Why do you call the Sylvan plane, mortal?"

"I am Ackdominel."

"I know who you are, mortal, and the state of your world. What is it you wish?"

Ackdominel swallowed. He had met many kings and queens, but never had he seen such nobility. He inhaled deeply and spoke. "To ask your aid. Soon I must lead my people to the haven the wizards of old prepared, and I will need bows to aid in our struggles. Also, I do not wish to surrender the mountain regions to the monsters uncontested. Thus I ask that you send me any of your people who wish to come. They may have the forest regions of the mountains, as a principality under my sceptre."

"You bargain fairly, mortal. I am King Aneleal, high lord of my people. My youngest son, Talion, is recently come to adulthood and desires lands. As well, there are those of my people who wish to hear the song of the bowstring. I will see what may be done."

"Thank you, Your Majesty. In the beginning, I must ask that you send no more than two."

"Fear not, mortal. I know your mind. I will send no more than you can feed." Saying this Aneleal disappeared.

Ackdominel stared at the trees in the triangles as they slowly moulded into new forms. At first, he wondered if Aneleal himself was coming. Then the wood shifted farther, and colour flowed into the statue-like forms. Ackdominel could now see one was a being like unto

Aneleal, save that its hair was black as midnight under stormy skies. Ackdominel looked to the other tree and what he saw took his breath away.

Within the triangle was a stunningly beautiful maiden. Her skin was a rich shade of tan, while her body was tall and slender, like a young birch tree. Golden hair fell to her waist, shimmering like sunbeams. The points of her ears were barely visible through her hair. Above all else, it was her face that captured his gaze. Her forehead was high but showed no crease, as if it had never known a frown. Her eyes were like two emerald pools. Her nose was slender, ending in a slight round over a pair of full, cherry-red lips and a strong chin. Both figures stepped from the triangles, their long green robes rustling on the grass as they did so.

Ackdominel forced himself to the task of the moment and, with a last look at the beauty of the elfin maiden, dismissed the elemental powers and opened his circle.

Turning to the male elf, he spoke. "Greetings, Prince Talion, may the stars shine brightly on our meeting."

The elfin maid giggled. The sound was like water falling on the parched earth. "He is well spoken, Talion my love."

"For one of his short-lived kind, Qulinea, for one of his kind!" replied the male elf, in tones that left no doubt about what he thought of humans.

"I assume you are the human I must pledge my allegiance to," continued Talion, making it sound as if he'd been told to follow the orders of a retarded baboon.

Gods! What have I brought upon myself? thought Dominel before replying. "Yes, I am King Dominel. Last of my line and."

"Yes, yes. Where is the patriation ceremony to be held?"

Dominel forced a smile. "There will be no formal ceremony. I am king in exile, as you know."

"Peasant race," muttered Talion, dropping to one knee. He drew the sword that hung at his waist and handed it hilt first to Dominel.

Dominel took the blade then after a moment's thought spoke the pledge his father had used with his vassal lords.

"Do you, Talion, Prince of the Elfin Realm, pledge to defend my kingdom and sovereignty against all threats? To be forever loyal unto me and uphold the laws set forth by my crown, as it is held by me and my descendants? Until the end of time?"

"I do."

"Then as is my right. I make you prince of the earthly elfin kingdom of the Barrier Peaks, ruler of its lands under me."

So saying Dominel tapped Talion on each shoulder with the sword and handed it back to him.

Talion rose to his feet and with an imperial look at Dominel demanded "Where is my castle?"

"You and your Lady may have the lodge under mine in the mountainside," Dominel gestured towards the lodges.

"You live underground, like some dwarf!" exclaimed Talion.

"Do not be ungracious, my love. He does not know our ways," soothed Qulinea.

"Very well," breathed Talion. "Your Majesty. It is not in the nature of my people to live underground."

"I am sorry my offer offended you." Dominel barely mastered his temper. "If you prefer, you may sleep under the stars, until a suitable dwelling has been made."

"This I will do. First, show me exactly where you dwell."

"A moment, Your Highness. Before anything else, we've a debt to pay. Bringing you into this world has cost the forest."

Saying this, Dominel moved to where the trees that had become the elves had been. Nothing was left of the trees but sundered leaves and wood chips. Sighing he picked up two potted saplings, which he proceeded to plant where the trees had stood.

"I took these from where many saplings were competing for life. They would have died without my intervention. I hope the nature spirits are appeased."

"You put us to shame. We, beings of the forest, forget our duty and a human remembers. Thank you, Your Majesty," said Qulinea.

Dominel beamed to hear the warmth and praise in her voice. Turning he led them towards the lodges.

Soon they stood at the base of the mountain stair. Dominel excused himself and entered the lowest lodge emerging momentarily with a selection of dried foods drawn from his remaining stores.

"You must be famished after your journey."

"Is this how you welcome royalty on your world, with dry old husks?" sneered Talion.

Dominel felt his temper rising and this time made no effort to control it.

"Who in the cosmos do you think you are? I've greeted you with the best I have. Given you every courtesy. The least you can do is be polite!"

"How dare you?" began Talion.

"Silence! If you did not notice, I am King! You are a prince under me. If you cannot abide this, I need not your help!"

"Why you arrogant clown! Call yourself a king! In my world, you wouldn't be a scullery drudge! I'll teach you a lesson you won't forget," screamed Talion, reaching for his sword.

Ackdominel looked at Talion and pushed with his mind.

"Put. It. Down!" Ackdominel commanded.

Talion gasped, sweat breaking out on his brow.

"Put. It. Down!" repeated Ackdominel.

With a cry, Talion dropped the sword.

"Good! Let us understand each other. It is clear your father sent you to me more of his will than yours. Furthermore, I can understand his motivations."

Talion made to interrupt, but Ackdominel silenced him with a gesture.

"Now what you must understand is that there are advantages to your situation. You can build a realm free of your father's rule. In addition, for many years after my people and I depart, you will be for all practical purposes autonomous of higher authority. What I offer you is freedom and responsibility. Now prove yourself a ruler and accept them both. I've no tolerance for spoiled children!"

Talion glared at Dominel before hissing a reply. "If my father knew how you have abused me he'd--."

"Laugh and say it was just what you needed," finished Qulinea. "I love you, that is why I came with you, but we must be honest with ourselves."

Melanie's acid edged voice called from above. "So these are our allies."

Dominel bit his lip and rolled his eyes skyward before speaking.

"Prince Talion, Lady Qulinea, I'd like to introduce my friend, the Lady Melanie."

Talion glanced towards Melanie, and all traces of hostility left him. He bowed deeply and spoke as he straightened.

"Greetings, Melanie, who is surely the fairest of mortal women."

Melanie descended the stair and stopped at its base, staring at Talion. Her cheeks flushed in the moonlight.

"Greetings, Your Highness," she breathed, dropping into a curtsy.

Dominel shook his head and slipped aside to where he could whisper to Qulinea.

"Is he always so militant?"

"Only with men. With women, I often believe I should get a leash and collar for him!" Qulinea smiled.

"Is Melanie in any danger?"

"Only if she wishes to be. I know our ways are not yours and you humans usually choose one mate at a time. I will make it clear to him that I do not welcome her into our marriage group. That will be the end of it. It is my right to bar any I do not wish to join us. Such is our law."

"Good!" remarked Dominel, with such obvious relief that Qulinea laughed.

A short time later Dominel and Melanie climbed the stairs to their lodge, while Talion and Qulinea, wrapped in blankets and Talion's cloak, settled beneath a tree.

Dominel fell into bed, while Melanie sat in the chair that adorned this lodge's sleeping quarters, brushing her hair.

"I didn't know they were so like us," she remarked.

"They're elves. They look like us outside, although the differences run deeper than it appears, much deeper." Dominel responded jealously.

"Oh, posh. They seem nice, and Talion is so handsome."

"He's elfin fair, and argumentative, and demanding!"

"I didn't find him so." Melanie smiled as she watched Dominel from the corner of her eye.

"Well, I did," spat Dominel, as he rolled over and punched the pillow.

Melanie's smile broadened as she stood and began easing out of her robe.

Dominel sat up in bed staring. "What are you doing?"

"Getting undressed, silly. Now that I've seen the elves and approve, we don't have anything to fight about."

Dominel shook his head but gave up any attempt to understand the situation when Melanie's lips pressed firmly against his own.

Chapter 10
Subjects for an Elfin Realm

Dominel helped Talion build a shelter from living pine trees trimmed to suit the elf's specifications. They finished on the day preceding the new moon leaving Dominel free of all other obligations when he entered the eleventh lodge.

Stepping into the lodge, he noticed that the main room was larger than in the lower lodges and the walls were draped with tapestries. He walked to the ceremony room and entered it.

Ackdominel froze. The other ceremony rooms had each contained part of a corpse. This room didn't. Instead, there was a silver circle on the floor, containing an empty throne. On the far side of the room, outside the circle, he could see a silver triangle, with a crystal in its centre.

Entering the circle, he traced it with his sword and summoned the elements before sitting upon the throne. The triangle before him began to glow and smoke rose from the crystal, coalescing into the translucent figure of a man. The man appeared to be in his mid-thirties, with grey-flecked, black hair, a narrow face, brown eyes and a wiry build.

"Greetings, Ackdominel, I am Kretras," said the phantom.

"Greetings, are you my teacher?"

"In a manner of speaking. I am here to aid you in realising what you already know."

"What do you mean?"

"You have learned what you must know, but you have yet to realise the extent of your knowledge. You are unaware of your potential. It is my task to help you explore your abilities."

"Very well. Before we begin, please tell me why this room is different from the ones before it?"

"You are now a master. It is unsightly for a master to kneel at the feet of another. Thus the throne is for you. As well, if you wished, you could speak freely with the dead. Your teacher need not have a physical form. Can you not see my spirit clearly?"

"Yes, I see you clearly. Could you tell me how to speak with the dead?"

"You already know. I will aid you to see what you know."

Kretras asked a series of questions that Ackdominel answered. A few minutes later Ackdominel knew how to visit the dead and the dangers involved in doing so.

As he continued his studies, he became calmer, and he saw the greater depths from which troubles arose. Once more life became routine, allowing him to relax.

It was nearly two months after Talion's arrival that he came to Dominel who lay sunning himself by the river.

"Greetings, Your Majesty."

"Greetings, Your Highness! How are you and your lovely mate?" Dominel emphasised highness.

"We are well. I need you to bring more of my people into this world to be my subjects!"

"Do you ask a boon of me? Prince, Talion."

Talion flushed. "I... I... ask of you a boon, Your Majesty," he replied through clenched teeth.

"Good, I will grant your request. After all, it's no good being a prince without subjects. Have you considered food and shelter for them?"

"My father will send provisions to aid in establishing this principality. It was discussed before I came."

"Good."

Evening found Ackdominel in a forest glade with twelve trees standing inside triangles at his circle's edge. Talion and Qulinea stood to one side of the glade, with a pile of saplings, awaiting the arrival of their people.

Ackdominel cast his spell. The trees took shape, hard wood becoming soft flesh. Minutes later twelve elves stood where the trees had been. Ackdominel swayed wearily in his circle. The elves stretched their long, slender arms, tan in the moonlight. Each was like unto Talion or Qulinea, as any human to another and all possessed an unearthly beauty.

"Prince Talion," said one elf stepping from his triangle. His hair was a mixture of silver and gold, and while no signs of age were apparent on his face, Ackdominel knew he was ancient.

"It is good to see you, Shalor," said Talion.

"As it is to see you, my Prince," replied the aged elf, who bowed. The oversized sleeves of his robe brushed the grass. "And you sir, must be King Dominel. Aneleal sends his regards." Straightening Shalor bowed to Dominel.

Ackdominel, having recovered somewhat from his efforts, bowed then spoke. "I am King Ackdominel, and I greet you. Is all well with your noble ruler?"

"He is well. He wishes me to give you this gift." Shalor handed Ackdominel a fine wooden box.

Ackdominel opened the box reverently. Within was a pair of bracers wrought from the finest gold and jewels. Each was covered by a design of interlocking rings.

"They are beautiful! I wish I had a gift to give in return."

"You have already given his son a realm to rule. That was the greatest gift any could give."

"Thank you." Ackdominel paused, where he'd touched the bracer his hand tingled. "There is more to these than meets the eye."

"Yes. King Aneleal would not share their secrets with me. If Prince Talion allows, you and I can together delve their mysteries."

"Are you a sorcerer?"

"Of my kind. My spells are of a nature that would do little to aid you in your present need. I can, however, summon my brethren to this realm."

"Hu hum," interrupted Talion. "If you two are finished?"

"Oh, of course. After you, Your Highness," said Ackdominel.

Talion led Dominel about the circle of elves, introducing him. They then planted saplings to take the places of the trees that had formed their bodies, as Dominel wearily made his way to the lodge and his lesson.

Weeks passed, and with each day Dominel felt his competence as a wizard increase. One day, as he emerged from the ceremony room, Melanie confronted him.

"One of those creatures from the mine came here last night," she growled.

"Oh. What do the dwarves want?"

"I don't know! It said it wanted to meet you at the mine's entrance."

"Hmm... I wonder what they could want?"

"I told you I don't know! I'll tell you one thing. I don't want those miserable malformed creatures parading up here constantly!"

"It's the first time one of them has visited us in months. I'd hardly call that constantly."

"Too often for my liking! Those things shouldn't even be on this world!"

Dominel shook his head and left the lodge. He found the dwarf in the shadows behind the cavern's door and smiled when he recognised Tuck. "Greetings. Melanie didn't tell me it was you."

"I be not surprised about that. She's a mean one she is."

"I'm sorry if she said anything to offend you."

"Not to be worrying yurself, Yur Majesty. Yur the one who be important to us, and you treat us kind."

"Thank you. Why did you want to see me?"

"Well, Yur Majesty, I've a wee bit of yur tithing."

"Already! I was expecting you to set the mine in order first!"

"That we did, Yur Majesty. If it be pleasing yur, we dwarves be fast workers and stone be our element. We can smell a vein of ore through the stone and call the rock to ease us on our way."

"Excellent! May I see the weapons?"

Tuck unrolled a long slender bundle of cloth. Within were five swords and several daggers. Dominel hefted a sword. After so many years the blade felt strange in his hand. He tested its balance then flicked the metal with his fingernail. The blade gave out a pure high-pitched ring.

"Beautiful!" he exclaimed, as he sent the sword whistling in an arc over his head.

Tuck beamed. "Aye considering we don't be having all the tools we be needing, it be a fair job."

"Fair? These are some of the finest weapons I've ever seen! If this is fair, your good must be wondrous!"

Tuck's chest inflated with pride, and his height seemed to increase.

"I must show these to Melanie. They'll win her over for sure."

"I be doubtin' that, but yur can be trying. We'll be having more soon. Prince Tom be letting more of our people in now we be having things arranged."

"Good. What are your numbers?"

"We be nigh three-hundred."

"Do you need anything?"

"No' that I can be thinkin' of. Our fungus farms be fine, and while I don't be speaking again' the food of yur kind, I be liking the dishes me mother made."

Dominel chuckled and rolled the swords back into the cloth. "Thank you for the swords." He hefted the weapons under one arm.

Tuck turned and strode into the darkness of the passage.

Chapter 11
Friends and Enemies

When Dominel entered the lodge, Melanie was waiting for him.

"What did it want?" she demanded.

Dominel shrugged before replying. "They just wanted to drop off a portion of their tithe. Nothing you'd be interested in, dwarfen blades would be beneath you."

"Swords!"

Melanie snatched the bundle from Dominel's arms.

"Are you sure you want to see them. After all, dwarves made them?" teased Dominel, as she unrolled the bundle on the floor. She knelt staring at the blades for a long time. Lifting one she swung it experimentally.

"The balance is excellent," she remarked. Then she flicked the blade with her fingernail, "The temper is good."

"Yes. It will be interesting to see their work when they have all their equipment together."

"I'm going to see the elves about making scabbards for my blades."

"Blades?" commented Dominel, as his eyebrows rose.

"Of course. I'll need a sword and several daggers."

"Melanie, I believe it's polite to say please."

"Don't be silly," chided Melanie, as she left the lodge.

Dominel stared at the three remaining swords. Melanie had taken all six daggers as her own.

"I think when I move to the next lodge, I'll let her keep this one, alone," he murmured before going to bed.

Dominel had barely closed his eyes when a noise awakened him. Rising he moved to the door of his sleeping chamber. Melanie stood in the lodge's doorway, sword in hand, holding back an unseen foe. The sound of metal striking metal filled the air. Dominel scanned the shield, it was intact. He leapt to a place behind Melanie. Sweat dripped from her, mingling with the blood from a cut on her thigh.

Ackdominel flared with rage. Words spilt from his lips and Talion was jerked back to dangle in mid-air beyond the balcony's edge. Ackdominel stepped forward and turned to Melanie.

"Are you hurt badly?" he asked.

"No. This is your fault! You invited these horrid elves!"

"Stop raving and tell me what happened."

"I went to the elf's village to get scabbards for my blades, and that filthy elf asked where I had got my sword from. I told him the dwarves living in the mountain.s He pulled out his sword, shouted he was going to kill you and ran towards the lodges. I caught up to him at the door to our lodge. That bastard attacked me when I wouldn't let him in to kill you! This is your fault for bringing elves into our world. I told you not to!"

Melanie strode to the sleeping chamber.

"Talion, what is the meaning of this?" Ackdominel turned to glare at the dangling elf.

"You lying trickster. You son of a viper. Put me down, and I'll teach you!" screamed Talion, flailing helplessly in the air.

"If you don't stop insulting me and start explaining yourself, I will put you down. Faster than you think!"

Talion looked beneath him to the distant ground and swallowed.

"You said this would be my land," he explained, a quaver in his voice.

"And so it is."

"You gave it to the dwarves."

"I did not. I gave them everything underground. I gave you everything above ground. Remember the wording of our agreement."

"You equivocating demon."

"Hardly. Just trying to do what's best for my kingdom!" Ackdominel gestured, and Talion drifted to the balcony. "I trust you are now ready to be reasonable about this?"

Talion snorted in reply.

Dominel continued in a soothing tone. "Your people do not mine, do they?"

"No."

"Of course not," said Ackdominel. Looking over the valley, he marked the approach of the other elves. "You are creatures of the sun and stars, of the open air."

"Well, yes." Talion found his temper mysteriously draining away.

"Dwarves are creatures of the shadows, who live in caves and mine the earth's secret riches. They can't even face the light of day."

"They can't?" Talion now felt calm.

"Of course they can't. In a way, I have done you a favour by inviting the dwarves to live under the mountains."

"How?" asked Talion softly.

"Because they can mine the riches of the world below and you can trade with them. Just think what your goldsmiths could do with the gold the dwarves can supply. You could be the richest prince in all the elfin realms."

"Yes, trade. But what?"

"Things made from wood. And wine. Dwarves love wine."

"Wood and wine. Dwarves can't get those for themselves, can they?"

I have him now. If only Shalor keeps silent, I might pull this off, thought Ackdominel. The first rank of elves was climbing the stairs, swords drawn.

"Talion, maybe you should tell your subjects that we have come to an understanding," suggested Dominel.

"What? Oh yes. Hold, my subjects! I have discussed what has occurred with this mortal and have found that he did us no ill. It was through the ignorance of his kind that a problem developed. We need not fight!"

The elves on the stair looked from one to another, collectively shrugged and sheathed their swords.

With minor variation, this act was repeated three more times, as new groups of elves approached and Dominel lead Talion to the base of the stair. Finally, when Dominel was beginning to breathe easier, Shalor arrived. Ackdominel moved towards the elfin sorcerer saying "Greetings, Shalor." While speaking with his thoughts, *Don't say anything! Let me explain.*

Shalor looked puzzled then glancing at Talion, saw the glow of wizardry. The elves who had charged to the attack were now milling about asking questions. Talion raised his hands for silence.

"My fellow elves, I have found there is no insult given us by having the dwarfen kingdom below. King Dominel has explained to me the situation. They hold claim to the places of stone below us, while we hold claim to the surface. Furthermore, we can turn this to our betterment. Within the earth is great store of gold and jewels, which we can trade for with common wood and wine," began Talion in an officious voice.

Dominel signalled for Shalor to follow him and stepped into the woods.

"Explain your actions and be quick or by all the gods, wizard or no, you're an acorn," threatened Shalor.

"I couldn't let him kill me, and no one wants a war among those who should be allies. My only choices were, force him to see reason, or drop him off the cliff."

"Will it have a lasting effect?"

"No. I only made him accept the advantages of having the dwarves below. The rest of his mind is inviolate."

"That I can believe. He's as long winded as ever," said Shalor, as Talion's voice droned on about trade with the dwarves.

"And as obnoxious. Manipulating him was not something I wanted to do. It was that or kill him."

"You need not worry. I shan't tell anyone of what you did."

"Thank you." Dominel shook Shalor's hand. "I could nearly kill for something to eat. Mind-warping is tiring."

"Especially on someone as headstrong as my Prince."

Shalor and Dominel began walking towards the elfin village.

"Hadn't I best return to the stair? I should be there when Talion finishes his speech," observed Dominel.

"You have an hour at the least, then another as he answers questions."

Shortly Dominel found himself sitting in a chair made from a split log, with a bowl of fruit in front of him. The room about him was formed by the interlaced branches of several evergreens. A bed made of soft grasses, growing impossibly close together, lay along one wall. A desk, made from a living plant trained by elfin skill into a new shape, stood against the wall opposite the bed. Two chairs and a low table of trained saplings completed the room's furnishings. Dominel noted that the desk was piled with books.

"How is the settlement?" he asked.

"We are well. Not many luxuries yet, but they will come. Tell me, when do you expect to lead your people from the mountains?" Shalor sat across the table from Dominel

"I'm not sure. I still have two lodges to pass through. After that, I'll need time to organise my people. It could be several years. Why?"

"This is not good. Talion wants to extend his sway beyond the valley next spring. He already has elves working on a way of descending the cliff to the pass below."

"Demon spit! Well, I've too many things to worry about today to concern myself with tomorrow. Do you think my spell will hold?"

"I have no doubt. When I looked, there was enough energy to light a coliseum!"

"You know, it is unfortunate your wizardry is different from mine. I could certainly use the aid of other practitioners of the art."

"You can't make a pine tree an oak, or a sparrow a hawk."

The two mages talked a while before Dominel took his leave to return to the lodges. As Shalor had predicted Talion was still talking, although the size of his audience had diminished.

Talion finished his speech and moved away from the stair, allowing Dominel to ascend to his lodge, where he was met by Melanie.

"Well, what happened?" she demanded.

"The elves have agreed to accept the dwarves. They're even talking about trading with them."

"What about my leg? That filthy elf tried to kill me!"

"Yes. He thought we had cheated him."

"I don't care what he thought! I want revenge!"

"Revenge, revenge, revenge. Don't you ever get tired of that word?" sighed Dominel, crumpling onto the bench by the entrance door.

Melanie glared at him and made to speak. Dominel cut her off with a wave of his hand.

"Very well, I will give you your revenge. Come here!"

She hesitated, a worried expression on her face.

"Come here!" ordered Ackdominel.

She moved to stand in front of him.

He laid his hand on her wound and chanted in a low singsong voice. When he removed his hand, the wound had vanished without a trace.

Melanie looked at her leg and smiled then she frowned and snapped, "You promised me revenge!"

"And I have given it to you. The great Prince Talion to have fought against a mere mortal woman and not even drawn blood. That will gall him."

"You call this revenge?"

"Yes." Rising Dominel shuffled towards his bedchamber.

"I'll challenge him. I'll cut him down like wheat. I'll--."

"You, will, not! You will leave him and his people alone! Do you understand this?"

"Who are you to order me?"

"King of this land! Your family's sovereign lord! Most of all, one of the last Adepts! You will obey me in this!"

Over the next few months, Dominel arranged a series of meetings between Talion and Tom, who, despite initial antagonism, agreed to a trade pact.

#

It was with a sense of quiet triumph that Dominel made his way to the twelfth lodge. He fingered the bloodstone on the gold ring he had received for passing from the eleventh. Stepping through the entrance, he examined the entry room. Tapestries covered the walls, while mahogany chairs sat about the floor. The room itself was half as large again as any of its predecessors. Turning to his right, he entered the ceremony chamber, which contained a central throne surrounded by a circle of silver. Ackdominel cast the circle and summoned the elemental forces before taking his seat.

As soon as he settled the room began to spin. He felt reality slipping away and found himself in a fogbound world. Only the area within his circle seemed solid. Shapes appeared, flickering in and out of the fog. Several forms stepped forward forming a ring at the circle's edge.

Ackdominel inspected the beings around him. All were human, but beyond that, they shared no resemblance.

"Who are you and why have you come?" he demanded.

"We have come from our places in the land of the dead, to teach you," replied one of their number, a large man with an oval face and powerful looking arms.

"Before I only had one teacher at a time. Why is this different?"

"Those teachers taught you the way of your order. We have come to teach you other ways," explained a petite woman, with chestnut coloured hair and a pretty face.

"How can I be expected to learn all of this before this body dies?"

"We will only introduce you to our orders, ignorant whelp!" sneered a tall, slender man with a weaselly face, clad in black.

"I know you," said Ackdominel, feeling an antithesis to this being.

"Of course you do, brother," replied the weasel-faced man.

"Brother?"

"Remember the cave, fool. Remember your past life. I am Xeron."

Ackdominel felt the name echoed through the passages of his mind. Images came to him of battles. Mystic duels that shook the mountains. "You are my enemy."

"Was your enemy! As much as I despise it, I need you."

"Very well. Let us begin."

At this Xeron began to lecture about an order called the Black Path, occasionally projecting images into

Ackdominel's mind; the deeds they'd performed or methods they used.

Ackdominel knew that this order and his own had been foes. It took all his will not to lash out at the sneering Xeron.

Aftcr scvcral hours the figures about Ackdominel faded, and he found himself back in the ceremony chamber. He rose, dismissed the elements and opened the circle, before making his way to the new lodge's bedchamber.

When he rose, he found Melanie in the central room.

"So this is our new dwelling. It's nice," she commented.

"Yes. It is nice," agreed Dominel. "Umm... Melanie."

"Yes?"

"I... Well, you see... I... Um... I would like to keep this place for myself."

"Of course we will. Until you move to the thirteenth lodge."

"No. I mean, I want this place, for me. No one else."

Melanie glared at him, tears welling in her eyes.

"You don't want me with you."

"I need to be alone for a while." Dominel tried to lay a compassionate arm about her shoulders.

Melanie jerked away from him and spat, "After all we've shared!"

"We can still be friends, but right now I need to be alone."

"You don't love me anymore! You used me. You never really cared!"

"That's a lie! I loved you once. At least I thought I did, and I do care. It's just that I can't be more than a friend. The lie would tear us both to pieces."

"What did I do wrong? Tell me. I'll change."

"You didn't do anything wrong. Maybe we weren't meant to stay together. We've both grown since our relationship began. We've simply grown apart."

Melanie rose to her feet, tears streaming down her face.

"You're a son of a slime demon!" she screamed then fled.

It couldn't go on. We were driving each other mad. Couldn't she see that? thought Dominel.

That night Ackdominel entered the ceremony room with a heavy heart. Again he found himself in a world of billowing mists. On this night his instructor was an old man, with a long white beard, dressed in a flame red robe. He spoke about the Brotherhood of Fire.

Weeks later Ackdominel found himself sitting in his circle, facing his last instructor. It was a woman with short, dark hair, a petite body, medium-sized breasts, smooth, tan skin, and muscular legs showing beneath a deer-hide tunic. Her face was round with blue eyes, full, red lips and an aquiline nose. He couldn't help but notice her attractiveness.

"So you are almost done with us," she observed.

"Almost. Though I admit, my mind is swimming with everything I've been told."

"That is natural."

"Aren't you going to tell me about your order?"

"That would be useless. You will soon know all you need know of us. You see, once our orders were great friends. We aided each other often. In fact, there were many marriages between your people and mine."

"How will this tell me of your order?"

"You will soon learn. I wish to request something of you, based upon our ancient friendship."

"What?"

"That when the time comes, you act as a friend. Oh, and tell my sister I like your current form even more than the last one. She is a lucky girl. Now I will go, farewell." The woman vanished. Ackdominel found himself in his ceremony room, all the mists were gone.

He pondered the woman's words before opening the circle. He searched for the gift with his mind. Energy called to him from the corner of the room. Moving to its source, he found a wooden box with a golden eye inlaid on its lid. Opening the box, he removed a silk wrapped bundle seven inches round. Inside was a mirror, or, at least, something like a mirror. It was glass formed into a bowl, coloured black as night. Ackdominel peered into the bowl, and the black gave way to flashing lights, which in turn formed an image.

He looked upon the world from a great height. Focussing his attention on one part of the image, he descended upon it. He moved the image to the area around the mountains. Encampments of monsters blocked all the passes. He shifted his attention to the mountains' interior regions. People crowded the land. Ackdominel drew his attention from the mirror and rewrapping it, placed it in its box.

"I must hurry. My people are crowded together like beasts."

Leaving the ceremony room, he placed his magic mirror on a table in the entry room and left the lodge to wander.

As Dominel walked, he noticed that the moon was dark.

"Tomorrow I will enter the thirteenth lodge." *I wish I could feel excited, but I've been through so many lodges.*

Chapter 12
Awaken Great Sleeper

When Dominel awoke, he descended to the eleventh lodge and braced himself for a chilly reception. He knocked, but nothing happened. Knocking again he called, "Melanie."

"Go away!" snapped a voice from behind the closed door.

"I just want to talk to you."

A minute passed before the door jerked open to reveal Melanie. Anger was apparent in every aspect of her being. "Talk," she commanded.

"I'm sorry I hurt you."

"Is that all you have to say?"

"No! I came to tell you I will be entering the thirteenth lodge tonight. If you want the twelfth, you can have it."

"I don't want anything from you! Is that everything?"

"No. I also wanted to know if you would like armour?"

Melanie paused considering. "Your old stuff, you maimed it, and it's too large."

"Not my old armour. I was going to ask the dwarves."

"Those disgusting little slugs."

"Do you want armour or not?" Dominel allowed some of his ire to leak into his voice.

"Of course I do!"

"Then be in the cave tomorrow morning to be measured," ordered Dominel, who moved towards the stair.

"Dominel?"

"What?" he turned to face her.

"I've missed you." Melanie clasped her hands behind her back and swayed her hips while biting her lower lip.

"I've missed you too."

"Maybe we could, well… You know." She smiled.

"No." Dominel stared into her eyes. "You are my friend and forever shall be, but it can't be more than that. We are too different!"

"Get away from me, you demon spawn!" Melanie jerked around and stormed into her dwelling.

Dominel descended the stairs. Upon reaching the ground, he heaved a heavy sigh and moved into the woods. As he walked, he noticed the changes his time in the valley had wrought. Many of the non-fruit bearing trees had been replaced by saplings. Where once tangles of young trees had competed for light, now saplings stood evenly spaced.

In a way, my coming was a death knell for this valley. I taught the deer fear. Now they're always on guard against the hunter's bow. It's not wild anymore. I've turned it into a park. I only did what I had to, but I regret it. He sighed and turned his footsteps towards the elfin village and the home of Shalor.

The elf village had grown to a mass of buildings, constructed from living trees. Dominel moved to the wall of saplings that surrounded it and walked to the main gate.

"Halt! Who goes there?" demanded a young voice.

"Don't be silly, Yreal. Who goes there? How many male humans are there in this valley?" chided Dominel.

"I am sorry, Your Majesty. I have orders from--."

"Prince Talion! I know. By the way, un-nock that arrow. You're making me nervous."

Dominel stepped through the break in the saplings to where he could see Yreal. The young elf was replacing an arrow in his quiver. He had a long, angular face and a build that was slight even by the non-demanding standards of his people.

"Do you know where Shalor is?" asked Dominel.

"The last I saw him, Your Majesty, he was moving towards his home, muttering something about a hard-headed, spoilt brat."

Dominel suppressed the temptation to ask if Shalor had just left Talion's company. "I'll see if he's still there."

"Certainly, Your Majesty."

"Very well... If, and when I get a proper court. I could certainly use a guard as diligent as you."

Yreal straightened where he stood, and a smile came to his lips. "Thank you, Your Majesty."

Reaching Shalor's house, Dominel knocked on the narrow, wooden door.

"Enter," called Shalor.

Dominel opened the door and stepped into the dwelling's main room. It was sparsely furnished with desk, table, bed and chairs. A pair of saplings grew against the northern wall so that their branches intermeshed to form a set of shelves, which held an abundance of books.

Shalor sat at his desk with his back to the door.

"Leave the wine on the table and get me some of the steamed fruit they're preparing in the kitchen," he ordered.

Dominel smirked. "Yes, great and glorious one."

"Oh, Your Majesty. I thought you were my apprentice. I'm quite sorry." Shalor leapt from his chair.

"Not to worry and please, call me Dominel. Talion 'Your Majesties' me to death."

"You know it's funny you should mention him. I was speaking to him only a few minutes ago."

Dominel tried with only partial success to stifle a laugh.

"What's funny?" Shalor looked perplexed.

"Nothing important. I do have a matter to discuss with you though."

"What?" Shalor moved to sit at the table in the room's centre while motioning for Dominel to do the same.

"You watch the warriors when they drill, do you not?" asked Dominel.

"Occasionally."

"I know Melanie drills with them. In your opinion, how is she?"

"As a warrior, excellent! There isn't an elf in the village she cannot defeat with sword, dagger or staff. However, few will spar with her."

"Why?"

"She doesn't control herself. She fights as if it was real, not a training exercise. Her opponents are afraid of being killed."

"Would you say she's ready for actual combat?"

"Definitely! Why?"

"Because tonight I am to enter the thirteenth lodge. We'll be leaving the valley soon."

"Congratulations, my friend! We must share a drink to your success."

"I'd like that. Will your apprentice be along soon?"

A sound at the door heralded an elf entering the room carrying a jug of wine. In human terms, the elf appeared to be maybe ten years of age.

"Finally. What happened, you vint it yourself?" chided Shalor.

The boy made to speak, but Shalor silenced him with a wave.

"Everyone needs an apprentice. For a bit of bread, a slice of cheese and the annoyance of answering an incessant string of inane questions, you need never fetch your own wine again," he observed.

"He's young for the art, isn't he?" asked Dominel.

"Somewhat. He's only seventy of your years, but he's a bright lad. When he bothers to apply himself."

Dominel shook his head. It was difficult for him to adjust his thinking to the elves' lifespan and the way it affected their view of things.

"Here," said Shalor, proffering a golden goblet.

Dominel took the goblet and examined it. "Nice work. Did the dwarves supply the gold?"

"Yes. I have an arrangement with the dwarf Prince. We sell spells to one another."

"Ah yes, the brotherhood of magic. Sometimes I think a wizard would sell his own mother for a spell."

"Some would. I actually heard of a case once where--."

Dominel and Shalor chatted most of the day. Evening was drawing in as Dominel made his way to the lodges. He collected the gifts that marked his graduation from the previous levels of his craft and climbed the final flight of stairs. When he stepped upon the thirteenth balcony the lodge's door swung open, and he entered. The common room was silent, and a white light that was everywhere but came from nowhere illuminated it. Carvings of wizards performing mighty deeds covered the walls.

Silently he moved to the door of the ceremony room. It opened without a sound. He stepped through, and it closed. At first, the room behind the door was dark, but gradually a light grew until it was as bright as a full moon on a clear night.

Ackdominel examined his surroundings. He was in a circular room five strides across. The door was behind him, and the wall opposite it was covered by a blue, velvet curtain. In the centre was a throne, situated so that whoever sat upon it would be facing the curtain.

Ackdominel was awed by the power radiating from his surroundings. He felt like a child that had crawled onto the throne of a mighty king. A jester, ordered to take the throne for the amusement of the court. Reluctantly he approached the throne. It shimmered as rainbows ran over its surface. He settled himself. The curtain before him pulled back revealing a mirror. Music filled the room.

Ackdominel stared at his reflection, surprised by what he saw. The image was no longer a battered young warrior, bloodied and defeated, weary in body and mind. Now he saw a mighty wizard king, wearing objects of beauty and power. As he watched, the dark blue robe he wore changed to white. The coronet of silver upon his brow flashed, and the golden symbol of power about his neck shone brilliantly.

He stared at his reflection for a long time before he noticed an arcane script above the mirror. It read.

"NOW SEE YOUR TEACHER."

Rising he walked towards the mirror. He noticed a crystal lain on a low table in front of the mirror. The crystal was like those used to hold the life essences of his teachers. He reached out, touched it and his world exploded. The room lurched from side to side then began to spin. Everything vanished into an explosion of light. Ackdominel found himself staring down the corridor of many lives that he had seen when he was summoned to the first lodge.

There was a slave struggling in the fields, a baron battling against his neighbour, a poet, a smith, a courtesan. Then life upon life filled with magic, learning ever more about the art. Order upon order he sampled, only to cast them aside after a life or two, until he found the Secret Way. The Secret Way had held him. This was the vehicle his spirit needed. Again life followed life, ever learning, ever striving. Each life being like a single day adding to the year of his totality, each death a night of slumber and restful dreams. Finally, he touched the wizard who had sacrificed his mortal incarnation so his order, and his world, might live!

Ackdominel's head spun, as the knowledge and wisdom of countless lives flooded through him. His being took the shape of each life, until he finally returned. He was no longer Dominel, although Dominel was part of him and didn't mind being left for something greater. He was now Ackdominel, a mighty oak sprung from the acorn of his mortal life. Every fibre of his being, every thought, every move was Ackdominel. Ackdominel, who had lived from the beginning of time and would witness its end.

Opening his eyes, he rose from where he lay upon the floor. The crystal that had held the life essence of his previous incarnation was shattered. His body felt strange. It was the one he had known all this incarnation, but it felt new to him. He thought of how before the teachers would have opened the doors to his memories over many years. Now there was no time for that. The mind of this life had been prepared as best it could in the short time available before the door to the past had been wrenched open. It would be some months before his psyche could accept all that had occurred. He knew he should rest, but he couldn't afford that luxury.

Returning to the crystal throne, he closed his eyes and concentrated. There was a sensation of air rushing past. When he reopened his eyes, he found himself in a large room containing a circular table.

All about the walls were doors, each bearing the symbol of a different order. Ackdominel noted that only his order's door bore the mark indicating it had been opened since the disaster. He also saw that many of the symbols he had known were no longer present. As he watched, a door disappeared from view. Along with the door went a chair at the table and the room shrank.

"I must hurry, but who to aid first?" he whispered.

He remembered his promise to the spirit in the twelfth lodge and with it came other memories. Memories of a laughing girl dressed in deerskin and a love cruelly cut short. His wife in his last life had taught him the ways of her order, and so when her sister came to him in the twelfth lodge, she had known there was no need to teach him more. Ackdominel sighed and moved towards the door marked with a stag's horns bedecked with acorns.

He paused in thought then spoke. "No. Not yet. I have a responsibility to my own people first. I shall return when I have set the exodus in motion."

Moving to his order's door, he stepped through. There was the sensation of wind. Once more he sat upon the throne in his ceremony room. Rising he exited the lodge.

When he emerged the day was dawning, and the birds were singing.

Ackdominel hesitated as if trying to remember something then called, "Melanie."

She came rushing out of the eleventh lodge then paused staring at him.

"Dominel?" she asked.

"No, but he is here, a part of me. Come, you must be armed for our journey. We will soon depart."

"Who?"

"I am all that was Dominel brought to the fore. I am Ackdominel. Join me. The dwarves await."

Melanie climbed the stair until she stood beside Ackdominel. An aura of power radiated from the man that made the hair on her arms stand on end.

"You have changed!"

"I have awakened!" He led her to the mine entrance and down to the waiting dwarves.

Prince Tom stood behind the door with Tuck and several others.

"It be good to be seeing yur, Yur Majesty," said Tom.

"It is good to see you also, my friend."

Tom fell silent as his mouth dropped open.

"I have awakened," Ackdominel replied to the silent question.

Tom fell to his knees and signalled for the other dwarves to do so.

"Rise! We are friends, good Prince. We need no such displays. Now let us get to the purpose of this visit. You have come to prepare my companion's armour."

"Aye, that we have."

"This is well. How stands the stockpiling of weapons?"

"I be having all me people armed, and I be having a fair tithe for yur to boot. There be good iron in these mountains."

"I am pleased. How stands your dwelling?"

"It be growing it does. We have nearly five-hundred pair of hands that be working on it. Soon we'll be bringing our womenfolk to be rounding out the place."

"Good! Soon I will be passing through your realm on a journey to the world beyond the valley. I shall be glad to see it."

"It'll be an honour to have yur, it will."

Through this Melanie had stood in broody silence as the dwarves measured her but now she interrupted.

"How much longer do I have to stand here with these?"

Ackdominel turned towards her. "Until they are finished! They are masters of their craft. If you cooperate with them, I am sure you will be more than amply rewarded by the results."

"Humph," replied Melanie.

Soon the dwarves finished taking measurements and vanished into their tunnel, leaving Ackdominel, Melanie and Tom standing by the door.

"Farewell, my friend. I will soon return," said Ackdominel.

"That be good. We'll be needing the missy here tomorrow to be fitting the armour."

"Tomorrow! It takes the greatest armourers in the world weeks to make a suit," Melanie objected.

"They don't be dwarves."

"I'll be here," snapped Melanie, who left in a huff.

"I am sorry she is like this with you, but do not concern yourself. Soon I will take her away from here, and she will never live to see the mountains again."

"What be yur meaning by that, me Lord?"

"Once we leave the mountains, it will be at least two-hundred years before we fight our way back. The monsters have claimed most of my world, and we are grossly outnumbered."

"So we'll have to be holding the beasties back for two-hundred years. That be a long time."

"I know, but there is nought I can do, and unless I move quickly, all may be lost. The strongholds are failing, and unless there are enough mystics to close and guard Haven, there will be nothing the rest of us can do."

"I be wishing yur luck, but if you'll be pardoning me, I must be getting back to me throne. No telling what me people be up to when I be gone."

"Farewell," said Ackdominel.

"And yur." Tom strode down the passage.

Ackdominel walked out of the mine into the light of day. He paused to look up at the pale-blue shield above him.

It will shrink soon, and my people will lack any space in which to live. I must gather them quickly, or thousands more will die, he thought. Taking a deep breath, he made his way to the thirteenth lodge and his day's sleep.

Chapter 13
Preparations

When Ackdominel awoke, the sun was sinking into the west.

Now it begins in earnest, he thought as he entered the ceremony room and felt its energies embrace him. Moving to the throne, he sat.

It took less than a minute for him to slip his astral form free of his physical body and send it flying over the mountains.

My first stop should be Mantan. It was the largest city in the mountains before the Storm engulfed them.

He pictured the house of the Baron of Mantan as he had seen it when he travelled with the royal entourage. As fast as thought, he was there. Mantan was horribly altered. Homeless and starving littered the streets. The dead lay among the living and the living envied them. Sickness stalked the refugees, and many showed open sores. Their clothing was in rags, and the stench was overwhelming. As Ackdominel watched, a cart drawn by two men rumbled down the street. These men were dressed in rags, but less starved than the human flotsam around them. Stopping they collected the dead and threw them on the cart.

Ackdominel followed the main street to the front gate and passed into the fields beyond. The pine forest that had surrounded the city was gone, replaced by piled stone shelters. The ground, which was more rock than soil, had been put to the plough. Outside the gate, there was a shallow pit into which bodies had been dumped. To either side of the pit were mounds, supporting young wheat.

Shaking his head Ackdominel rose and stared down at the stump littered mountain slopes. In isolated places, he saw bits of green, spared by their inaccessibility. He willed himself to a new location. It was a cottage barely within the shield's protection. A young man laboured in the garden, trying to squeeze a crop from the rocky soil. Ackdominel drew closer and was about to touch the man's mind when he saw the answer to his question. In the corner of the field were two flower-covered graves.

"This is merciful, my friends. You have been spared a long and perilous journey. Maybe when you are reborn, it will be a kinder world. Rest well, Emma and Jason, you shall be remembered," murmured Ackdominel. Returning to his body he strode to the lodge's door, summoning Melanie as he did so.

Melanie stood in a clearing of the forest, training with her sword, when the summons touched her mind. She resisted the call, but slowly curiosity defeated stubbornness.

Ackdominel and Melanie met at the base of the stairs.

"Greetings," began Ackdominel.

"How dare you enter my mind?" she ranted.

"I simply called you! I wished to tell you that we will be leaving the valley as soon as your armour is ready. We must rally our people for the push to the sea."

"And then what?"

"We will retreat to the place the wizards have prepared for us."

"Retreat! I want blood!"

"And you shall have it. First, we must move those who are not skilled in combat to safety. There must be some to bring forth the warriors of the next generation. You will see blood enough in guarding their retreat."

"Not blood enough for me, but it will be a start."

"Good! Now I must go to the elfin village and have them prepare their tithe of bows. After we leave the valley, I wish to move our people within the year."

"Year!"

"Yes, year! It will take at least that long to organise our people for the exodus. Do not worry, as soon as we have adequate warriors, I have a task for you that will give you your blood."

#

Talion sat upon his throne in a long hall made of interwoven branches. His throne was made from hardy plants of a golden hue and sat opposite the room's entrance.

"Greetings, Your Majesty," sneered Talion as Ackdominel entered.

Ackdominel walked the length of the hall in silence, stopping within two strides of Talion.

"Stand in my presence, insolent Prince!"

Talion snapped to his feet, surprised by the command in the mortal's tone.

"I have come to tell you that I will soon be leaving the valley."

Talion stood in shocked silence.

"I will need bows, and I will need them quickly," said Ackdominel, as a part of him rejoiced to see Talion brought to heel. "As well, I wish a quiver and two dozen arrows to companion each bow. This was the agreed tithing of your principality, and you have been delinquent. You are to prepare the tithe and leave them with Tom's people. Have you any questions?"

"Your Majesty, I...I...I... I did not know. I...."

"You did not realise that humans are more than we seem. Learn from this, Talion. Learn that all creatures of good heart are deserving of respect. There is room in the cosmos for us all. Farewell."

The Wizard King of Bani turned and swept from Talion's throne room.

Ackdominel moved to his lodge and was soon seated upon his throne. Thinking of the council chamber, he found himself sitting at his place at the table.

Now I may aid the others with a clear conscience, he thought.

Walking to the door bearing the stag's horns and acorns he hesitated. Touching the door, he let it swing open and stepped into the darkness beyond.

He stood in a blackness his mystic sight couldn't penetrate. Guided by memories of nearly a century before, he made his way to a door. Opening it, he stepped into a hallway that sloped gently downwards, with doors on either side. The hall was dimly lit by shafts that cut into its ceiling. He noted the smell of rot and looked at the ceiling of heavy beams, which showed signs of decay. Light stabbed into the hall from its far end, blinding him.

Fearing he had come too late to save this order, he pressed himself against the wall, trying to disappear into the shadows. A silhouette appeared against the light from the door. The figure moved a bow appearing in its grasp.

"Show yourself!" commanded a feminine voice.

Ackdominel felt an urge to comply but fought it down, instead he called from where he was hidden, "I come in peace, sister of the wood."

The silhouette moved as if looking for him and demanded. "How did you enter this shrine?"

"That is of little import. What is important is that I have come to aid you."

"Are you a teacher?"

"I am a friend of your teachers. A master from another order."

"Show yourself!"

Ackdominel moved into view of his assailant.

"I mean you no harm," he stated.

The woman hesitated, arrow in hand. "How do I know I can trust you?"

"Is the shield about your woodland intact?"

The woman fell silent then replied, "Yes, it is."

"Then you can trust me." Ackdominel moved towards her.

She held her arrow levelled at his breast before releasing the tension and returning it to her quiver.

"I knew there were other orders, but I never thought I would meet their members until we reached Haven." She led the way out of the passage into the wooded clearing beyond.

"I will be leaving my refuge and am in a position to let my own defences fall. This leaves my energies free to aid you," explained Ackdominel.

Outside he could, for the first time, see the woman clearly. She was short, the top of her head barely level with his chin, with a tan, well-muscled body. Her short, chestnut-coloured hair framed a rounded, pretty face, with a pair of mischievous green eyes. She was clad in a deerskin tunic that accentuated the gentle curve of her breasts and left her smooth, almost-hairless legs visible from mid-thigh downwards. Ackdominel's heart beat faster and a lump caught in his throat at the sight of her.

"Woodreana," he whispered.

"That is what the teachers call me."

"Then that is what I shall call you."

Wrenching his eyes from her, he looked upon the stronghold of the Children of the Wood. This was different from his mountain refuge. The shield encompassed a large forest. The Wizards' stronghold was an island formed by a split in a swiftly flowing river. Behind him were the training chambers, within an earthen hill.

"Your realm is beautiful," he remarked.

"Yes, it is. But it is also shrinking."

"That is why I have come." Ackdominel heard rustling in the bushes. Reaching with his mind, he commanded the creature to reveal itself. A moment later a small beast ran towards them. The creature had the lower body of a colt, with the torso and head of a boy of seven rising from it.

Ackdominel drew his blade and moved between the centaur and Woodreana. The little beast stopped two strides from Ackdominel, tears running down its face.

"Put that thing down," commanded Woodreana.

"But it is a centaur? They are part of the Storm."

"Not this one." Woodreana pushed past him. "What is it, Chiron?"

The creature held up a cut finger and sobbed, "Mommy, I hurt myself!"

"Oh, you poor thing. I'll take care of it."

Woodreana kissed the wound and, gesturing for Ackdominel to follow, led the way to a stone cottage that blended into the hillside. On one side of its single room was a rope bed with a dresser beside it. Opposite this was a table and chair, while across from the entry door was a well-equipped hearth.

Upon entering Woodreana picked up a bowl of water and washed the centaur's cut. She then bandaged the wound and, with an admonishment to be more careful, sent Chiron out to play.

"I never thought…" began Ackdominel.

"Oh I'm sure that's not true," objected Woodreana. "You'll have to excuse me. It has been three years since I've spoken to anyone but Chiron or my teachers."

"How did you tame him?"

"He's not tamed, just loved."

"In that case, how did you find him?"

"That's a long story."

"I have time."

Woodreana motioned for him to sit in the chair while she sat on the bed.

"It happened on my way to the forest. I escaped the sacking of my village," A shadow of grief passed over her face, and she paused. "I was travelling towards the woods, having heard rumours that they were safe, when I came upon Chiron. He was standing in a stream, his hoof caught between two boulders, sobbing. I couldn't leave him. I found a staff of wood and used it to pry the boulders apart. After I bandaged his leg, he followed me and has been with me since."

"Fascinating, did not he call you mommy?"

"Why not? I've raised him."

"How did he pass through the shield?"

"My teachers say it was because his heart was pure. Many of the monsters are not intrinsically evil. They have been corrupted by the Covetous God."

"True enough. I had best do what I came to do and strengthen your shield."

"Yes of course. Will you be returning on other nights?"

"Of course I will! Have not I...." *Careful she does not yet remember. I must be on my guard. It will be hard to have her so close and not be able to hold her as my wife,* he thought.

Ackdominel became aware of Woodreana staring at him. He smiled. "Sorry. I will return. There is no way the two of us could maintain your shield. It is too large."

"Oh."

"Shall we begin?"

"Yes."

Woodreana led the way down a forest path until they came to a grove of oak trees.

"This is my place of power," she stated.

Ackdominel closed his eyes and felt around himself. Energy was everywhere.

"It is marvellous," he remarked.

"Yes, it is," agreed Woodreana, a sultry huskiness coming to her voice. "Shall we begin?"

Woodreana led Ackdominel about the clearing ringed by the trees. Their motion quickened and took on rhythm, becoming a dance to music that only adepts can hear. A dance to the rhythm of the world's life beat. As they moved energy built, roaring and surging about them. Contained by the trees, drawn from the earth, directed by the will of the dancers, the power grew. Both dancers stopped and directed the gathered force skyward. The energy contacted the shield, feeding it, making it strong. The pale green of the shield darkened. Exhausted the mystics collapsed.

"Gods and demons! I have not worked that hard since we put the shields up," panted Ackdominel, as his head swam and he fought to keep his stomach contents down.

Woodreana lay on her back looking into the branches above her. "You built the shields?"

"Yes, in my previous life. So did you."

"I don't remember." Woodreana closed her eyes in hopes that it would stop the world from spinning. "We're lucky we were born as humans again."

"My order believes that once you are born as a human, you are always human."

"Mine says you can always be born as anything. Do you think you're better than a snail?"

"Not better, more spiritually developed maybe."

"So you're better." Woodreana's world had stopped spinning, but she had no intention of trying to get up. "And because you're better you can do to the lesser creatures whatever you want."

"No. With development comes a responsibility to look out for the less developed creatures. Like an older brother for a younger. Could we discuss something else? I am not capable of arguing at the moment."

"Yes. That's a good Idea. I feel the need to sleep."

"Yes, sleep," mumbled Ackdominel, drifting into unconsciousness.

The sun had just risen when Ackdominel awoke to discover that a tree root had worn a hole in his back. He groaned as his muscles protested any attempt at movement. Using one of the surrounding oaks for support, he stood.

I must return to the valley. Melanie will be having her armour fitted soon. The last thing I need is for her to cause an incident.

He began breathing deeply, allowing the pain and stiffness of his body to flow out on his exhalations, while he inhaled health and well-being. Soon he felt more like himself.

"Thank you Franlor, your body control lessons are wonderful."

Ackdominel moved to Woodreana's side and lifted her in his arms. She stirred, nuzzled against his chest and was still. Taking care to make no noise he carried her like a sleeping child to her shelter, where he tucked her into bed.

He stared at her face then kissed her forehead before leaving her cottage. Once outside he ran to the seventh of the teaching chambers that had been prepared for Woodreana. He stopped only to speak the word of command that caused the lodge's door to open. Entering the room beyond, he found himself in the council chamber. Closing the door behind him, he walked to his order's entrance and stepped through.

#

Melanie awoke with the dawn, dressed and made her way to the mine entrance. As she descended the stairs into the sloping passage a deep, gravelly voice hailed her.

"Hello, missy. I be waiting on yur. I have yur suit fer yur to try."

Melanie stepped past the entrance door and paused to allow her eyes to adjust to the darkness. Soon she saw three dwarves and with a scowl noted that Prince Tom and Tuck were two of them. She recognised the third dwarf as one of those from the previous day.

"Now if yur will be standing still, we'll be about placing the armour fer yur," said Tom.

Melanie stood sullenly as she felt the hands of the dwarves buckling the straps that secured her armour. After what seemed a long time Tom announced, "It be on. Try moving in it will yur?"

Melanie moved. The armour fit like a gown tailored for her alone and moved like heavy cloth instead of hard steel.

"It's incredible!" she exclaimed. Picking up her sword she swung it experimentally. "It feels as light as a feather, but will it stop a blow?"

"That it will, lass. The blows be glancing off they do. The secret be in the angles," replied Tom.

"Excellent! Thank you. Thank you very much," said Melanie. Bending down she kissed Prince Tom's cheek.

Tom stared at her in astonishment.

"Now I'll make those monsters pay! I'll have their blood! Now they'll be the ones to suffer!"

"I be begging yur pardon. Can I take it that yur no longer hate us?" asked Prince Tom.

"Hate you? Not in the least! So long as you keep me supplied with arms and armour like this, how could I hate you?"

"We'll be keeping yur armed we will."

Ackdominel entered the cavern.

"Is all well?" he asked with apprehension in his voice.

"Of course. The dwarves are our friends, and they're going to keep us supplied with armour and weapons. How soon can we leave this place and attack the Storm?" demanded Melanie.

"Tomorrow. Before I go, I have a job for you and your people, Prince Tom. After I leave, this door will be permanently closed. I want you to start work on another exit."

"That I can be doing."

"Good. Also, the elves will be bringing shipments of bows to the cavern's mouth. I ask that you transport them to the other entrance for me. Can you do this?"

"Of course we can be doing that fer yur. We'll be having a feast ready likewise, fer when you pass through me kingdom."

"Alas, I cannot stay."

"Now, laddie, yur will be having to sleep and eat on the way. So won't be slowing yur. Now I must be going if I'm to be overseeing me smiths, as they be about making those arms fer yur."

Tom and the dwarves disappeared into the darkness while Melanie and Ackdominel returned to the light.

"Are we really leaving tomorrow?" asked Melanie.

"Yes, and as soon as you are able to gather and equip a troop of warriors, I have a task for you."

"As I'm able?"

"Of course. What are generals for?" Ackdominel led her into the thirteenth lodge.

"General?"

"Think girl. I taught you more than how to swing a blade. I taught you everything I know about tactics. The elfin commanders did the same. You will be one of my generals!"

"One of?"

"Of course, one of! If warriors from my father's army escaped to the mountains, I have to give them a place. Generals have a nasty habit of surviving. It is called hiding behind the lines."

"I won't! I want to see those bloody-handed beasts die on my sword!"

As they spoke Ackdominel led Melanie into the lodge's kitchen and sat her down.

"Tea?" he asked as he picked up a kettle from his hearth and with a moment's thought caused the water in it to heat.

"Yes, but not the pine needle type, it makes my mouth burn. So what are the preparations?"

Ackdominel added herbs to the hot water and poured two cups. "We will need packs of food, any extra clothing we have and anything we wish to take with us. I will be returning to the valley before we depart, but I will have other burdens to carry then."

As he spoke, a smile grew on his face.

"What are you smiling about?" Melanie sipped her tea.

"Nothing really. It is simply, you do not seem to hate me anymore?"

"Hate you?" She paused and looked at herself. "Gods, sitting here drinking tea with a man, who a month ago I was thinking of ways to kill. I am so fickle!" She began then she sobered. "You didn't, did you?"

"No wizardry, simply friendship."

"Nothing more?"

"No. Is not friendship enough?"

"Yes. Yes, I think it will be. Let's finish planning for tomorrow."

Soon everything was arranged. Packs jammed full of supplies stood in the entrance to the thirteenth lodge, alongside Melanie's armour.

Ackdominel wandered through the woods, enjoying their beauty, knowing that between the valley and the sea nothing like them still existed. As the sun drew to the west, he turned his steps towards the stair. He was on the lowest step when a voice hailed him. It was Shalor and beside him stood Talion and Qulinea.

"Greetings," said Ackdominel.

"Greetings, Your Majesty. We have come because of your imminent departure," said Talion with a low bow.

"For a time. I will return at least once before I leave the mountain range."

"This pleases us! We are here to see that something is done," remarked Qulinea, her soft voice caressing every word.

"What?"

"It is the wish of our king that you don his gift in our presence," said Shalor.

"Why?"

"We do not know," explained Talion.

"As you wish. I will retrieve the bracers from my chambers if you will await me here?"

It took only moments for Ackdominel to collect the bracers and return to the elves. All eyes were upon him as he lifted the lid of the box that contained the elfin king's gift. The bracers glistened in the rays of the setting sun. He lifted one and placed it upon his wrist then reluctantly closed the box containing the other.

"What is it?" asked Shalor.

"I can feel the bracer's power. Your good king lamented the short span of years of my kind. Thus, he has given me a gift of years to this life."

"Why don't you complete the spell?" asked Talion.

"The one bracer gives me life five times that of others of my kind. Would you have me live those years alone?"

Talion stared at Ackdominel then comprehension dawned. "I see."

"This is a great gift. I had lamented that I would only see the beginning of my world's rescue. Now I will see many lands freed of the Storm's filth before my years are spent. This gift does not, however, help my victory and for that, I must rest. Farewell, my friends."

"Of course, Your Majesty," replied Qulinea. "May the sun and moon be forever your protectors."

The three elves bowed and disappeared into the wood.

Chapter 14
Earthy Hospitality

Ackdominel and Melanie stood at the mine entrance. Bracing themselves, they descended into the darkness, where they were met by Tuck, who was carrying a lantern of glowing stone.

"It be good to see yur, Yur Majesty, it does," said the dwarf.

"I am glad to be passing through."

Ackdominel and Melanie shouldered the packs they had left at the door and followed Tuck along the passage.

A couple of hours later they came upon a party of dwarves laying four tracks of iron running parallel to one another.

Tuck yelled, "Yur can be slowing down, he beat us to it. This here be King Ackdominel and the Lady Melanie."

The dwarves bowed then returned to work.

"It won't be long 'afore the going be easy," remarked Tuck.

"What do you mean?" asked Melanie.

"Well, if it be pleasing yur ladyship, we be about setting up our own way of getting about."

Soon they came to where two of the branching tunnels had been expanded to form a chamber. Here the parallel lines of iron stopped, and another pair started three strides down the passage. A large wheel stood at waist height between the two sets of tracks with a cable looping around it. One end of the cable was lost to the darkness of the passage the other attached to something that reminded Ackdominel of a hay cart that sat on the tracks. A dwarf leaned against the cart.

"Bap, you lazy frub! This be King Ackdominel and the Lady Melanie, now be acting proper," snapped Tuck.

The dwarf straightened and bowed saying, "Tis an honour and a privilege to be meeting yur, Yur Majesty."

"It is a pleasure meeting you as well. Please tell me what this cart and these iron strips are for?"

"This is a mover," replied Bap.

"A mover? How does it work?"

"That be simple, Yur Majesty. Yur see this cable," Bap gestured to the cable going around the wheel, "connects this cart to the one below. When this cart be loaded, we let loose the break, and the one below be dragged up by the weight of this one rolling down."

"But what do you do when you want to bring something up the passage?" asked Melanie.

"Aw, that's the thinking part of it. There be a water tank under the seats. So we set up a catchment fer the rain on the mountainside and run pipes to all the stations. We still need to be setting that up fer this one. When we want to be a bringing somit up, we fill the tank, and up she comes."

"Ingenious," said Ackdominel. "We should climb aboard."

"Do I have to?" asked Melanie.

"It should be easier than walking."

"I doubt it." She boarded the cart.

Once they were in, Bap pulled a lever, releasing the brake.

The cart bumped along at a sickening pace, rocking from side to side. After the first cart came to a stop, Tuck hurried them into another like it.

At the fifth mover, Ackdominel signalled a halt. Both he and Melanie were green, and neither of them was sure they could keep their breakfast down.

"'T aint it a grand way to travel. It be only two more cars, and we be at the throne room. How that be for speed?" said Tuck.

Ackdominel focussed on the dwarf, shook his head then examined his surroundings. The tunnel had become spacious with an arched ceiling supported by pillars of rock.

"You have come a long way in a short time," he observed.

"This be nothing. It be only started. Wait a couple more stations. That be a place to be proud of."

Two stations later lines of doors opened off the main passage, and there were walkways to either side of the tracks. Dwarves moved about their business and shops opened onto the cavern.

"This be merchants' row," explained Tuck. "We don't be near what we were having back home, but here one don't have to be givin' it up to the king's foul taxes."

One stop later Ackdominel and Melanie staggered from the descending cars, blessing the fact that it was over.

Prince Tom approached them as they stood before the lake chamber's doors. The humans were awed by their surroundings. The structure of the passage was the same as earlier, but here there were statues of dwarfs doing mighty deeds along the walls.

"Greetings, Yur Majesty, Lady Melanie. It be a pleasure and an honour to be having yur here," Tom greeted them.

"Oh yes, thank you, Your Highness." Ackdominel moved closer to Tom and whispered, "Can we make this short? I need a drink!"

"Carts be doing the same thing to me, they do, but it be quicker, and yur can't be all day getting to yur back door. Now can yur?"

"I guess not."

"It's a horrid way to travel!" remarked Melanie, from where she leaned against a pillar.

"Well, if yur will be following me, I'll be takin' yur to me palace. Yur can be leaving yur packs here. Tuck will see they're waitin' fer yur at the tother gate."

Tom stepped up to the door of the lake room and opened it. Fires burnt in the braziers on either side of the chamber's central lake. The stone trees reflected the light like a forest after an ice storm.

"Me palace, it be off this hall." Tom led them around the outside of the crystal chamber. He stopped in front of what appeared to be an ordinary piece of wall.

"This be me door, now watch, this be worth seeing." Tom made a deep rumbling sound. The wall opened revealing a chamber beyond.

"It's not magic, is it?" asked Ackdominel.

"No. It be simple good engineering. The door be triggered by the sound. It were a wee bit tricky to do. We weren't about to be marrin' craftsmanship as fine as this chamber. Dwarves be appreciating fine work. No matter who done it."

Ackdominel stepped into the room beyond the door. His breath caught. The low walls were marble. A table of jet, with a glowing stone lantern on it, filled the room's centre. About the table were three wooden chairs. Doors of opaque stone opened from the side of the room opposite the lake chamber.

"This be me private entrance and study," explained Tom. Picking up a brass bell he rang it. "Be having a seat."

Seconds later a dwarf entered with a flagon and cups.

"Yur should be having some of this. It be helping yur recovery from the carts." Tom poured the wine.

"Those are um, interesting. Really most... ingenious." Ackdominel accepted a goblet.

"It's all right for rock!" Melanie stared at her wine like it was going to bite her.

"I be with yur, lass."

"They are fast though. If I did not feel so wretched, I'd be tempted to press on to the outside today," said Ackdominel.

"Now yur not to be doing that! I've a feast planned fer yur."

After Ackdominel's and Melanie's stomachs settled, Tom led them to a chamber easily fifty paces across by a hundred long. Pillars of stone rose through circular tables, to support the ceiling, which curved up from a stride high at its edge, to two stories at the centre. The pillars looked like tree trunks and branched out like living boughs at the ceiling. Fire burned in braziers at each end of the room, and there was a breeze that wafted through the chamber from some hidden vent.

"This be our great hall. What do yur be thinking of it?" asked Tom.

"Incredible!" stated Melanie.

"It be hardly half done. It were a job to be joining the shafts yur people left, but we were about saving a mess of time by using them."

"It is difficult to believe that this was ever a mine," commented Ackdominel.

Tom smiled and led them to their seats at a rectangular table on a dais overlooking the room.

Ackdominel and Melanie sat at the table's centre, flanked by Tom and Tuck. Dwarves began to file in, taking seats at the tables below. Soon over a hundred dwarves filled the room.

"This here be our nobles. They be our master craftsmen, they do," said Tuck.

Ackdominel looked over the throng. Most wore clothes better suited to working a forge than a court dinner.

"Why are they dressed like that?" asked Melanie.

Ackdominel turned an angry eye on her.

"They be in their best," Tom replied hotly.

"And they look fine," added Ackdominel.

"That they don't, but it be all we can be doing. When we came, we couldn't be bringing what wee bit of finery we were having. Dwarves be masters of metal and stone, not cloth, so cloth be precious to us."

Ackdominel rose and spoke so all could hear.

"Prince Tom. You undoubtedly have the finest court I have ever seen. I have known many a noble, but how few I have found with any knowledge of what those who serve them must do. Here I see beings whose hands have known labour. Who through their own efforts have risen to high station. I salute you one and all.

"My most worthy friends and allies. To the dwarves, earth dwellers, long and well may you live."

Raising his glass, he took a long swallow. The dwarves cheered and clapped.

The feast began.

The first remove was of bread made from a blending of several types of powdered fungus. It was sweet and quite filling. Then came a variety of soups and stews, featuring several types of fish that Tom said lived in the river system that cropped up in the mine. The next remove consisted of a meaty fungus. Before long Melanie had a variety of untouched food in front of her.

As the revellers ate, various dwarves came before them to perform. One juggled daggers, another tumbled, and another entertained the crowd with a hilarious, if lewd, story about an elf searching for a tree to relieve himself behind in the desert.

When Ackdominel awoke the next "day" the taste of fungus was heavy on his tongue. He sat up in his pitch-dark room, felt for the bell left on the marble night table beside him and rang it. Seconds later his door opened admitting the dwarf assigned to attend him carrying a lit candle.

"What can I be a doing fer yur, Yur Majesty?"

"A bite to eat and a bit of heated wine. What is your name?"

"I be Gug, if it be pleasing, Yur Majesty," said the dwarf as he disappeared through the door, leaving the candle on the nightstand. Moments later he returned bearing a platter covered with steaming dishes. Ackdominel ate heartily.

"Do you know if Melanie is ready to go?" he asked, pulling on his robe.

"The lass, I be thinking she still be abed."

"Gods and demons! We will never get out of here at this rate. Could someone wake her?"

"If that be yur royal decree, I be willing to be doing it. But if yur don't mind me saying, she won't be a liking it."

"She doesn't like much of anything. I want to reach the surface quickly."

"Now what be this I hear about yur running off?" queried Prince Tom entering the room.

"I have to be going. Delays could prove disastrous."

"And move yur shall, but I've a wee bit of a surprise fer yur before yur be off." Tom gestured for Ackdominel to follow him. They walked along the corridor stopping at a metal door.

"It be in here." Tom threw open the door. Ackdominel entered the small room beyond. Half of the room was taken up by a bronze tub of steaming water. A cauldron of water bubbled on a hearth beside the door, and rough towels hung from the walls.

"Tom, I really...."

"Now don't be shunning me hospitality. Gug will be about bringing yur some soap fungus. I'll be seeing about waking the Lady Melanie. She'll want to be about eating and bathin' before yur set off. So yur has time. In the world outside the sun don't even be up yet."

With a sigh of resignation, Ackdominel stripped and climbed into the tub. When he finished bathing, he called for Gug.

"I be here," said the dwarf, hurrying into the room.

"Good. I want you to lead me back to the main passage."

"That I can be doing. Oh by the by, yur lady friend be up now and be resting in her tub."

"Gods! I'll never get away now."

Smiling and chatting, Gug led Ackdominel to the chamber of the lake. Fires burnt in the braziers and the room was empty save for a dwarf who stood on the pier beside the boat.

After a long wait, Melanie arrived. She was dressed in her armour, but now her hair fell down her back in two braids.

"Shall we go?" Ackdominel asked impatiently.

"Let's," she replied and stepped into the boat. Ackdominel followed her and finally the dwarf that had been waiting on the pier boarded.

"I be ferry master. I'll be taken yur across," explained the dwarf.

Tuck burst into the lake chamber calling, "Don't be leaving without me," as he ran towards the boat.

Ackdominel stifled a chuckle as the irrepressible dwarf pelted across the stone floor. He was dressed in a pair of grey pants, held up by blue suspenders, and a bright-green shirt, that was only half buttoned. His boots were in his hands.

"You don't have to guide us. I know the way out," said Ackdominel, when Tuck came within speaking range.

"That I be knowing, Yur Majesty. But sure yur understand. I've been made yur guide, and I must be doing fer yur."

"Very well, climb aboard."

The boat ride allowed Tuck to finish dressing. Thus, when they set foot on the opposite shore, they were ready to move on.

The passage on this side of the lake showed little change from Ackdominel's memory of it. They walked a short distance before coming to the first cart station on their upward journey. Here an armed and armoured dwarf stood by the wheel that held the cable.

"Why is he set for war?" asked Ackdominel.

"Prince Tom be thinking it's good to be getting us prepared fer when the beasts be coming. The other side of the lake be more or less safe, but here we be fixing fer a fight."

Ackdominel reluctantly climbed aboard the cart.

Melanie stood staring at the cart. "Do I have to?"

"Yes."

"Please? It's a lovely time for a walk."

"Get in."

"Sure, it be a great way to travel. The wind in yur face, it be grand," said Tuck.

Melanie glared at him, as if he had slithered out from under a rock, and settled into her seat.

The brake was released, and in seconds they were careening along as fast as a horse could gallop. Seven carts later Ackdominel signalled a halt and slumped to the floor with his back against the wall. Melanie crawled to his side and collapsed.

"I am never going to do this again!" she gasped.

"It's the only way in or out of the valley," remarked Ackdominel.

"I don't care."

"It be a nice time to be stretching one's legs, now don't it?" chirped Tuck.

"Can I kill him?" asked Melanie, as she slouched against the wall.

"Maybe I can turn him into a toad?" mused Ackdominel. "Tom would probably object."

"What be the matter? If I did somit to offend, I be sorry."

"You have done nothing. Does not riding in those things bother you at all?" Ackdominel managed to look Tuck in the eye.

"No! Why? It be pleasant it be."

Ackdominel glared at the dwarf then shook his head.

It took half an hour for them to recover sufficiently to resume their journey. One cart ride flowed into the next until it seemed the unpleasantness would never end. Then the last cart rolled to its apex and stopped.

"We have to be walking from here, Yur Majesty," said Tuck.

Ackdominel was too busy trying to keep his feet to cheer. Melanie sat by the tracks looking sick and embarrassed. When the two humans recovered, Tuck led them to the stair they had descended years before.

"Be holding a moment. I'll be showing yur somit," said the dwarf.

Ackdominel and Melanie paused as Tuck disappeared into a chamber cut into the cavern's wall and pulled a lever. Spears leapt from the passage's walls, filling the length of the stair.

"It be part of our defence," Tuck remarked from the side cavern as he pushed the lever up and the spears disappeared into the walls.

"Impressive," said Ackdominel.

"Very," agreed Melanie.

"That don't be all, and we only be startin'," said Tuck.

When they reached the top of the stair, they found the passage blocked by a heavy, iron door, bolted and barred from the inside.

"This be our front gate. Nothing be coming through it without a fight," exalted Tuck.

Ackdominel nodded his agreement. Noticing doors in the walls to either side of the main gate he asked, "What are the small doors for?"

"Those be archer runs and guard rooms. We be having a wee passage cut along each side of the main one, with only wee holes big enough to shoot through between 'em. This way we can pepper any who wants to beat on our door until they be hedgehogs."

"Sound strategic design," remarked Melanie.

"No one's getting in less we want 'em in. We already be keeping a watch in the guard rooms, but I won't be disturbing them, meeting yur is a treat. It be a punishment to be stationed here."

"As you wish, my friend, but here we must part. I will be returning at some point to gather the remainder of my things from the lodge. Please thank Prince Tom for everything."

"Sure-un I'll be doin' that," said Tuck, as he unbolted the door.

Ackdominel walked up the tunnel, which looked exactly as it had when he first saw it. In moments he emerged into bright sunshine. Melanie followed him, and they started down the trail.

Chapter 15
A Wolf in the Fold

"I'm cold," complained Melanie as they crunched through the high mountain snow.

"Humm. I'm quite comfortable. Then again, that is a property of my cloak. What are you wearing under your armour?" Ackdominel continued walking.

"My blue tunic and britches."

"Anything else?"

"No."

"In that case, you deserve to be cold. Put on some furs." Ackdominel stopped and shook his head.

"I guess that would be a good idea." Melanie moved to a place where a cliff face broke the wind and unbuckled her armour.

Ackdominel looked skyward then moved to help her. Soon they were on their way again, with Melanie's armour loosely fastened over several layers of hides and cloth. As evening approached, they came to Solin's hut. Ackdominel knocked on its door.

"Go away! I don't want to hurt you! So go away!" ordered Solin from within.

"I do not wish to harm you either, Solin. It is," Ackdominel paused awkwardly then finished, "Dominel. We visited a few years ago."

The door hide was pulled back to reveal Solin, his face badly beaten and his arm in a sling.

"Dominel! You're back. What happened to you and who's the warrior woman?"

"In good time. First, what happened to you?"

"Refugees! Please step inside, I'll tell you the whole story."

They entered the shelter. Ackdominel took a seat upon the only chair, while Solin and Melanie sat on the bed.

"Tell us your story," said Ackdominel.

"What I feared came to pass. As the refugees flooded the mountains, people moved closer to my hermitage. I couldn't help myself. Each full moon I would run towards the nearest settlement, drawn by the smell of human blood. One night I reached them. I don't remember what happened! Others tell me they found the torn and bloodied bodies of an elderly couple outside their hovel. Searches were organised, but they never found anything. For a time I was safe. The fear of the unknown beast kept people away. Memories grow short when the belly is empty. Soon people were living near me again.

"I tried tying myself up. Even putting myself in a cage. When I recovered my true form, the rope was gnawed through and the cage broken. It was during the last full moon that it happened. I had tied myself securely and locked the cage.

"My nightmare began with my body shifting and my mind clouding. Normally I am spared remembering, but not this time! Oh, Gods. Not this time! The pain was incredible. Then I was a snarling, snapping beast filled with blood-lust. I gnawed through the rope that bound me then threw myself at the cage door. The door held against my first blow, cracked with my second, then exploded into splinters with my third. I was out!

"The scent of blood was on the wind, and it made my mouth water. My mouth actually watered...." Solin swallowed, and a shudder ran through him. "I... I charged through the night towards the smell. It was a shepherd boy minding a small flock. He couldn't have been more than eight. I leapt at him and sank my teeth into his shoulder. His blood tasted sweet." Solin fell silent. The others sat quietly while he composed himself. After a few moments, he continued.

"Something struck me. It hurt unlike anything I'd experienced before. I faced my attacker. He was armed with a silver-tipped staff. I leapt at him. He struck with his staff, sending me to the ground. He rushed me, swinging again and again. I ran away as fast as I could with a broken foreleg. The man didn't follow. He must have stayed behind to care for the lad. I wish he had finished me!"

Ackdominel watched Solin with silent pity before speaking. "Lycanthropy is a horrible curse. I am sorry. I must ask, would you know the boy if you saw him?"

"Yes, I believe I would. Why?"

"This only happened at the last full moon?"

"Yes. That still doesn't answer my question."

"There might be a chance if we hurry. Solin, I think I can save the boy from your curse."

"What?" said Solin and Melanie in unison.

"You have infected him. Anyone wounded by a lycanthrope, who does not die, will become a lycanthrope, unless treated promptly."

"But what can we do? There are no wizards to aid him," objected Solin.

Melanie smiled and looked towards Ackdominel.

"Don't be too sure of that!" she remarked.

"You?" asked Solin sceptically.

"You wanted to know our story," replied Ackdominel.

Ackdominel and Melanie quickly recounted the tale of their adventures and by the time they finished, night had closed around them. They spent that night under Solin's roof, but Ackdominel did not sleep. Instead, he feigned sleep until the others were lost in slumber.

If I use conventional means, we will never find the child in time, he thought. Forcing his breathing to become deep and steady he let the tension flow out of him. In moments his thought body had risen from his flesh and drifted out of the shelter.

His astral-self moved across the land, in seconds reaching a collection of ramshackle buildings made from piled stones. He searched these, but the only child was a girl who, aside from hunger, was well. He felt a need in his body that slowly grew. He ignored his body's call until he came upon a stone hut. Entering he found a boy, soaked with sweat and writhing in agony. His arm was wrapped in a dirty, grey bandage. Ackdominel marked the position of the hut in his mind and returned to his body. When he arrived, his throat was dry. After drawing a ladle of water from Solin's barrel, he settled to sleep.

He awoke to the smell of meat frying and fresh herbal tea. Rising he exited the dwelling into a clear sunny day. Melanie and Solin crouched by a small fire with a grill over it.

"Good morning," said Ackdominel.

"Good morning, my friend." Solin came to his feet. "Melanie has been telling me more of your experiences in the valley. It's hard to believe you are a wizard returned from the dead to aid us."

"We all return from the dead, and my destiny was planned years ago." Ackdominel smiled. "But destiny doesn't make the mouth water. Is the food ready?"

Moments later he was sitting by the fire holding a slab of hard bread heaped with fried strips of meat in one hand and wielding his eating dagger with the other.

"Where will we start looking for the boy?" asked Melanie.

"I found him last night. He's in a hut in a box canyon a few miles from here. There is a pond at the canyon's end, fed by a small waterfall. Do you recognise it?" asked Ackdominel.

"Yes, I think I do. It's only half a day's walk from here," replied Solin.

"Then let us go."

The journey to the canyon went swiftly. The sun was at the noon when the three of them approached the stone cottage that served as the boy's home. Sheep bleated in a pen to their right. Reaching the cottage door, Ackdominel pounded on it and called.

The door creaked open, revealing a powerfully built man in his mid-twenties. He towered over Ackdominel and was clad from head to foot in rough worked sheepskin.

"Who are you, and what do you want?" he demanded.

"I am Ackdominel, and I have come to help your sick boy."

"How do you know about my child?"

"That is unimportant. What is important is that he contracted the illness from a werewolf's bite. If you do not let me help, your son will have a life of agony."

The big man stared at Ackdominel then his gaze strayed to Melanie and Solin.

"Aren't you the hermit from up yonder?" He gestured in the direction of Solin's hut.

"Yes, I am. I led this healer here when I learned of the boy's condition."

"Please, forgive me. We've had trouble with strangers. Come, Erum is asleep on the cot," invited the man. The dark circles under his eyes spoke to his exhaustion.

Ackdominel entered and moved to where the boy lay on a bed of sweat-soaked sheepskins. "It is almost too late."

"Please, don't let him die. He's all I have left of my Heidi," pleaded the big man.

"I will do all I can. With luck I am in time," said Ackdominel. Turning to Melanie and Solin, he added, "I need an iron pot, wolfsbane, rowan leaves and quiet."

"I have an iron pot," said the shepherd. He pulled a battered caldron from a corner of the room.

"Good man, Orlor."

"How did you know my name?"

"I'll explain as we gather the herbs." Solin took Orlor's arm and led him from the cottage, with Melanie behind them.

Ackdominel laid his hands upon the child, his right upon the boy's brow and his left over the child's heart. Stillness filled the room, and Ackdominel began to chant. He felt the ecstasy of energy flow through him. His spirit filled with power. The chant grew stronger, and the child's lips moved to mimic Ackdominel's. The world around Ackdominel dissolved. He found himself standing at the entrance to a bleak and barren valley. Weird, shadowy shapes flitted to and fro at the edge of vision and a cold wind, bearing a carnal stench, wafted from the valley's depths. The air seemed to mutter threats and curses.

I should have known. The valley of vengeful spirits. What else would be the power centre for a lycanthrope? thought Ackdominel. Steeling himself, he called, "Erum."

"Help," replied a small voice from deep within the ravine.

Ackdominel strengthened his mystical shields then strode into the depression. As he entered their domain, the shapes became clear. Beings of strange and grotesque aspect danced on all sides, clawing against his shields. A creature shaped like a curvaceous woman with the head and mottled skin of a venomous snake blocked his passage.

"You are mine, man thing. Hiss." The snake woman stared at him with glowing green eyes.

Ackdominel felt the attraction of those eyes but fought it.

"I am my own! By the power of the lords and ladies of light and love, I command you begone!"

The snake creature hissed and leapt away as if stung.

Ackdominel moved deeper into the valley. All the creatures crowded against his shields.

"Help me," called Erum's voice, now close at hand.

The creatures stopped crowding around. Ackdominel stepped into a clear area with a large, slab table in its centre. Erum lay upon the table, bound hand and foot, while a large she-wolf with a blood-red coat prowled about him. Her eyes glared malignantly at Ackdominel.

"No farther, man-beast," snarled the wolf.

"I have come for the boy," stated Ackdominel.

"He is mine! You cannot have him." The wolf's hackles rose.

"He is of the human race. I come to claim one of my own. By what right do you prevent me?"

"By right of revenge!" The wolf glared at Ackdominel. "I once had a body upon your world. A mate, cubs! We hunted the woods, rich in deer game. Always we followed the law and ate what we killed. Then one of your kind came. I had left to search for a better den for the coming winter. My mate was with the cubs.

"The man-beast slaughtered my cubs! My mate called me. I ran arriving in time to see him bludgeoned to death over my cubs' bodies. My cubs had not even seen the cold season. My Fang, my Tumbler, my Brush Tail, and my dear, dear Snarl. I leapt at the man thing in anger and hate, thirsting for its blood, but one of its fellows sent a feathered shaft through my heart. Then, did the man thing follow the law? Did he eat our flesh? Did he wear our hides? Did he even pray to the wolf spirit for the sake of our souls? NO! He took my Snarl and filled his hollow shell with stuffing to adorn his den. He left my darling cubs and me to rot. I hate all your kind, man thing, and will forever for that."

Ackdominel stood silent. He brushed his face and felt a tear trickling down his cheek. For the sake of the living, he knew he had to harden his heart to the injustice of what he'd just heard.

"That was not this boy. Can one be held responsible for the actions of others of his kind?"

"One you say! How many of my kind have died and suffered from your kind's cruel disregard of the sacred laws?"

"Still, is this child guilty of any crime against you? Is the blood of your cubs on his hands? He is someone's cub. If you take him, surely your paws will be as bloodied as any man's!"

"I care not! I will have my revenge! I swore so by the great wolf spirit. And I will have it!"

"Then we are foes, and it will be a trial of strength. I wish it were different. Would you accept a sacrifice in the child's stead?"

"No! He will be mine!"

"Then foes we are. Fear not, Erum, I will return." Saying this, Ackdominel focussed his mind and returned to his body in the cottage. His leg was cramped from the position it had been in, and he had much to consider.

Ackdominel was sitting quietly in front of the cottage when Melanie came running towards him.

"I have them. I found the rowan leaves," she yelled.

"That is good, but try to be quiet. Erum is sleeping. He will need all his strength for this evening's trial."

It was a short time after Melanie's arrival that Solin and Orlor returned with several clumps of wolfsbane. Upon seeing Ackdominel, Orlor dropped to his knees and pleaded, "Mighty wizard, great king, please help my son."

Ackdominel looked skyward and shook his head.

"Get up, please. Wizards have never been much on bowing and scraping, and I was born the youngest son this life, my brothers were the ones people bowed to."

Orlor rose to his feet.

Ackdominel continued, "I think I can help your son, but it will be difficult. The spirit that seeks to possess him is powerful and implacable. I will have to fight it in its own realm, where its strength will be greater and mine less." He fell silent and stared off into space.

Melanie lead Solin and Orlor away from the cottage allowing Ackdominel to spend what remained of the day meditating, building his mystic strength. He finished his preparations as the moon topped the horizon. Placing Orlor's caldron over a bed of coals on the cottage's small hearth, he filled it with water and set the wolfsbane and rowan to brew. In minutes the cottage was filled with a pungent aroma. Laying his hands upon Erum, Ackdominel whispered a chant.

Once more he stood before the valley. The sense of malice was even greater than he remembered. He waited for the wolf spirit to appear. It moved towards the valley, across a rocky, barren plain, carrying what looked like a child in its jaws.

"Halt!" called Ackdominel, and the very rocks echoed his command.

"What! You. Stay out of this, man thing!" said the she-wolf, dropping the child.

"No!"

The she-wolf snarled and sprang.

Ackdominel raised his hand and focussed his will. A beam of force leapt from his palm, striking the wolf, slamming her into the ground.

"Desist! Give up vengeance. I do not wish to hurt you," called Ackdominel.

"Die, man thing!" snarled the wolf, blood spattering from a cut lip.

Ackdominel staggered back. The force of the malice in those words was like a spell. His shields had barely blunted its effect.

He drew his sword and called out, "By the power of my blade and the servants of light. I command you to thy valley and abjure thee to remain there a year and a day."

The wolf shifted indecisively then laughed, the darkest, most malignant laughter Ackdominel had ever heard. "Maybe in your own realm you could command me, mage, but we are close to my realm. You haven't the right or the might to banish me here." The wolf leapt towards Ackdominel's throat.

Ackdominel's warrior training was all that saved him. Of its own accord, his body pivoted and slashed out with his blade, leaving a deep, bloody, gouge down the she-wolf's flank.

"You cannot win," snarled the wolf. Its eyes were mad with hate and pain. "This is my place. Here I can call on all that is vengeance. All that is anger. All that is hate. Here I am the master!" As the wolf spoke, it grew larger and more ferocious, until it stood three times Ackdominel's height. With a snarl, the beast leapt, and Ackdominel barely avoided being crushed by a paw.

"Gods of power, gods of light, I summon forth thy holy might. By all the powers of the light. Help me win against vengeance's might," called Ackdominel.

Energy flooded him. His body shone like a firebrand. Raising his hand and focussing his will he channelled the force, becoming a conduit for the god force that enveloped the wolf in flame. The wolf howled in agony and bolted into the valley.

"My lords and ladies of the light, I thank thee," prayed Ackdominel. Kneeling he bowed, touching his forehead to the ground.

Rising, he moved to the child and lifted him in his arms. With a thought, he was back in the cottage, and the fragment of Erum's spirit he had rescued was returned to the child's body. Ignoring his exhaustion, Ackdominel filled a cup with the broth bubbling in the cauldron and lifted it to the boy's lips.

"I must give him enough to prevent the wolf from trying again, but not enough to still his lungs," he murmured, as he forced the child to drink.

Erum sputtered, gagged and tried to push the cup away.

"I know. It smells almost as bad, but drink it anyway."

After the child drank half a cup, Ackdominel laid him upon the furs. Erum's eyes closed, and he fell into a peaceful sleep.

Smiling, Ackdominel lay beside Erum listening to the child breathe.

Hours passed before Ackdominel let sleep steal over him. He awoke to Melanie shacking him the next morning. Orlor and Solin both stood behind her.

"Will my boy heal?" demanded Orlor, before Ackdominel had focussed his eyes.

"For the most part."

"What do you mean, for the most part?" Orlor sounded desperate.

Ackdominel glanced at Solin and noticed that the werewolf looked sick. "Solin, you fool, get out of here before the wolfsbane fumes overcome you, and we have to carry you out."

"What do you mean 'for the most part'?" repeated Orlor, as Melanie led Solin from the cabin.

"Your son was attacked by a werewolf. That opened the door for another of its kind to enter our world. Each night since the attack a vengeful wolf's spirit has carried off a portion of your son's spirit. If the process had continued, he would have had a spirit half human and half wolf. The wolf side would have seized control when the moon was full and gone marauding over the lands. I broke the cycle. Now Erum has more of a human spirit than a wolf's."

"And what does that mean?"

"Probably that he will be able to control the wolf within himself. I am really not sure, but at least he won't be a werewolf."

"Thank the gods for that."

"You don't know how much."

Chapter 16
Call to Arms

Ackdominel awoke late that morning. Rising he stretched and made his way outside. Solin sat on a stone a little away from the door talking to Erum. Ackdominel scanned the landscape and saw Melanie farther down the valley, practising her sword strokes.

"Good morning," said Ackdominel. "Where is Orlor?"

"He took the sheep to where there's better grazing. He hasn't been able to take them very far of late," answered Solin.

"Y... Y... Your Majesty," enquired a small voice, as Ackdominel drew close to Solin and the boy.

"Yes, Erum?"

"I. Well. I wanted to say thank you."

"You're more than welcome. How do you feel?"

"Better! I don't feel sick at all now."

"Good. I'm glad to hear it. I am sorry, but we have to go."

"Where?" asked Solin.

"To town. If I am to raise an army, I will not do it sitting around here."

"I guess that's true."

Ackdominel collected his pack and called Melanie to his side. Minutes later they were on their way.

It took them over two hours to reach the nearest of the new mountain communities. This was a shabby affair made out of piled stone houses, surrounded by a waist-high wall.

They were forced to circle the defensive wall until they came to a low wooden gate.

"Who are you and what's your business?" demanded a rough, grubby looking man, clad in rusty chainmail, from behind the gate.

"I am Ackdominel, last of the line of Otinerus, rightful King of Bani. I have urgent business with your leader, whoever he may be."

The grubby man placed the battered remains of a cap helm upon his head and drew a notched sword.

"You must be joking. Everyone knows the royal family died in the battle of Duran Pass," snapped the man, eyeing them suspiciously.

"Not all. I, the youngest son of Otinerus, was left for dead on the field and thus escaped my family's fate."

"Can you prove what you say?"

"Only with this," said Ackdominel. Removing his backpack, he pulled out the remains of the tabard he had worn over his armour. The royal arms were visible on the cloth.

"That don't prove nothing!"

"I can give you one more reason to let me in."

"Oh? And what in the names' of the gods is that?"

"I'm a wizard."

"You're a real jester aren't you, funny mannnnnnn," said the warrior. With an effort of will and a flick of his wrist, Ackdominel levitated the man his own height off the ground.

"Gods and demons and my sweet dead mother!" screamed the man.

In seconds the village was running towards the gate, nearly forty people.

Ackdominel waited for them to approach then called out loudly. "I mean you no harm. I am Dominel, King of Bani, and Ackdominel, wizard of the Secret Path."

As he spoke, he lowered the warrior to the ground. No sooner had the man settled than he fell to his knees and presented his sword to Ackdominel hilt first.

"My service to you, son of my king." As he spoke the words, new strength entered his voice.

Ackdominel took the sword, raised it high and handed it back to the man saying, "Serve me well for your pledge I accept. I need to speak to your town's leader."

A balding man with loose skin stepped forward.

"I am Frall, the seneschal of this village, Your Majesty. I'm afraid we've little to spare."

"I have brought my own food. We must speak, and I will need your people to help spread the word of my arrival. First tell me, how many warriors of able-body do you have here?"

"Only Trom there."

"Melanie," ordered Ackdominel.

She walked towards the guard and signalled for him to follow her away from the crowd of villagers.

"Now Frall, we have much to discuss," said Ackdominel.

Frall led the way to one of the stone huts and pulled back its deerskin door flap. Ackdominel entered a single-room shelter. Hides spread about a central fire-pit were its only furnishings. Ackdominel took a seat and began to speak before Frall had fully settled himself.

"You know the shield is failing."

"Yes. Are you going to fix it?" asked Frall, hope leaping to his eyes.

"Not possible. It's too large for one wizard to maintain."

Frall's face fell.

"I do, however, have a plan. Actually, it would be truer to say we have a plan. There is a land awaiting us in the western sea. It is rich enough that it can support all the remaining human population and it can be shielded against the Storm."

Frall stared at Ackdominel. "The coast is a long way away. How would we win through? Even if we reach it, it might be held against us."

"It is not! I have seen the coast. It is still held by men. Although, I cannot say for how much longer."

"But how will we ever reach it? There are thousands, hundreds of thousands of monsters in the way."

"We will reach it with high magic, low cunning and the valour of the desperate, leaving a trail of blood in our wake!"

"But," began Frall.

So it went into the afternoon until they emerged from the hut and Ackdominel began ordering the people of the village. He sent runners to the neighbouring villages, to announce his arrival and call all warriors and village leaders to a moot. After this he sought out Melanie and found her at the village gate, watching Trom put a fresh edge to his sword.

"I see you have already started ordering your troops," remarked Ackdominel.

"Yes! I'll soon give those murderous beasts a surprise they won't forget!"

"I am sure of that. There should be more warriors here within the next few days. Soon we will be able to move to the opening of one of the major passes and begin raiding."

"Good! I'll... We'll cut them down like wheat!"

"Just don't forget you're raiding for wheat. You're to plunge in; capture supplies and equipment then get out again. No foolishness!"

"Yes, of course," replied Melanie, in a way that said the more I gut the better.

The next day the village leaders arrived with several men at arms. Most suspected a trap, since raiding for food was common. Ackdominel spoke with them, and they quickly lost their fear of treachery.

The next night runners were sent to more distant villages, from where the news could be spread.

Melanie soon found herself with a troop of nearly fifty men armed with old, battered weapons and armour. A week after their arrival at the village Melanie and Ackdominel sat at a small, dung fire.

"I'm going to have to get better equipment for my troops before we do anything," remarked Melanie.

"Yes."

"I think I'll take them to the dwarves."

"What?" gasped Ackdominel, who'd only been half listening.

"They need their arms and armour repaired. The dwarves can do that. They do, after all, owe you a tithe."

"You are right. By the way, what happened to the rest of the swords they gave us that day?"

"I left them in my lodge. You'll have to bring them when you come back the next time."

"Are not you coming with me?"

"Of course not! I've an army to command, and there is nothing that would make me ride those carts again!"

"Very well. Get your men properly armed, but do not show them the entrance to the Dwarfen Kingdom. Take them to within a short march of the cave and have the dwarves meet them at your camp."

"Fair enough."

"Oh, and Melanie. Tell them what to expect. I don't think anyone's quite ready to deal with Tuck. Much less if they don't expect him."

Melanie smiled then continued to talk about her plans.

Ackdominel ignored her and thought about the shield growing weaker and that it would soon shrink again.

Five days later he led Melanie and her troop of sixty, fully armed and armoured, men down the mountain towards the main pass. An unarmed reserve followed the troops, pulling carts piled with the remnants of battered equipment they collected along the way.

Their progress was slow because Ackdominel stopped at every village they came across to rally people to their cause. When they did reach the main pass, both Melanie and Ackdominel paused in silent horror. The once beautiful mountainsides were nothing but barren slopes, littered with ramshackle huts. The shallow soil now sprouted stunted crops. The smell of human waste filled the air, and stone cairns marked the fate of many.

"Merciful gods! All this in four years," whispered Melanie.

"It's hard to believe," breathed Ackdominel.

Slowly they made their way down the pass. People on all sides of them stopped and stared. Many followed the soldiers in their armour. They moved on for half an hour before stopping. Ackdominel walked up the mountainside a short distance.

"Good people," he called.

There was a babble of voices.

"Good people," he repeated, his words booming, bringing immediate silence.

"I am your King, come to deliver you to a new land, but you must help in your own salvation. Spread the word! I need all who can wield bow or blade. Let it be known that I will feed all who serve me and their families."

"Food," cried one voice.

"Food," echoed others.

"There will be food for those who earn it. Is there a smith nigh?"

A burly man of average height stepped forward. His face was scared with a thousand little burns.

"I'm a smith."

"Good! I have armour to be repaired. Where is your forge?"

"Yonder," said the smith, with a gesture to his right.

"Melanie, have some of your men haul the carts of old armour to this man's forge. We will sleep the night here and hopefully add to our troop."

The next morning the ranks of Melanie's troop had swelled to over a hundred, although only eighty could be equipped. Each day the scene was repeated, and each day their ranks grew until they drew near the edge of the shield. By this point, Melanie could field a force of nearly two-hundred infantry, with a partially equipped reserve of equal size. Two smiths had joined their company, working at piecing shattered bits of armour into whole suits.

#

Ackdominel stood within the shield wall staring down at their foes that crowded the pass' mouth. He sighed thinking, *It is nearly impossible, but we have no choice*.

Putting all other thoughts aside, he turned his attention to the reason he had come. Undoing the latches on the box containing his black mirror, he propped it up before him and stared into its depths. At first, everything was cloudy, as the image cleared he found himself looking at the enemy camp from a great height. Moving his vision closer to the camp, he searched until he found the object of his quest, a tent full of supplies. Nearly half of the tent's contents were unsuitable for human consumption. The other half had been pillaged from towns or grown by human slaves. Ackdominel moved his gaze to the tent's exterior and noticed that it was little more than fifty strides from the monsters' front rank.

"Almost time," he murmured. He replaced his mirror in its carrying box.

That night he ordered Melanie to prepare her troops for a foray. He passed on the location of the supply tent, and enemy troop strength then left organising the raid to her.

He climbed the mountainside to a plateau and sat staring into space. All that night clouds gathered over the pass as the wind rose to a threatening howl. By morning the air had a chill, and a storm threatened.

"Do you think we should fight in this?" asked Melanie, while she and Ackdominel sat at breakfast.

"Fairweather soldier, are we?" Ackdominel stirred his pitifully small bowl of gruel.

"No! Rain could endanger our position."

"I guarantee you, this storm will do nothing to us that won't hurt the monsters far more."

Realization filled Melanie's face, and she smiled. "Yes, Your Majesty." She left to oversee her troop's preparations.

The storm struck as Melanie's troop began advancing upon their foes. Lightning laced down into the monsters' camp, killing many and setting tents ablaze. The monsters' ranks milled about in confusion.

Ackdominel stood on the mountainside watching the scene below. Occasionally his hand would move, and he'd speak a word, as if orchestrating the storm.

The human troops moved towards the monsters who formed themselves into a ragged line. The forces met, and a balance was struck, spears were thrust, and axes swung, shields dented, and the clamour grew loud.

Ackdominel, seeing the two lines meet raised his arm above his head then snapped it down.

Hail poured from the clouds beating against the monsters' faces and eyes, half blinding them while it glanced harmlessly off the human force's armoured backs. The wind ripped through the monsters' camp, sweeping lightning kindled flame from one tent to another, while knocking the fattest ogres off their feet.

#

Melanie rejoined her troops minutes before the battle.

"What are our orders?" asked Trom.

"We attack," said Melanie.

"But the weather?"

"Is, it would seem, Ackdominel's to command! I don't know what to expect, but I've no doubt something will come of it."

Trom shrugged. Melanie looked up the mountainside to where the small, white figure of Ackdominel clambered to a higher vantage point. She smiled and moved to the head of her troops.

She arranged them in a double line, shieldmen to the front, spear and axe men to the rear, with one spearman to three shieldmen. Behind these were a collection of half equipped warriors, carrying empty sacks and wheeling carts.

Melanie took one last look at her troops then signalled the charge. As they progressed, lightning flashed in the enemy camp, lighting fires and killing monsters in a seemingly random pattern. Soon they were met by the monstrous line, and the battle was joined.

Melanie lashed out, her dwarfen blade slicing through the horny hide of an ogre like butter. The beast fell only to be replaced by another. Something clunked against her helmet. In seconds hail was driving into her enemies' faces. A piece struck her third opponent, a hill troll, in the eye. While it was distracted, she slit its throat.

"Now for blood, death, glory and vengeance, strike, strike hard and boldly," she screamed, pressing forward at the head of her troops, leaving a bloody swath in her passage.

Her troops hearing her cry and seeing her move fell in behind her, forming a wedge that drove through the monsters' ranks. Shield men to the outside, spearmen next and cart bearers in the middle. They pushed forward with Melanie at the driving point. Some of the carts now bore wounded men, but they pushed on. The hail had stopped, as soon as their wedge was complete, but winds still whipped to all sides of them, disrupting the monsters' ranks. Rain pelted down. It was deflected by the humans' visored helms, but the monsters, with their reliance on bone and hide, were blinded. The toll extracted by the humans mounted as they approached the supply tent.

The human ranks enveloped the supply tent and halted. Men with carts and bags went to work, taking anything of use as the warriors kept the monsters at bay. In minutes they were done, and the human wedge moved towards the safety of the shielded mountains.

Breaking free of the monstrous horde the warriors reformed their defensive line, while the cart bearers hauled their burdens up the pass. Step by step the warriors fell back. Spats of hail began to fall from the abating storm, although helpful, they now lacked the force to disrupt the beasts. A horn sounded to the humans' rear, signalling that the cart bearers were safely behind the shield. The human line began an orderly retreat. The monsters lagged behind until only a handful remained. Melanie cut two of them down, the others fled. Smiling she decapitated one of her fallen foes.

"A prize," she stated as she picked up an ogre's severed head.

As Melanie approached the safe area, she noticed a rotting stench. Glancing at her trophy, she dropped it in disgust. It was as if the work of weeks of putrefaction had taken place in seconds.

"So that's how the shield works. Pity about my prize."

Chapter 17
Eagle's Call

Ackdominel stood on the mountainside overlooking the remains of the monsters' camp. The creatures were already reorganising. The gale still howled but he could feel it ebbing. Casually raising his arm, he sent a bolt of lightning crashing into a minotaur. A wave of dizziness swept over Ackdominel. Gathering his strength, he descended towards the troops below. Melanie met him at his tent. Her hair was matted with sweat, and her armour was gore-spattered. An unwholesome light gleamed in her eyes.

"We did it! We must have killed hundreds of those miserable things," she exulted.

"Yes, you did. Did you gather the food?" asked Ackdominel.

"Of course. That's what I went for."

"Good. How many did we lose?"

"Only three dead. We managed to save their armour. A few others were wounded. Little loss."

Ackdominel stared at Melanie with a feeling of disgust.

"Your father undoubtedly killed many monsters. Was his death little loss?"

"My father. How dare you!" snarled Melanie.

"I dare because those men who were little loss might have had daughters of their own, or sons, or wives, or parents. Do you think I fight this war because I want to? I have no choice!"

Ackdominel fell silent, and tension hung in the air as Melanie looked to the ground.

"Take me to the wounded men," he ordered.

Melanie led him to the hut they were using to house the wounded. Ackdominel paused at its entrance gathering his strength then, taking a deep breath, stepped in. Only the most severe cases were inside. Those with minor injuries treated themselves. Six men lay on a row of cots.

Ackdominel knelt by the closest man. He was in his middle years and had a large gash across his stomach.

"Lord Wizard, Your Majesty. That storm. I didn't really believe until I seen it," said the man.

"Lie still. Save your strength," instructed Ackdominel.

"No use. Can't live with a belly wound like this. I'm soldier enough to know that."

"But I'm wizard enough to know you can."

Pulling the ring from his finger, Ackdominel placed it stone down into the man's wound. At first, nothing happened then as he drew the ring from the wound the tissues became whole. In minutes the injury had been reduced to a nasty cut.

"Rest now. You must finish the healing naturally. I have only so much strength to spend, and others are in need." Ackdominel wiped sweat from his brow and moved on to a man whose leg had been severed mid-thigh. A chirurgeon had seared the stump and stretched the skin to cover it, Ackdominel could do no more. He spent the next hour doing what the chirurgeons could not. Finally, he stepped from the clinic's confines.

"How are they?" demanded Melanie, who had waited for him.

"The death count went up by one. There is a man with no leg, another missing an arm. The rest will fight again!"

"You look awful!"

"Used too much energy." Ackdominel staggered and caught himself before falling.

"You have to eat something."

She took his icy hand and led him to the supply hut.

"Yes. Food might help."

Melanie entered the hut, emerging with a loaf of hard bread, half a cheese and a skin of wine.

"Eat," she ordered.

Ackdominel began to eat then asked, "Wine?"

"They grabbed whatever was handy, don't worry, we've enough to feed an army for a while."

"We'll need more soon."

"Yes, but tomorrow is the time to worry about tomorrow. For now, eat. A dead wizard is of no use to anyone."

After eating Ackdominel staggered to the small tent that Melanie had had erected for him on the flat by the pass's central road.

The next day he awoke to ravenous hunger. Rising, he stretched then exited his tent into a bright, clear day. Walking to the food tent, he bullied the quartermaster into releasing a triple ration. Melanie found him sitting on a rock enjoying the sun and eating heartily.

"Something's going on at the shield," she panted.

Snatching up his last bit of bread and cramming it into his mouth Ackdominel followed her to the shield's edge.

The monsters crowded into the pass, almost pushing into the shield's area of effect. Ackdominel examined the shield with wizards' sight. The barrier flickered between dark and light.

"Demons of the abyss!" he swore. "Get your warriors. Form a defensive line where the pass narrows. Have everyone else retreat up the pass. Empty the camp and put bowmen on the mountainsides so they can shoot down when the Storm moves forward. The shield is about to shrink!"

In minutes word spread through the camp. Those with armour prepared for battle while the rest moved the camp farther up the pass. Melanie deployed her troops behind a sweating Ackdominel who fought to hold the shield in place.

#

Ackdominel felt his energies flowing into the vast shield wall surrounding the mountains. It was like a child emptying a bucket into the sea. The shield snapped back, leaving him stunned. He fell against the troops who passed him behind the lines and stood ready. Bows sang from the mountainsides, killing many monsters as they charged.

The monstrous ranks crashed against the human defenders, driving them back step by step. A screech sounded above the human line. Beasts with the heads and breasts of hideous, old women and the bodies of vultures swept down upon them.

"Harpies! I must do something," gasped Ackdominel, who was recovering from his attempt to hold the shield.

Gathering his strength he directed his will inwards, picturing the eagles that flew over the valley of wizardry. He could feel bone and muscle shift and mould. Hair became feathers and sprouted all over him. With a cry he leapt into the air, spreading his mighty wings.

Catching the ascending thermals, Ackdominel circled higher and higher, until the humans below looked like ants. He could see that the shiny humans were being driven back. It wouldn't be long before the monsters reached the people that scurried up the pass carrying bundles.

Ackdominel, the eagle, focussed his eyes on one of the harpies and folded his wings. He plummeted towards the earth, the wind forcing the feathers of his neck hard against his skin. When he struck, his talons bit deep into the creature's flesh. The jolt snapped its neck. The eagle dropped the limp form and used his momentum to swoop up higher than the harpies could fly. Keening, the harpies beat the air, trying to reach the eagle who continued to climb. Again the eagle dove, killing a harpy, another followed then another. Climbing again the eagle folded his wings and plummeted through the harpies' ranks. Levelling his flight, the eagle soared across the sky, keeping to the low altitudes obtainable by his foes. In a rage, the harpies chased the eagle over the monster occupied lands.

When his momentum abated, the eagle climbed above the harpies' ceiling and flew back to the mountains. His wings ached, and he felt tired. His sole desire was to return to his nest. Flying over the humans, he looked down. The humans were behind the blue wall the sour tasting creatures couldn't pass through. Many of the shiny humans were being carried, and there were red stains on them.

The eagle shook his head, he felt the need to find his nest but couldn't remember where it was. Whenever he tried, a picture of a man nest came to mind. One human, with brown snakes dangling from its head, attracted him. The eagle flew closer and landed before the human with the brown snakes.

"Urnit ithing wohon ving," funny sounds came from the human.

"Quokgody, Ackdominel, can you hear me?" asked Melanie. She held her helm in her hand her twin braids dangling over her shoulders.

"What?" Ackdominel was in a daze, as his body shifted from eagle to man.

"Are you all right?" asked Melanie.

"What happened?"

"You turned into an eagle and fought the harpies."

"I did?"

"Yes!"

"Oh yes, I did, didn't I? Thank the eagle spirit."

"Three cheers for King Ackdominel," called Trom, who stood to one side nursing a small arm wound, "Hip hip hooray."

The cheer was quickly echoed by the troops.

"The food! Did you save it?" Ackdominel tried to piece human and eagle memories together.

"We saved everything, just. We lost more men, and many were wounded, but all our gear is safe," replied Melanie

"Good! If you bring me a nice, juicy, fat rabbit, I'll do what I can for the wounded after I have eaten."

"A rabbit, and how would you like that done?" Melanie raised her eyebrows.

"Done? Fresh killed. Mmm, a nice meadow hare!"

Several of the men in earshot began to chuckle. Seeing that Ackdominel was in earnest, their faces became as grave as Melanie's.

"Ackdominel, you're human. Human!" prodded Melanie.

Ackdominel looked at her incredulously then shook his head.

"I'm sorry. It is harder to come back than I thought it would be. Some cheese and bread please."

Smiling with relief, Melanie left to fetch him the food.

Chapter 18
Journey to the Heights

Later Ackdominel treated the many wounded, collapsing before dealing with half the cases. He was carried to a seat beside the fire.

"I am exhausted!" he stared into the flames.

"Who isn't?" countered Melanie, who sat beside him.

"At least everything is organised."

"Until the shield shrinks again."

"We will have warning next time. I intend to keep watch on the shield. We will know at least two days in advance of the next shrinkage."

"That's something."

"The troop is larger, is it not? I saw unfamiliar faces."

"Yes. I've had fifty new recruits since this morning. Seems news of yesterday's success has begun to spread. Though I admit, some are sceptical about my command after today's events."

"How so?"

"Several of them arrived during the retreat. Their first experience of my command was to have a bundle of something thrown at them and be ordered to run farther up the pass with it."

Ackdominel chuckled, "Impressive." Groaning, he moved his arms.

"What's wrong?"

"My arms. I must have pulled every muscle in them."

"Too bad you weren't a pigeon. You could have let them know what we think of them."

Ackdominel laughed shifting into a more comfortable position.

"How are you dealing out the food?" he asked.

"I can't feed everyone! I've been using it for my troops and their families. It gives an added incentive to join us."

"That's good." Ackdominel closed his eyes and settled in a lying position. "I am surprised their families are coming with them, considering how close to the shield we are."

"Some are already building stone huts up valley."

"I will spread the word of your glory when I return to the lodge."

"You're going so soon?"

"Within the week. These men need arms and armour. Tom can supply those. Not to mention the bows that should be waiting for us." Ackdominel smiled. "Besides, I have a tryst with a cute little Druidess named Woodreana."

"Sure you do. Seriously though, I need the rest of my troops armoured. As things stand, I'll need all the men I can muster."

Ackdominel's reply was an incomprehensible murmur. Melanie looked at his sleeping form, wrapped his cloak about him then walked towards her tent.

Over the next few days, word of Melanie's raid spread and men thronged to her banner. Some brought with them rusty swords and battered armour, some nothing more than a sling and a bag of stones, but all came drawn by the promise of food.

It was six days later that Ackdominel left the now large encampment. A troop of one hundred men to be armed and armoured accompanied him. Trom came to act as Ackdominel's lieutenant.

As the troop drew near Orlor and Erum's cottage, Ackdominel ordered Trom to lead them up the trail until sunset then make camp and wait for him. Filling a pack with dried meat, Ackdominel walked towards Orlor's cottage, reaching it by dusk.

"Hello."

"Who is it?" demanded Solin's voice.

"It is Ackdominel."

The deer hide that acted as a door was pulled aside to reveal Solin.

"It is good to see you, my friend," said Ackdominel.

"And you. Orlor should be back soon with the sheep, and Erum is fetching water."

"How is the boy? I have worried about him."

"He's no werewolf, but he has changed."

"How?"

"Come, see for yourself." Solin led Ackdominel outside.

The two men waited for a few minutes before the boy walked into view, a puppy chasing him.

"A dog! I thought they had been eaten?" said Ackdominel.

"Most were. Some were spared because they were useful to the shepherds. One of the neighbouring shepherds couldn't bring himself to roast his dog's pups, so we accepted Wolfsbane."

"Wolfsbane?"

"Wolfsbane. The dog isn't the change I mentioned. Watch this."

Solin called for Erum to hurry up.

"Yes, Uncle Solin?" The boy ran towards them. With a bow he added, "Greetings, Your Majesty."

"I taught him that," remarked Solin. "Erum, I want you to ask Wolfsbane to roll over, run around in a circle three times, jump up on a rock, wag his tail and bark, in that order. Please."

"He's tired," objected Erum.

"Please do it," said Solin.

Erum paused then the little dog began. It rolled over, ran in a circle and when the pup stood barking and wagging its tail Ackdominel commented, "Nice trick."

"It's no trick, Your Majesty. Dogs do what I tell them. Even Uncle Solin."

"What?"

"It's true," said Solin. "Orlor guessed about my curse and helped tie me up last full moon. I was snapping and growling when Erum spoke to me. I understood him. He told me they were my friends and to stop behaving badly. Then he started petting me. There was no way I could hurt him, and I knew I'd do anything he asked."

"Does he have this effect on all canines?"

"As far as we can tell."

"Useful... I wonder?"

"What?"

"Just a thought."

When Orlor arrived the four of them settled for a meal from Ackdominel's supplies. After eating Ackdominel examined Erum, and satisfied with what he found, left to rejoin his men. By this point, it was full dark, and he could barely see. Speaking a word of command, he caused the gold buckle on his belt to glow lighting his way. When he reached his men, they were settling for the night.

Ackdominel yelled, "Trom."

"Yes, Your Majesty," said Trom.

Ackdominel smiled and spoke. "By tomorrow evening the troop will be as close to the entrance of the dwarfen realm as I dare bring them. The day after that, I want you to come with me to the gates of the dwarven kingdom. You must keep the way there secret. Do you understand?"

"Yes, Your Majesty! Thank you for trusting me. I saw the dwarves that came to armour us. Fine folk, though passing strange."

"Part of the reason I chose you to lead this troop is Melanie said you accepted the dwarves well. Treated them with respect were her words. Continue to show respect to our allies, and in future, I will ask you to bring other groups here to be armoured."

"As I may best serve my king," said Trom, pleasure apparent in his voice.

"Good. Is my tent prepared?"

"Yes, Your Majesty, over there."

Trom pointed towards a small tent close to the camp's centre.

"Good. We march one hour after dawn."

The day that followed was uneventful except that Trom chose a man to command his troop during his absence. When the camp settled for the night, they were high along the mountain trail.

The following day dawned cold and so misty that Ackdominel could only see two strides through the fog. He waited at the edge of the encampment whistling a child's tune as Trom approached him.

"Are you prepared?" asked Ackdominel.

"Yes, but demons it's cold," remarked Trom, looking enviously at Ackdominel, clad in his white robe and light cloak.

"Cold?"

"Yes. Don't you feel it?"

"No. Of course, that is one of the properties of my cloak. Foolish that it should slip my mind."

Trom's teeth chattered as he hugged himself.

"Here, wear this." Ackdominel unfastened his cloak and draped it across Trom's shoulders.

Immediately Trom felt warm. Ackdominel now felt the cold breeze cut through his thin robe. He shivered then willed his body temperature to increase and led the way up the trail.

They walked for over an hour before reaching the entrance to the old mine shaft.

"This is the place," said Ackdominel.

"This? How could anything live in this? It's a dreary hole! Besides, it's pitch black in there. How will we see anything?"

"It goes deep, and you have not seen past the front gate. As to light, I'll see to it." Ackdominel touched the golden belt buckle he wore, and it began to glow. Then closing his eyes, he focussed his thoughts and touched Trom's scabbard. It began to shine in mimicry of the belt buckle.

"Magic," breathed Trom.

"A waste of power. If I had any sense, I'd have brought torches. Still, it will do." Entering the passage, Ackdominel moved to the iron door that formed the first defence of the dwarven kingdom.

"I am King Ackdominel, and this is my loyal subject. We have come to collect my tithe," he called into the air.

"King Ackdominel be yur? I'll have to be seeing a bit of proof of that," replied a gruff voice from behind the wall.

"Call Tuck or Prince Tom, both of them know me, or Gug."

"There be no need to be doing that. Yur can be coming in," said the voice, now taking on a friendly note. After a few moments passed, the iron door opened.

Trom and Ackdominel stepped into the dwarven realm and were greeted by a plump dwarf who appeared from the shadows by the door and bowed.

"Yur Majesty, it be fine to have yur back among us, it be."

"Thank you. Could you send word to Prince Tom of my arrival?"

"Sure, the message be sent it does." The dwarf pushed the door to and bolted it.

"Good. I'm curious. How did you know I was who I claimed to be?"

"That be simple. When yur mentioned that no-good layabout, Gug, yur had to have met him. People they be remembering kings and high officials they do, Gug 't aint either. Truth to tell, Gug 't aint much of anything, 'sept lazy."

"Oh. Could my guard stay with you while I start down the passage?"

"Now I be not one to say yur can't be moving freely in yur own kingdom. I'll be a warning yur though, there be a change or two since last yur were here."

"Changes?"

"Aye, we be adding to the cart system we be, and we also be putting in talker tubes."

"Talker tubes?" queried Trom.

"Aye, yur see like this one," said the dwarf as he led them into a small chamber on the passage's side. The room was so short Trom and Ackdominel had to duck walk to avoid the ceiling. As they entered, two dwarves, who were watching the entry tunnel through cracks in the wall, waved.

"This be a talker tube," said the dwarf pulling a steel cap off a narrow pipe that disappeared down the tunnel. He blew into the pipe, his cheeks puffing out as he did so and waited. After a time, a faint voice issued from the pipe.

"High station here, what do you want, guard room?" it demanded.

"His Majesty be starting down. Be passing the word along," said the dwarf into the pipe.

"Fascinating. How does it work?" asked Ackdominel.

"The pipe it goes to the first station where the attendant be posted. When I be blowing into it, a whistle be sounding, so he knows to come. Then when either end talks into the tube, the message it be carried. The attendant sends it along to the next station and so on."

"Useful." Ackdominel returned to the main corridor. "Trom, you are to wait here so you can guide the dwarves to our men. I will rejoin you at the camp before the armouring is complete."

"Your Majesty, shouldn't I stay with you as guard," objected Trom.

"No. I wish to move quickly. You would slow me down." Ackdominel turned and started down the stairs into the dwarfen principality.

Hours later Ackdominel staggered through the entrance the dwarves had cut into the wizards' valley.

"Thank the gods Tom agreed to put off the feast until I return. If I had to eat anything!" He fell silent as the mere thought brought his stomach contents to his throat. "I hate those carts! At least Tom agreed to have his dwarves start on the armour immediately."

Chapter 19
Magic Brethren

Forcing his nausea down, Ackdominel descended the stair to the thirteenth lodge. Entering, he sat until his stomach had settled then strode to the ceremony room and moved directly to his throne. Focussing his will, he pushed against the barrier of space and in seconds was in the magic users' council room. He noticed that now only twenty chairs sat at the table, and slumped into his seat shaking his head.

"So many," he murmured. He noticed that a door, other than his own, bore the symbol of opening. Searching his mind for the representation of a silver wave that marked the door he matched it to an order.

"The order of the Changing Sea. They are from the southern archipelago and their magic deals with controlling weather, wave, and sea life," he whispered.

Moving to the door, he traced the wave symbol to summon the other master. In minutes the door swung open and a burly, weather-beaten man, in his mid-twenties appeared. He was shorter than Ackdominel, though broader in the shoulder and deeper in the chest. His sandy-blond hair fell in an unruly length about his shoulders, and his face had a harsh, angular cut.

"Greetings, brother." Ackdominel inclined his head.

"Greetings. I am Searun. Why did you not come when I summoned?" Searun surveyed Ackdominel with piercing grey eyes.

"I was too far from my throne to hear the summons. Shall we sit?"

"Yes." Searun smiled.

"How stands your shield?"

"It will hold long enough. We have only lost a few of the outer islands. Though the gales that occur when those beasts draw nigh have sunk many a ship. We will last until we can reach Haven."

"Good! I plan to leave soon myself."

"It would be easier if we could bring the power keys through the council room."

"Yes. It is a pity their energy would disrupt the enchantment, but there is nothing that can be done about it. They must be brought through the physical world or not at all."

"I still think we should have explored the possibility of shielding the keys more."

Ackdominel's past life memory of Searun came to the fore at that. He groaned as he recalled hours of argument on the issue of the power keys. "It was a debate for another life. Decisions were made, and it's too late to change them. Let's move on. How stand things with our other brothers and sisters?"

Searun shook his head. "Poorly! Many shields have failed, as you can see, and many of those left are weakening."

"When I was here last, I helped Woodreana to strengthen hers, but it undoubtedly needs more." Ackdominel's tone was an invitation.

Searun smiled. "Then, brother, we shall give it more. I, until today, have been too busy with my own affairs to aid any other. Tell me though, is she as lovely as she was in her last life."

Ackdominel smiled, "If anything more so."

"You're a lucky man, my friend, even if your views on magical shielding are wrong-headed." Searun laughed. The two men rose and moved towards the door adorned with stag's antlers and acorns. They paused to gather their strength then stepped through into total darkness.

"Stand still. I will open the door and let some light in," said Ackdominel.

"This is well. I cannot see a thing."

"Neither can I. I remember where everything is." Taking a step, Ackdominel barked his shin before reaching the door. Opening the door gave enough light for Searun to move to his side.

"Where is she?" he asked.

"Either in a training lodge or her hut, I imagine. I should warn you, she has befriended a young centaur."

"Interesting! Did I mention the mermaid that visits my island?"

"No. I have elves and dwarves forming principalities in my mountains. I am beginning to wonder if we are saving the world or giving it away."

"Both!" replied Searun, as they exited the lodge's corridor into the starlit night.

Ackdominel led the way to Woodreana's cabin where they found her poring over an old text.

"Ackdominel!" she exclaimed then noticing Searun she added, "Who did you bring with you?"

"Searun of the order of the Changing Sea," Ackdominel introduced his fellow master.

"Have you come to help strengthen the shield?"

"Yes. You sound anxious, is it preparing to collapse?" demanded Searun.

"Yes. As you know, my order's magic draws strength from nature. With so many refugees in the woods, nature's balance has been disrupted. The shield is failing. I also fear that the refugees might break through to my island. That would mean the end of the last area where nature remains intact. The shield would crumble immediately if that happens."

"We will do what we can," Ackdominel assured her.

Soon they all stood in the oak grove.

The ceremony to strengthen the shield was the same as before save that a third line of force joined the spiral of eldritch energy. The shield seemed to snatch at the power, dragging it from the mystics.

When they finished the ritual exhaustion overtook them, and they fell to the ground and slept.

With morning Ackdominel found that his old friend the tree root, or one exactly like it, had been hard at work excavating another hole in his back. He rose with a groan and looked about. Searun was gone. Woodreana stirred and opened her eyes. He was abruptly reminded of his manhood. She looked vulnerable and inviting. She lay on the forest floor, her hair in disarray, looking at him with her large, green eyes. He swallowed in a dry throat.

"Did it work?" she asked as she stretched, which did nothing to alleviate his discomfort.

"You can check it as easily as I can. I am sure it must have, or I would not feel this drained."

"You have a point." Coming to her feet, she leaned against an oak tree.

Ackdominel followed her lead, taking comfort from the sense of life in the tree.

"I must go. I have a lot of work to do," he said.

"As do I."

Woodreana took a step forward and stumbled.

He caught her before she fell. Her body rested against his as they leaned on each other for support. He looked down at her. She raised her face to his. Their eyes met then their lips. The kiss was at first tentative but soon grew earnest.

Woodreana pushed away and stared at him.

"I feel. I feel. I hardly know you... But it seems so right with you. I...," she wondered.

"You know me far better then you think!" said Ackdominel. He once more bent to kiss her. She responded with no hesitancy. Turning they walked arm in arm to Woodreana's cottage.

It was past noon before Ackdominel rose and dressed. Woodreana stared at him from the bed.

"Must you go so soon?"

"I am afraid so, my love. In our world there can be little rest for such as we."

"True." Woodreana stretched leisurely upon her bed. "I must prepare myself anyway. My teachers have summoned me for a lesson."

"I hope I did not take you from last night's lesson."

"You didn't. My teachers call me when I am to go to them. They didn't call last night. Perhaps they knew you were coming."

"Perhaps." Ackdominel pulled his cloak over his shoulders and knelt by Woodreana's bed to kiss her.

"Why does it feel so right with you?"

"Are you in your sixth lodge?"

"Yes."

"You will have your answer soon. Until then take care, my little chipmunk."

"Chipmunk," repeated Woodreana, with raised eyebrows.

Ackdominel shrugged. Leaving the cottage, he walked to the seventh of Woodreana's teaching rooms. Without pause, he opened the door and stepped through into the mystic's council chamber. Striding to his orders door, he opened it and was immediately sitting on the throne in his ceremony room. Rising he ate then gathered everything from the lodges that might be useful to his people. Wrapping the items in blankets, he carried them to the entrance to the dwarven realm.

He was checking the lodges for anything he might have missed when Shalor hailed him from below. Ackdominel met Shalor on the balcony of the tenth lodge.

"Hello, my friend, it is good to see you once again," remarked Ackdominel.

"I couldn't let you leave without wishing you farewell." After a long pause, he added, "You look awful!"

"Why thank you, and you're looking fine as well."

"Seriously. You should rest a night before returning to the outer world. You look exhausted."

"I have no time. Tonight I will sleep in the dwarven city and be on the other side of the mountains by tomorrow afternoon."

"You're the king. Tell me. Will we see you again?"

"That depends on how quickly the monsters are driven back."

Shalor nodded.

"Anything left in the lodges after sundown tonight is yours to do with as you please."

"I would rather you stay, but that is not to be. Pity though, Talion is becoming impossible."

"I can imagine. He has always been impossible. It will not be long after the monsters attack that he will change."

"Yes. That will sober him, and many of us."

"I thought that if you died on this plane of existence, you were simply forced to return to your own?"

"If you had ever experienced it, you wouldn't say simply! It is something to be avoided. After such a death it is a long time before one can plane travel again. I'd rather not be put in the situation."

"Oh." Ackdominel extended his hand.

Shalor accepted the hand and shook it, saying, "Live long and happily, elf friend."

"May joy and peace of heart be yours."

Both men returned to their separate duties.

It was nearly sundown when Ackdominel returned to the thirteenth lodge's ceremony room. The crystal throne sat upon the floor, glowing dimly in the darkness. Beginning a chant, he stroked the chair's armrests. It drew in upon itself, growing smaller and smaller. Sweat broke out upon his brow. The throne shrank until it was the width of his palm. Wrapping the throne in silk, he placed it in his pack as the lodge grew dark and cold.

He solemnly climbed the stairs towards the entrance of the dwarfen principality, pausing on the highest balcony to look over the valley. It was different than he remembered. Its magic had changed. No longer was it the enchantment of man. Now the strange magic of the elves pervaded the air. He looked one last time at the beautiful scene below then plunged into the darkness of the tunnel.

Chapter 20
A Bed for the Night

When his eyes adjusted to the dark, Ackdominel noticed Gug.

"It be nice of Yur Majesty to be coming. I be thinking yur would be missing the feast," remarked Gug.

"I said I would come. Can you help me with my belongings?"

"Sure I can be helping. If yur will be passing me yur pack, I'll carry it fer yur."

"There's more than my pack. I will have to carry my parcels out of the sun. You can put them in the cart." Saying this Ackdominel left, returning momentarily with a heavy bundle.

"If you'll be pardoning me asking, how many loads are yur bringing?"

"Ten."

"Couldn't you be about magickin' them into the cart so's we can be gettin' to the feast? We be running late yur see."

"I am too tired to maintain a spell like that. We are going to have to do this the old-fashioned way."

Gug stood mouth agape as Ackdominel left the cavern and returned with another load.

"If it be pleasing, Yur Majesty, I have a thought."

"What is it, Gug?"

"I be thinking that maybe we should be getting to the feast. Prince Tom can be sending a team to be moving yur belongings to the far entrance."

"Is that wise?" asked Ackdominel, a smile playing at the edge of his lips.

"Aye. Me back be none too good. I don't be wanting to throw it out."

"Very well."

It took less than a minute for them to walk to the start of the cart system. Ackdominel grew to loathe the carts more with each journey, but due to their speed, he arrived at the feast only slightly late.

Tom sat at the head table with an untouched loaf in front of him. Ackdominel entered; then all rose calling, "Hail to the King."

Ackdominel walked to his seat at the head table, bowed and sat.

"Wine?" he asked. A goblet of the elves' best was thrust into his hand.

"Yur were getting late," remarked Tom, once Ackdominel had drained the goblet.

"Too much to be done in too little time."

Gug approached the head table and bowed before speaking. "Begging yur pardons yur lordships, but I be thinking His Majesty be forgetting his possessions at the elves' gate."

"Ahh yes. Prince Tom, could you please have some of your people transport my goods for me? They are at the valley entrance to your realm. I would appreciate it if you could have them taken to the other entrance."

"Sure I can be doing that. Gug yur to be taking a group of folk and be seein' to His Majesty's goods."

"But… But... Yur Highness, won't I be needed here to serve His Majesty?" stammered Gug.

"I don't be thinking His Majesty will be needin' much beyond a bed. If yur hurry, yur can be back for when he be waken'."

"Yes, Yur Highness," sighed Gug, who slunk away.

"A good lad. Lazy as a tunnel worm, but a good lad still the same," stated Tom.

For Ackdominel the feast dragged endlessly. Finally, Tom led him to a room containing one of the rope beds from the lodges. Ackdominel barely covered himself before falling asleep.

He opened his eyes. Above him, the trees of a woodland glade swayed. A brook babbled to his left, and the air was sweet.

"Hello, old friend," said a strong, baritone voice.

Ackdominel rolled over and saw a man step out from between the trees. The man had long, silver-grey hair that fell about his white-robed shoulders. A beard covered his face, save for a well-proportioned nose, rosy cheeks and piercing green eyes.

"Hello, Geran," said Ackdominel, rising to his feet.

"I have come to warn you. Our foes are planning a magical attack against you."

"What is its nature?"

"I do not know. We cannot penetrate their defences well enough to discover more than I have told you."

"Probably another mind feeder."

"Maybe, but do not be too sure. There are many beasts with power. I must go. You have been warned! Prepare!"

"I shall! Peace to you and thank you for the warning."

Geran faded from view.

Ackdominel awoke feeling refreshed. After dressing, he exited his room to find Tom waiting for him.

"Yur be wishing to be off now?" remarked Tom, leading the way along the corridor.

"Yes, I wish I had more time."

"Don't be worrying yurself. Yur will come back when yur come back. I be wanting to have a word with yur about that armour yur be wanting."

"What is it?"

"We need to be setting the limits of the tithe. No offence to yur, but most of me dwarves were coming here to escape our old king's taxes. Were it a mistake for them to come?"

"You are right. Is twenty new suits annually until the War of the Storm is over acceptable? After that, you'll only have to arm the royal household."

"That be fair enough," agreed Tom, as they turned into the main passage of the dwarven city and walked towards the lake chamber.

"Is that everything?"

"Aye, that be all of a princely nature. As yur friend, I be wanting to see yur off."

"I appreciate that, but I can't make you ride in the carts. There's no reason we both should suffer."

"I be appreciating that!"

"Farewell, my friend," said Ackdominel, as he boarded the small boat to begin his journey to the surface world.

"Farewell," called Tom, as the ferry dwarf untied the boat's bowline and pushed it into the lake.

Ackdominel emerged from the dwarfen principality to find his possessions piled at the cavern's entrance. Muttering a spell, he levitated the awkward bundles and, with them trailing behind him, started down the trail. He reached his camp at sunset and was challenged by a sentry dressed in dwarfen chainmail.

"It is King Ackdominel," he replied.

"The king approaches," called the sentry, whose mouth then dropped open.

"What is it, man? What is the matter, you look like you have seen a ghost?"

"Y... Y... Your Majesty, I think I have," stammered the sentry, pointing towards the floating bundles.

"Do not worry. That is my doing. I have brought some equipment from my stronghold. Take a blanket."

The man stared at the heap, swallowed then darted forward, snatched a blanket, and leapt back.

"Was that so difficult?" Ackdominel walked to the camp's fire and deposited the pile of goods beside the cook.

"I suggest you add the stores I have brought to your larder. Most of them are not suited for travel, but as long as we are here, you can put them to good use."

The cook stared at Ackdominel then at the pile. Taking a deep breath, he separated the provisions from the other goods. More men crowded in to snatch up useful items as Ackdominel went to rest.

He had just lain down when Trom approached. With a sigh of resignation, Ackdominel opened his eyes and sat up.

"You certainly made an entrance," remarked Trom.

"I guess I did. Hopefully, that will end the rumours that I am a fraud! Did I surprise them?"

"Not everyone. Some here saw that storm you whipped up, but most nearly fouled their britches."

"Good! How many of our men are armoured?"

"Five, why?"

"I cannot wait for the rest of the troop. Have any who are armoured meet me at sun-up, the day after tomorrow. I will be at the village you were living in. They are to be my personal guard."

"You, a bodyguard?"

"Best not to tempt fate, and I have to keep up appearances."

"As you wish. Why the day after tomorrow?"

"Because today is the last chance I will have to rest for a long time. Tomorrow I am going to be persuading a friendly werewolf and a boy who can control him to join us."

#

The next morning Ackdominel travelled to Orlor's cottage, arriving before noon, to find Erum sitting by the door watching Wolfsbane chase his tail. At Ackdominel's approach, the boy froze and sniffed the air.

"Greetings, Your Majesty," he called.

"Greetings. Where are your father and Solin?"

"They're looking after the sheep. They left me to guard the cottage."

"You are doing a fine job of it. Maybe it is for the best you are here. I really came to speak with you." Ackdominel took a seat on a rock.

"To me?" breathed Erum, who cocked an ear listening.

"What is it?"

"A bat. Something woke it."

Ackdominel stared at the child, before continuing with his proposition.

"I have an idea that I need your help with."

"You need my help? But you're a wizard, and a king, and I'm, well I'm."

"Able to command dogs."

"Well yes. I think so. Dogs like me."

"Did you know some of the monsters are like dogs?"

"No. Does this mean dogs are bad?"

"No. Only the monster dogs are bad. Like humans are good and ogres are bad."

"Not all humans are good. There are lots of bad men."

"You are right, but for our purpose they are good," explained Ackdominel.

"Whatever you say."

"Do you think if you asked these bad dog things to fight on our side, they would?"

"Maybe. I would have to see them to do that."

"I know. I want to take you, Solin and your father to where we are battling the monsters. We can find out if the dog monsters will obey you there."

"Could Wolfsbane come?"

"Of course! We might even have a use for him."

"You're not going to eat him?"

"Of course not!"

"The last time someone said they had a use for Wolfsbane they were carrying a spit," explained Erum.

The arrival of Orlor and Solin, driving the flock, saved Ackdominel from more eight-year-old explanations. He helped herd the animals into their pen before any words were exchanged.

"To what do we owe this visit?" asked Solin.

"I will tell you inside," replied Ackdominel.

When they were seated behind bowls of mutton soup Ackdominel explained his plans.

"Let me see if I understand this. You want me to become a werewolf at night and prowl through the enemy camp. You must be mad! I could get killed!" objected Solin.

"Yes and I'll not have my boy's life risked," added Orlor.

"I know it sounds strange, but think of the advantages. Enough food and Solin could be among men again. All Erum would have to do is say kill monsters, not men. You could appease your bloodlust with no human the worse for it."

"That is true," commented Solin.

"What about my boy. King or no, you'll not put him at risk while I live to have a say about it."

"Erum will be safe. I guarantee it. In the beginning, all we would do is ascertain if he can control the monster dogs."

The discussion lasted the rest of the day and into the night. The next morning when Ackdominel left, Solin, Orlor and Erum accompanied him, driving their flock before them.

When they reached the closest town a one-armed man, dressed in battered scale armour, with a sword at his side, stood at the gate.

"Greetings, Your Majesty, I am Slall, guardian of this village," spoke the man, as he bowed. The empty arm of his armour dangled from his shoulder.

"Greetings, Slall. Why are you guarding the gate? Are towns still raiding each other?" asked Ackdominel.

"Haven't had an attack since you passed through. The seneschal thinks it's better safe than sorry. I was stuck with guard duty because I was the only fighting man left in the village."

"I see. Have my honour guard arrived?"

"Yes! Quite a sight to see! My old armour never looked the half of what theirs does."

"How much do you want for your old suit and blade?"

"If I gave up my armour, who would guard the town?"

"Soon the town will not need guarding, and I need every scrap of armour I can lay my hands on."

"Well. It was given me in the King's service, so it's really yours already."

"Good. I will take it with me when I leave. Is this all the armour in the town?"

"Let me think. There's Borin's old, hardened-leather suit. He fell off a cliff. I think his widow has it."

"Is that Josha?" asked Orlor.

"Yes."

"Tell her I'll trade my cottage and sheep for the armour."

"As you wish." Slall left to remove his own armour and fetch the other suit.

Orlor and Solin herded the sheep into a pen beside the gate and slaughtered one to appease the hungry villagers. Ackdominel collected his guards, returning minutes later with five men dressed in plate armour. They all waited at the gate until Slall returned with Josha and the armour. Promising better days ahead, Ackdominel led his troop from the village.

It took four days for the party to reach Melanie's camp, which had swollen to nearly fill the mountain pass with a litter of rude stone huts and tents. Ackdominel wove his way through the camp to the huts that served as the officers' quarters. In the centre of this, he found Melanie sitting on a crude chair.

"Ackdominel, you're back. Where's Trom and his men?" she asked as he approached.

"They are coming. It takes even dwarves time to make armour."

"Demon spit. I need that company."

"Why? It appears you have more than enough manpower?"

"Men I have. Equipment I don't. I've two thousand warriors and only enough equipment for five hundred or so."

"That is bad. Have you thought of buying suits from the refugees? I gathered two suits on the way here that way."

"I've been doing that. I pay a good half a lamb for a suit of chain, but equipment is slow in coming, and there's only so much in the mountains to start with."

"How progresses the raiding?"

"Acceptably. I've managed to keep my troops and their families fed, but each time the resistance is tougher, and the supply tent farther off. Soon we'll fail at a raid. Then we'll begin to starve."

"Would the beasts guarding the other passes be easier prey?"

"I've been waiting for Trom to return. I want to place half the force under him and start raiding at other points while keeping a force here to threaten them. That way I can keep their main force occupied while he brings in the food."

"That is a good strateg-- arrrrrg! Arrrrrg!! Arrrrrg!!!" Ackdominel screamed clutching his head and falling to his knees. Fire exploded between his temples, and his stomach writhed like a snake.

"Gods!" he exclaimed then the pain struck again.

The pain subsided, and he seized his chance. Focussing his will, he thrust against the shattered remnants of his personal mystic shield, forcing them into a whole. His shield wavered then, as he placed the full force of his will behind the shield, it grew strong. Another attack lashed him, but this time his shield held. Sweat broke out on his brow, then as quickly as it had come the attack ended. With a groan, he collapsed into unconsciousness.

Chapter 21
Wizards at War

The light that filtered through the canvas wind hole cover of his stone hut woke Ackdominel. His head throbbed like a drum, and the inside of his mouth tasted like an aviary's floor.

"Whatever I was drinking should be banned," he griped.

"You're awake," remarked a rail of a girl, who sat beside him wearing a tattered dress. She was dipping a cloth in a basin of water.

"I must be. I hurt too much to sleep."

The girl laid the cloth across his brow and let her hand rest for a second touching his face. He felt a tingling sensation and noticed his headache lessen. She removed her hand, and the sensation ended.

"I have to summon General Melanie. She told me to call her as soon as you awoke," said the girl. Pulling red-brown hair away from her face, she moved to leave the tent.

"Tell her to bring food when you see her."

Minutes passed before Melanie barged in carrying a tray.

"What happened? One minute you were fine, the next you were screaming," she demanded, taking a seat.

"An attack more powerful than anything I have encountered in all my lives." Ackdominel accepted the tray.

"An attack, but the monsters don't have sorcerers strong enough to challenge you! Do they?"

"Not that we have met! Tell me how long have I been unconscious?"

"Most of a day. I had Elin, the healer you saw just now, attend you when I couldn't."

"I want to get to know that girl."

"That's sick. She's hardly more than a child!"

"Not for that reason! She has a talent for the art. She already instinctively uses low-grade, energy healing. Properly trained she could be formidable."

"I doubt she'd be interested. She's totally dedicated to the healing arts. There's not a hurtful bone in her body. That's why I assigned her to you."

"Why should that matter? A mystic healer is a precious thing. In the days before the Covetous God, there were entire orders dedicated to healing. This is for the future. Now I must prepare. Pass me my sword then leave this tent and place a guard at the door. No matter what, no one is to enter until I emerge. No one. For any reason; on peril of their soul! Do you understand?"

Melanie looked at Ackdominel fearfully. A malevolent strangeness seemed to emanate from him. She nodded, passed him his sword and left the hut.

Ackdominel rose, trembling with the strain. Unsheathing his sword, he began to chant. His voice rose to a shout then he drove the point of the blade into the ground. He collapsed onto his cot without seeing the huge black dog that appeared beside him.

Melanie stood outside Ackdominel's door flap, trembling.

This is ridiculous. I know him. He's my friend, was my lover. Ogres and trolls scare me less than this. She inhaled deeply, steadying herself. *It's his power. It's like a knife. It can heal in the hands of a surgeon or kill in the hands of a murderer. I never saw how dangerous he could be until now. I can understand why the followers of the Covetous God feared the wizards so. Thank the gods Ackdominel is benevolent, or he could be worse than the Storm itself.*

She hailed a pair of passing soldiers and ordered them to guard Ackdominel's tent.

#

Ackdominel awoke into darkness. He struck the flat of his sword with his palm while intoning a thank you. Rising, he donned his robe and exited the hut into the light of a nearly full moon. He was hailed by a pair of pale-faced guards.

"Your Majesty, are you all right?" asked the bolder of the two.

"Yes. What happened while I slept?"

"The demon thing in the tent, it howled and snarled. No one dared go near. Even without the general's orders, no one would have disturbed you. We thought you were done for."

Ackdominel smiled, in a way he hoped was reassuring, but the moonlight turned it into a death's head grin.

"All was well. That was simply my watchdog. You are dismissed."

The two men bolted.

Ackdominel shook his head and returned to his tent where he put on his remaining possessions. When he emerged, false dawn had arrived. He made his way towards Melanie's tent and was drawing near when he heard a voice hailing him from his right.

"So, you are alive. You've been in your tent for two days. We were becoming concerned," said Solin. His chest was blood-flecked, and his face was smeared with gore.

"As well you might. The force that struck me was enough to level a mountain. What has happened since I withdrew?"

"Bad luck, everywhere! Swords breaking, people slipping, fires getting out of hand. Can you explain it?"

"Our enemy has a skilled sorcerer. A being who knows how to penetrate our shields. He, she, or it, is responsible," explained Ackdominel as they walked towards the cook fire.

"Monster sorcerers? I thought that was impos--."

"Not impossible. Rare, but not impossible. Not many types of monsters can produce them."

When they reached the cook fire, Solin ladled water from a steaming caldron into a basin and washed.

"We can help. I'm sure Melanie could mount an offensive, and we could fight our way through to your foe," he suggested.

"No. This is my battle. I must face this challenge alone. This is, in part, why my order exists. Besides, my enemy could be half a world away."

"Is there anything we can do to help?"

"One thing."

"What?"

"Feed me! I am starved!"

Once he had eaten Ackdominel left the camp in search of a private place suited to his needs. Finding a deserted plateau on the mountainside, he prepared for battle. By sunset he was ready.

A circle of power dominated the flat area, and Ackdominel's tools lay upon an east-facing altar of piled stone. Taking up his sword he lifted it above his head and called, "I challenge thee, follower of the dark ways. Come thee forth and face me."

He waited, feeling like a bowstring, pulled tight in anticipation of the arrow's flight. He was preparing to call again when a thin voice issued from the air.

"I, Malose, the undead Mage of the desert, hear the challenge and come to answer."

A lich! I should have guessed. I wonder how many centuries since this mage's spirit should have gone to the land of the dead, thought Ackdominel, but he only said, "You will fall!"

"Never! I almost crushed you before. Now I shall destroy you," said the voice, growing stronger with each syllable.

"You surprised me, demon spawn. Now I am prepared!"

Ackdominel focussed a line of mental force against his opponent, which glanced harmlessly off the lich's shield, as did the force directed against his own shields. The preliminaries dealt with, Ackdominel began the battle in earnest. Raising his wand, he called, "Spirits of wind that scream and blow. I call on thee to fell my foe."

Wind screamed about the lich, pulling at its robes, dragging the skeletal remains of its physical body towards the edge of its protective circle.

"Enough!" cried Malose and the wind subsided.

Ackdominel stood awaiting his enemy's counterstrike. The earth beneath him began to quake and heave. Boulders fell from the surrounding cliffs, while Ackdominel struggled to keep from being thrown outside the protection of his circle. Clutching at his staff for balance, he screeched a spell.

"By the mirror, that to the source returns. This spell of earth shall now be turned."

#

Malose posed arrogantly in its circle as its spell struck the ground about Ackdominel. Suddenly, the floor beneath Malose's feet began to tremble and quake. The creature raised a skeletal hand, and all grew quiet.

"Use my own spell against me, little wizard. Taste flame as your reward," it spat.

#

Fire leapt up about Ackdominel's circle. Smoke filled the air as the temperature soared. He fell to his knees as he struggled to gasp out the spell that would save him.

#

Malose waited within its circle for many minutes before lying on the ground. It separated its mind from its decaying, physical form. The mental nature of Malose flew across the distance separating it from Ackdominel. Reaching the mountains' shield, it paused as if adjusting its nature then passed through.

Ackdominel lay in his circle, the ground about him scorched and blackened by the flames. The lich moved closer and watched for movement. No breadth seemed to stir Ackdominel's still form.

"Pity! He would have made a formidable lich, but he was too foolishly noble. It wouldn't have mattered anyway, none can defeat the undead Mage of the desert," Malose gloated, as it backed away from the circle's edge.

The lich returned to its body. Straightening the blood-red robe that covered what remained of its physical form, it stepped from the circle.

Energy bombarded the lich, smashing its personal shields and washing the fragments away like wood chips upon the sea.

Ackdominel pounded into the stunned monster's mind, driving his will deeper and deeper into his enemy's psyche. Finally, he reached the connections that held the lich to its decaying earthly form. With an effort of will, he tore the connections free. The lich screeched as its spirit went careening into the plains of the dead, leaving its bones to clatter onto the ground.

#

Ackdominel leaned upon his staff within his circle, silently thanking every teacher who had drilled body control into him. They had taught him how to slow his heartbeat and breathing so that he appeared to be dead. He took a deep breath and straightened. The last thrust had drained his carefully hoarded reserves. With meticulous care, he took down his magical circle then slowly returned to the camp.

It was well past dawn when he arrived to be met by Melanie.

"What happened?"

"I won." Ackdominel walked towards the nearest cook fire.

Later he recounted his tale to a rapt audience.

"What exactly is a lich?" asked one of the crowd.

"A lich is a sorcerer who refuses to die. He or she turns their arts upon themselves, transforming themselves into a member of the undead," explained Ackdominel.

"It's hard to believe that anything that was once human would join with the monsters," remarked Melanie.

"Once is the important word," said Ackdominel.

Chapter 22
Escape

Months passed. The number of warriors under Melanie's standard increased until she could field a force at every pass leaving the mountains. As Melanie ordered the army's deployment, Ackdominel prepared the populace for the exodus. Finally, the human population stood ready, nearly a quarter million strong. Many chose to stay behind, feeling that escape to the human-held territories was a foolish fantasy.

Ackdominel stood on the mountainside, overlooking the non-shielded areas. The view resembled an anthill, swarming with the creatures of the Storm.

"Fathers of wizardry, grant me strength," he whispered.

Melanie clambered to his side.

"Is everything ready?" she asked.

"As ready as it's likely to be. We will begin in the morning. Is Trom's force engaged?"

"The runners report since dawn. Question is, did we give the monsters enough time to transfer their forces from the other passes to this one? They have to think the major offensive will be here or Trom won't break through."

Ackdominel bit his lip as he thought. "If I were their commander, with the forces we have allowed them to think we have, I would suspect we had emptied our garrisons to muster this many warriors."

Melanie nodded. "If… when Trom breaks through, clearing the other passes should be simple enough. He can lead thousands out of the mountains before our enemies realise we're the feint."

Ackdominel closed his eyes and seemed to look inward for a second. "He will break through. I can sense that."

"Good. Now it's up to us to clear the main pass. I worry that once we're out, we may not have enough troops to protect our people."

Ackdominel snorted. "Of course we don't have enough troops to guarantee a safe passage. Once we're out, it's a sprint to the coast and gods help those who fall behind."

Melanie nodded. "Now to why I'm here. There are a lot of troops out there." She gestured to the monsters crowding the pass. "How are we supposed to break through that?"

"Fight as well as you can. Keep our foes' forces here away from Trom. When the time comes, I will take a hand. We will escape. One way or another!" Ackdominel stared at the ground and shook his head disparagingly.

The next morning dawned blood-red. Melanie led her troops in a charge against the monsters. The forces met with a crash, but soon the humans were being driven back. When the human line seemed ready to collapse, Ackdominel strode forward with Erum on his back. Arrows whistled about them, but any time one approached it would deviate to one side or the other. When Ackdominel and Erum stood just behind the lines of fighting humans, Erum made a series of yapping and yipping sounds. The canines among the monsters went mad, attacking the beasts of the Storm. The humans rallied, forcing their opponents back. Other humans surged forward with wheelbarrows and stretchers, collecting the wounded and dead. Once behind the shield the fallen were stripped of their armour.

Ackdominel stayed well back from the battle, biding his time. It was as evening fell that a messenger ran into the human encampment. Her breath came in gasps, and the light tunic and leggings she wore were sweat drenched. She was passed a water skin by the communications officer then brought before Ackdominel.

"I've a message for General Melanie," the girl gasped her slender form starting to shake with chill and excursion.

"Give it to me," ordered Ackdominel.

"I was ordered to give it to the general."

"I am King Ackdominel. If you want Melanie, you will have to go get her." He gestured to where the fighting was thickest.

"Please, Your Majesty. I meant no disrespect. I can tell you."

"Smart girl."

"Commander Trom has broken through the Pine Valley pass. He's split his troops and is leading the first group of refugees out of the mountains. He's left five hundred men to attack the other passes from the rear and has ordered the armour from the wounded to be sent to you. It should start arriving sometime tomorrow."

"Good! Very good! Maybe we do stand a chance."

The battle raged until dusk when the retreat sounded. Step by step the human force fell back to the protection of the shield.

As soon as Melanie entered the camp, Ackdominel approached her.

"Trom has broken through and is heading towards the coast. He has left five hundred to help open the other passes," he said as he helped her remove her dented, blood-spattered armour.

"Good! Have you been to the casualty huts?"

"On and off all day. It's bad! We have lost a lot of good people, and many are maimed."

"Demon spit, I need all the experienced troops I can muster. My reserves are green as grass."

"I know. Trom is sending armour. It should arrive tomorrow. For now, have one of the helpers give you a rubdown. You will have to fight again with the dawn."

The next day was little more than a repetition of the first. Though now the monstrous dogs had all been killed or driven off. About noon messengers began to arrive saying that other passes had been cleared of the Storm. Ackdominel tallied the numbers. Nearly a hundred thousand had escaped.

With sunset the troops returned, more weary and bloody than the day before. The dead piled just outside the camp formed a grizzly hill where ravens feasted.

Melanie came to Ackdominel before the evening light had faded. "We can't keep on like this! We've nearly exhausted our trained reserves. Soon I'll be sending able bodies into the field. Even the best of us are ready to drop."

"I know. I will take a hand tomorrow. As many of the other passes as can be opened have been. We flee with the dawn."

"What can you do? A storm is helpful but will hardily win out against these numbers."

"I have abilities you do not suspect. I have not used them because I will have to draw energy from an outside source. The only thing nearby with enough energy to supply my need will be depleted."

"What?" began Melanie then realisation dawned, "The shield?"

"Yes! It will shrink. Also, I cannot guarantee I will kill all the monsters in our path. The spell has a limited range. I had to use you to force them to commit their reserves. Draw our enemies close tomorrow. I will do the rest."

Ackdominel spent the night amid the injured. In the wee hours, he ordered the wounded moved up the valley and joined the troops massing for their third day of battle.

Dawn found him standing before the double line of human warriors at the shield's edge. The monsters gestured and threatened him in a tightly packed jumble. He raised his arms and began to mutter.

#

Shalor sat in his tree house, eating a loaf and fruit when he felt a flux of energy. Running out he looked at the shield, which shifted and changed as if a great current was drawing all its force to one point. "Ackdominel. Soon my people will join your war," he whispered returning to his breakfast.

#

Energy built about Ackdominel then surged through him towards his enemies. Flames leapt from the earth searing monstrous flesh from bone. Three-quarters of the beasts were destroyed in seconds, while others writhed at the edge of the flames' embrace. The stench of burning flesh filled the air then the flames were gone. The shield retreated up the pass until it was a distant shimmer.

#

Melanie stared at the mass of scorched flesh before her.

"Gods of my fathers! He killed the lot of them," swore a man to her left.

A shudder ran through her as she forced herself to the task at hand. "He left some for us. Piper, sound the charge!"

The sound of the bagpipes echoed off the pass's walls as the humans rushed through the smouldering remnants of the monsters, crashing into the disordered creatures beyond, routing them. The refugees, some pulling ramshackle carts of supplies, followed close on the warriors' heals. The humans raced onto the plain and turned west to the sea.

Chapter 23
Trudge

The charge of escaping humans slowed to a walk then degraded to a trudge. They moved across the monster-held lands, straining themselves to the limit, driven by fear of attack. Children who collapsed were carried; the human tide marched on. The scattered groups of monsters they encountered fled upon seeing armoured troops.

Soon groups that had escaped from the other passes began joining the main force of refugees. They travelled until they were too exhausted to continue then made a camp that consisted of piles of humanity huddled together for warmth, watched over by exhausted guards.

Ackdominel looked towards the lighter grey clouds that marked the sunset.

"Cursed demon clouds," he muttered then turned to Solin and Erum who stood beside him. "Do you understand what I want you to do? Just prowl about the edge of the camp, killing any monster you find."

"Don't ask me if I understand. It's Erum who has to instruct my wolf form. After the transformation, I'd as soon rip your throat out as an ogre's."

"I understand. I hope that uncle doesn't get hurt," said Erum.

"So do I." Ackdominel gestured that they should begin.

Solin removed his clothing and dropped to all fours. A growl escaped his lips as they curled back around his teeth, which were growing longer and sharper. His eyes snapped open, an insane light tinting the irises red. Fur bristled all over his body, as muscle and bone shifted. In minutes a huge, snarling wolf stood where Solin had been.

Erum yipped and yapped a few times. The wolf bounded into the darkness.

"Poor Solin, I wish I could aid him," muttered Ackdominel. He returned Erum to Orlor.

The next few days passed in a blur of walking until the group could walk no more then collapsing into sleep.

#

Melanie, Solin and Ackdominel gathered at the edge of camp behind a hill.

"I am troubled by our progress," opened Ackdominel.

"Unless you want us to sprout wings we're doing well for a large group on foot. I expected to be held up by a series of skirmishes, but so far there's been nothing. I'm getting bored!" countered Melanie.

"That's what concerns me. Why haven't we been attacked?"

"Yes, it's strange. I know the monsters are watching us. My stomach's been too full for me to eat anything since my night patrols started." Solin scanned the barren landscape.

"Is there a bottleneck we have to pass through. They could be planning an ambush," said Melanie.

"You know the maps as well as I do. The only land that isn't prairie this side of the human-held territories are the Twin Sisters," replied Ackdominel.

"It can't be there. The gap between those two escarpments is half a day's march wide. Even the Storm couldn't block that much terrain," observed Solin.

"They might have a garrison there that could harry us. They wouldn't need a solid line to challenge us," said Melanie.

"Their commanders are smarter than that. We have already proven we can defeat them with hit and run tactics. They will try to force a line battle," stated Ackdominel.

"Where?" demanded Melanie.

"I must find that out. I have avoided using magic because it would open me up to the monster sorceries, but we must know what lies ahead. I'll need a guard around the base of this rise to see I am not disturbed."

"I'll do it personally," offered Melanie.

"Be careful," said Solin, as Ackdominel climbed to the top of the hill.

Sitting, Ackdominel extracted his magic mirror from its box and stared into it. A grey mist crept across his vision and figures moved before his eyes. With an effort of will, he sent his sight over the trail before him, seeing nothing until he came to the gap of the Twin Sisters. The gap had changed. What had been an area of farms and shallow gullies was now a quagmire.

"How could this happen?" he whispered.

Image after image of dammed streams flashed before his eyes.

"Demon spit! Their leaders must have realised the strategic importance of the gap and done this to block it."

Examining farther, he found that the lands hugging the escarpments on either side were dry, but blocked by crude, stone forts, teeming with monsters.

Feeling like a mouse in a trap he shifted his vision away from the gap and looked back the way they had come. Approaching from the rear was a huge force of beasts.

Feeling a mystical intrusion Ackdominel cast a spell of deflection and swiftly drew his will from the mirror.

"We are between the hammer and the anvil," he muttered. "**Melanie!**" Ackdominel replaced his mirror in its box and descended the hill.

"What is it?" demanded Melanie reading the concern on her friend's face.

"We have a problem."

"This is news worth shouting?"

Ackdominel explained their dilemma.

"What should we do?" she asked.

Ackdominel stood, grim-faced, staring at the map of the situation he had drawn in the dirt. "We might have a chance, not much of one, but a chance. I have an idea, but it will take time to make it work, and I am worried about the beasts behind us. Maybe Erum and his dogs can help."

"I'll get him. He's probably curled up with that pack of mongrels he's been attracting."

"That pack of mongrels might prove more useful than you know, but don't call him yet. I have to think some things through."

The next day the refugees continued their eastward march but stopped when they reached the swamp that filled most of the gap.

"What a stench!" exclaimed Melanie. "Must those beasts poison everything they touch?"

"They are making it more homelike," explained Ackdominel.

"Homelike! No wonder they're so foul. Now that we're here what do we do?"

Ackdominel walked to a supply cart and pulled out a smoked haunch of mutton.

"Monsters ahead of us, monsters behind us, a swamp blocking our only route of escape, and you're going to eat?"

Ackdominel shrugged and threw the mutton into the swamp.

There was a sudden commotion as the water exploded in a confusion of horrors then subsided.

"That rules out wading," he remarked.

"In truth!" Melanie went pale.

"It is, however, what I was hoping for. I have a plan."

"What?"

"You will learn soon enough. First I want you to call Erum and tell him to bring along his largest dogs. As well, order men to cut any branches they can find large enough to sweep away a trail. Hurry, time is short."

Melanie shook her head and left to comply while Ackdominel took a seat by the water's edge and studied it intently.

Erum arrived with a collection of nearly a hundred motley curs. These dogs ranged from the monster dogs to the ragtag descendants of once proud royal-hunting hounds.

"Erum, I have a job for your dogs. It is very important."

"Will they get hurt?" asked Erum.

"They might, but if they do not help us, the monsters will kill all the people and probably the dogs as well."

Erum looked at his feet and asked, "What do you want them to do?"

"I want them to take the sticks that Melanie is going to bring and drag them behind them as they run around this swamp to the north."

"Yes, Your Majesty, is that all?"

"No. Tell the monster dogs when they see the other members of the Storm they are to attack them."

"Yes, Your Majesty," Erum agreed sadly.

Minutes later Melanie's men appeared dragging a collection of dead branches. These were, with the help of Erum, distributed amongst the various canines who, after a few yips from Erum, ran to the north dragging them.

"Now it is our turn. Melanie, order some of your men to wipe out our tracks. Try to keep the people in a narrow band. I will travel up front to see what I can do with wizardry. We move to the swamp's southern shore then continue east along it."

They walked through that day and into the evening. They camped that night at the mouth of the dry spit of land running between the southern escarpment and the swamp.

Ackdominel lay awake, focussing his will on the moisture and soot-rich clouds that accompanied the Storm.

Chapter 24
Opening a Way

Rain fell, drenching everyone and everything. Ackdominel sat watching the dark waters of the swamp as they began to rise.

"So far so good. Now if only the rest of my plan works. Demon spit, I am tired! The last few days have been too much, I feel grey inside. Maybe I am getting ill. No, it is just the strain of all the magic," he muttered. Rising he strode to where his blanket lay on the ground and settled for what remained of the night.

By morning the swamp had flooded to cover a quarter of the trail between it and the escarpment and the rain still pelted down. Melanie sent scouting parties ahead to deal with any observers the monsters might have in place then the humans began to march. It was less than two hours before they stopped behind a rocky out-jut that hid them from the monsters' keep.

"What now?" Melanie demanded of Ackdominel, as they stood at the front of the column.

"Ready your troops. Tell them the beasts will be busy fighting fantasies. Our men are to leave none of them alive. I will signal when to attack."

The rain poured down but the swamp, having reached its level of drainage, had stopped expanding.

Ackdominel stood silently focussing his will. Drawing the black crystal from his pack he held it and imagined its essence creeping over the monsters' keep.

#

Garzug looked at the brush marks that led to the north, while her troops gibbered and cantered about her. She raised her hand, everything fell silent, and all save her personal guard moved away from her.

"This human is good but did not count on having Garzug, Countess of the Lamia, to deal with. This little ploy would have fooled any of the lesser races, but not me."

The beasts about Garzug nodded, knowing better than to disagree. She'd inherited her mother's title in the traditional way, single combat to the death, and had defended it several times since. Her lower portion was a cross between a donkey and a jungle cat, with front paws capable of cutting an ogre in two with a single blow. All present had watched her pulp the skull of an incompetent troll with a kick from her hind legs. Her physical skills though were not her most formidable asset. Garzug's torso and head were those of a dark, exotically-beautiful woman, with long midnight-black hair that fell covering full breasts. Her face had delicately sculpted features behind which lived a mind that had conquered worlds.

"They have sent a contingent of their people north as decoys. Probably the old and sick, useless baggage! See how the tracks have been badly swept out. The rest have gone south, covering their tracks well, but there are still signs of their passage."

"That is a brilliant deduction commander. How do we proceed?" whined a pug-faced goblin with slaver dripping from between its fangs.

"These are my orders. Dispatch the goblin contingent to the north. We are better rid of you useless wastrels. Old and wounded humans shouldn't be too much for you to deal with. The rest of my troops will go south. As I have spoken, so now let it be."

#

Ackdominel kept concentrating. It had been two hours since he had begun and the only change was that the monsters in the keep seemed to be massing on the battlement. More time passed, and the guards outside the keep's gate huddled against the stone wall of the escarpment. One of the beasts bellowed and clutched at its ankle. Falling to the ground, it pushed itself towards the water while looking as if it was trying to crawl away from it.

"Now," whispered Ackdominel to Melanie, who sat beside him.

Leaping from her perch on the rocks, she signalled the attack. By this time all the monsters on the wall had turned to watch the inside of the keep. A horrendous din rose from behind the defensive wall. Several of the beasts on the rampart seemed to be grappling with imaginary opponents.

Melanie's archers let fly, slaughtering the creatures on the rampart. A wounded troll clutched at an ogre, toppling them both from the wall. The ogre landed with a thud, screamed then started beating at itself as if trying to knock something away. Moments later it was dead.

Another flight of arrows drove the last of the beasts from the ramparts. A group of partially armoured men rushed the gate, carrying a tree trunk. The crude ram drove against the steel reinforced beams until, with a crack, the keep's gate flew open.

The human troops rushed forward. The beasts of the Storm sat upon the roofs of the crude stone buildings that littered the ground behind the gate. Many bodies lay dead in the dirt.

"Swordsmen, spearmen, clear the palisade. Archers deal with the beasts on the roofs," ordered Melanie.

#

Ackdominel's body was shaking with effort, and he was drenched in sweat. With a cry, he dropped the crystal and lapsed into unconsciousness.

#

Things in the keep changed. The monsters looked down from the roofs, bewildered then bellowing leapt to attack the humans. So ferocious was their initial assault that Melanie's troops were driven into a defensive line, but the monsters had lost too many of their number. In minutes the beasts lay dead or dying.

Melanie, chest heaving, moved back to the stone where Ackdominel lay.

"You, wrap that crystal in a cloth and bring it along. You and you, prepare a litter and get him onto it. I want to be moving in ten minutes," she commanded, jabbing her finger towards the refugees.

"I'll take care of it," said Orlor, who came striding up with an empty supply cart.

"Good! I'm glad to see there's someone with sense here. I--."

"General Melanie, they're attacking our rear," cried a young man who charged up and collapsed before her.

"Scum loving, skaggy," began Melanie. She cut off her tirade to command her troops.

#

Garzug laughed as she watched her troops massacre the poorly armed humans.

"This will take care of their little uprising. Foolish of them to try! They're like the rest of you mongrel races. Only fit to be slaves. This is too easy though. There's no challenge. Where are the troops and that wizard?" she remarked to her ogre lieutenant.

Before the ogre could reply, a force of humans, nearly five hundred strong, attacked Garzug's army from the rear. In a rage she ordered her defence, deploying her reserves at the rear of her column. Minutes later armoured humans appeared from amongst the refugees and formed a defensive line.

#

After Trom left the mountains, he led his men east until they came to the gap of the Twin Sisters and found it held against them. Seeing no other option, they established a camp in caves along the northern escarpment and started raiding for supplies.

Three days after making camp one of the scouts reported seeing dogs, dragging branches, running towards the monsters' stronghold. Trom, guessing at the meaning of this, ordered his men to march towards the southern pass. As they moved they avoided a company of goblins and soon came upon the tracks of a much greater force. Following these, they intercepted the main force of monsters as they massacred the refugees at the rear of Ackdominel's lines.

#

Melanie raced to the rear of the column of refugees, leading a company of her troops. She left the looting of the monsters' camp to Orlor.

I have to think of a way to hold those beasts back and stall their pursuit so we can escape, she thought. A stitch in her side forced her to slow to a walk. She waved her troops onward. She noticed that the strip of land between swamp and escarpment was narrower here than farther along the gap and smiled.

She pulled a couple dozen able bodies out of the column of refugees and gave them orders. "I want you civilians to dig a trench blocking this passage. Make it at least two-man lengths wide and knee-deep. Keep an earthen wall against that swamp. When it's dug, get out of here fast. Understand?"

"Yes, Lady General," said a ragged man, who began to dig with his hands. The others joined him as the refugee column filed past. Melanie ran towards the battle.

#

Trom led his warriors in a charge against the monsters' disorganised rear. The land between the swamp and the escarpment was nearly fifty strides across here, which allowed both sides room to manoeuvre. Trom's companies hit the monsters, driving into their force. The humans manoeuvred into a closed wedge formation, cutting deep into their enemy's ranks. Soon they were surrounded. The monsters rallied against the enemy in their midst, forcing the humans to a standstill. All seemed lost until Trom saw a line of figures charge down the trail between escarpment and swamp.

"She's come, and she's brought the whole gods loving army with her. Fight me boys, fight like you've never before," Trom cried.

#

Melanie's troops took up a rotating line formation, which meant new rested fighters were always being brought to the fore.

#

The battle raged, and more of Trom's men fell to the centre of the triangle formation, wounded or dead. The monsters seemed endless. Trom stood at the point of the wedge, fighting like a demon. Step by step they drew closer to Melanie's troops. Soon they were no more than than eight strides apart. Escape seemed possible and hope flared in Trom. An ogre, with a spear, thrust towards his leg, forcing him to drop his shield to block the blow, as a troll clawed at his sword arm. Pain burnt through his arm. He fell back gasping. Dropping his shield, he pulled a dagger from his belt and let it fly, striking the troll in the chest.

"Got you, you bastard," he muttered as he moved to the centre of the wedge formation, trying not to look at the bloody stump where his right arm should have been. When he was clear of the front rank, he wrapped his sword belt about the stump, stanching the flow of blood.

A combined push from Melanie's force and Trom's troops closed the gap between them, crushing the monsters in the way like flies. Then began the long, slow retreat up the trail.

#

Ackdominel lay on the cart, which jigged and jogged along the uneven ground. His first sensation was of pain.

"When will I learn to stop over straining?" he muttered opening his eyes.

Everything was blurry, but slowly his vision cleared to reveal something he could hardly believe. A full moon shone down from a clear sky.

"How long have I been unconscious?" he demanded.

"Nearly five hours," replied Elin, the girl healer who had treated him in the mountains.

"Only five hours. We can't be in the human-held lands so quickly, but the sky?"

"Grew clear after the rain stopped. Now rest."

"Where is Melanie?"

"Rest."

"Tell him, girl. He has to know," ordered Orlor.

"He has to rest!"

"If something is wrong, you better tell me now!"

"We were attacked from the rear. Melanie went with the troops to fight them off. No one's seen them since," explained Orlor.

"Demon spit!" Ackdominel racked his aching head for an answer. "Elin, I need your help."

"My help?"

"Yes. You have the inner strength to practice the art. I will teach you later. For the moment, I must borrow your strength. To take it without asking would be evil, but I am too weary to aid the troop as I am."

"I, I, guess I could help, Your Majesty. I, I mean will it hurt?"

"A headache when you awake is all."

"Well... Do what you must, Your Majesty."

"Orlor, stop this cart."

Ackdominel clambered from the cart and placed his left hand across Elin's brow.

"What in the name of the dark gods!" exclaimed Orlor.

"Catch her when she falls. Care for her as you would me. You are in charge until Melanie or I return," ordered Ackdominel. He chanted in a low voice. Seconds later Elin fell into Orlor's arms.

"Thank you, child. I took nothing that will not regrow. Now I must help our troops." Ackdominel strode towards the west.

#

Melanie's troops slowly gave ground before the superior numbers of the monsters. When the civilians were well away, the human troops fell back until they reached the trench Melanie had ordered dug across the trail. Water had already oozed into its base through the wall of earth that separated it from the rest of the swamp. This made the trench's bottom a quagmire that sucked at the legs of the humans as they plodded across. On the far side of the trench, the warriors formed new lines and waited. When the defensive line behind the trench had formed, the human front line allowed itself to be driven into the trench.

The defensive line backed away from their foes, while some troops tore at the earth separating the trench from the swamp. No sooner had the humans climbed free of the ditch than water spilt into it. The battle raged at the trench's lip until an ogre cried in agony, followed by a hill troll. Within seconds the monsters were thrashing wildly, ignoring the human defenders as they struggled to reach the shore. Melanie watched as an ogre, twice the size of a man, was hauled into the swamp by a huge, orange tentacle. Other beasts screamed as small, wiggling things enveloped them, leaving nothing but bones behind. A cheer rose from the human lines, but it was cut short by the twanging of bowstrings. Melanie's forces bolted down the trail as fast as their legs could carry them.

#

"Filthy, little human. If she thinks this is going to stop me!" raged Garzug, pacing the length of the trench.

"Yes, mistress," agreed a brutish centaur with blood-red hair.

"Silence, fool. I want all those useless little diggers put to work filling this pit. I want to be across it within the hour. We cannot let those humans escape!"

"Yes, mistress," agreed the centaur, who left to order the Kobold companies.

"I'll get you yet, wizard! You'll all be in the mines before I'm done!" muttered Garzug, as she watched the retreating human line.

#

Ackdominel walked in silence. It disturbed him to see how little progress his people had made while he was unconscious. It disturbed him, even more, to see that they were breaking into separate groups, with the fast not waiting for the slow.

There is nothing I can do to remedy it. I have to help the soldiers, without them the refugees do not stand a chance. Once the army is safe we can regroup for the final march, he thought. Halting his musings, he cleared his mind. He needed to build on the energy he had taken for it to be of any use.

Trudging silently, he appeared to any who saw him to be dazed and wandering. No one hailed him or tried to discover why he was walking the wrong way.

By the time Ackdominel reached the fortification that blocked the trail, the sun was high in the sky. He could feel its warmth and energy beating down upon him. Looking up he saw that the blue sky was already tinted dirty grey. Taking a deep breath and slowly releasing it, he took a seat upon the monsters' battlements and began constructing a collection of mental images.

#

Melanie stood at the rear of her troops, watching the monsters' activity at the trench. The beasts were filling it with rocks, dirt and anything else they could find. It was only a matter of time before they would cross.

"Accursed beasts!" spat Melanie. "Everyone except my elite guard, retreat to the monsters' fortification. Try to repair the gate. Tear down those shacks and use the stone to strengthen the palisade. When you're done sound the retreat. We'll try to hold here until then. If the beasts break through, hold them back as best you can. Lieutenant Fraze is in command, now move."

Melanie's troops split, with all but fifty moving as swiftly along the trail as their weariness allowed. Melanie watched the monsters filling in the trench. Looking up she noticed the sun rising over the opposite escarpment.

The air split with a screech.

#

Garzug paced impatiently.

"Useless slug races, will nothing make them work faster?" Garzug hissed to herself. "Maybe I should give them another example, they seem to have forgotten that slow-moving troll I threw into the trench. It is almost as if they fear the human troops more than they fear me. That must be it! I know how to correct that!"

Smiling evilly, she reached into a pocket of the pack she wore strapped about her animal portion and pulled out a whip and a jar.

"This will show those lesser creatures whom to fear," she muttered. Dipping the end of the whip into the jar she drew it out, dripping with a yellow liquid.

She sauntered towards the line of beasts carrying rock and dirt towards the trench and bellowed at them.

"Afraid of the humans are you! Working slowly to avoid a fight? I'll teach you what to fear!" Garzug let the whip fly, striking an ogre across the back. It yelped then froze. Froth gathered at its mouth, and its body shook all over then it stood perfectly still.

"You will bring rocks to fill the trench," ordered Garzug.

The ogre mechanically obeyed, while the other beasts looked on in terror. The pace of work increased.

"Superstitious fools. They will think I've taken the ogre's soul. Now they'll obey me. Spine fish venom, such a simple ploy." Garzug laughed.

Screams split the air. A goblin in front of Garzug froze in its tracks then crumbled into sand. On all sides of Garzug creatures either returned to the matter from which they were formed or fell to the ground, scrambling blindly in search of shadowy places.

"What?" she snarled then looked skyward. The sun had just crested the escarpment's edge. "Curse that rain, it cleared the sky!"

As Garzug watched an ogre stumbled into the deadly swamp.

Hissing between clenched teeth, she stormed into the midst of her troops to try and mitigate this latest disaster.

#

Melanie formed her troops into a line and waited. For some reason, fewer of the monsters were filling the trench now, and she was thankful for the time to rest. She wished her archers had arrows, but the shafts were all long since spent. The retreat sounded breaking her reverie. Wondering at how quickly the blockade had been repaired she ordered her troop into a column and marched them towards the crude fortification.

As she approached the keep, her breath caught. Spread across its top was a troop of human warriors.

"What!" she exclaimed.

"Quickly, behind the wall," ordered a warrior who approached them from the fortification.

Melanie ran the last few paces to the shattered gate of the keep, which was being filled in with wood and stone pulled from the huts.

As soon as she entered the keep, she surmounted the battlements and addressed one of the soldiers.

"I am General Melanie. Who is your commander?"

The soldier said nothing. Melanie noticed that none of the warriors moved. Not a shuffling of feet or a shrug of shoulders.

"What's going on?" she demanded.

A young warrior, wearing battered leather armour, explained. "King Ackdominel came back to help us. He made this army and told us archers to wait behind the wall. The monsters had a stock of arrows in one of the huts. We've divided it amongst us. His Majesty sent the others ahead to gather and protect the civilians."

"What does he hope to accomplish with an army of pictures?"

"I intend to scare them into delaying their attack. The longer they are delayed, the better the chance our people have of escaping." Ackdominel moved to Melanie's side, great strain was apparent upon his face.

"Why don't you use the dark crystal to make them see their worst fears again?"

"An illusion must be believable to be accepted. Otherwise, it has no power. Besides the touch of that horrid thing is costly."

"To the crystal?"

"To me!"

"Oh." Melanie joined the rest of her troop leaving Ackdominel to refine the illusion.

\#

Garzug frothed at the mouth. She looked to the sky, which had betrayed her. It was slowly darkening as clouds rolled in

"It will be late afternoon before these light blighted fools can do more than grovel in a hole. Maggot races! I will have to attack with my strength halved. At least that cursed ditch is almost filled. When this world is fully taken, I'll kill every creature in that swamp. That will be a fitting punishment for interfering with my plans," she grumbled.

When the trench was filled, and Garzug led her troops across.

When I find the little creature that commands the humans. I'm going to rend her limb from limb, personally, as payment for the trouble she has caused me! thought Garzug.

\#

Melanie sat behind the fortification and tried to sleep, but she was too keyed up. She noticed that most of her troops didn't share her situation.

"Enemy approaches," came the cry from the battlement. It was late afternoon, over four hours since Melanie had arrived at the monsters' old keep. She rose and with a few gentle kicks awoke several of her men. These men turned to the task of waking their fellows.

The monsters approached, marching in file, heedless of the possibility of archers. The column drew closer then stopped. The keep was manned by a strong force of, apparently, fresh troops. Ackdominel's bowmen let fly, and monsters fell like wheat before a scythe. Panicked, the beasts fell back, but the arrows flew again before they were out of range.

#

"Where did they come from? Who are they? What is this?" demanded Garzug, punctuating each question by kicking the escarpment's side with her hooves.

"I do not know, mistress. What are we to do?" asked the burly centaur.

"Do! We have no choice. We must wait for the clouds and attack with our full strength. Send a messenger to those fools in the rear and tell them to come as soon as possible. Until they arrive, we must wait."

#

"Do you think that scared them off?" asked Melanie.

"I hope so. Now we must leave quickly. You will have to guide me so I can maintain the illusion," replied a sweating Ackdominel.

"Of course." Melanie gave the signal to move then took Ackdominel's arm and guided him as if he were blind.

It was nearly two hours later that Ackdominel tripped over a rock and fell to his knees.

"Run! Find the others. Meet at the Valley of Floods. The illusion is gone," he commanded. He followed behind his troops.

#

Garzug stood fuming at the delay when the figures on the battlement vanished.

"What? No! It's the wizard!" she exclaimed. "Troops, prepare to charge."

In less than three minutes Garzug's force was advancing towards the battlement. They quickly breached the makeshift barricade and stood in the middle of the abandoned keep.

"No! No! No!" howled Garzug.

She lashed out with a hoof, killing the closest of her troops.

"After them. Run. We must overtake them. Run, you fools. A hundred pieces of gold to whoever finds the human scum."

Garzug took off at a gallop.

Chapter 25
Border Crossing

Upon reaching the hills beyond the Twin Sisters escarpments, the human troops split into small groups and dispersed. Ackdominel and Melanie, with ten warriors, followed the most direct course towards the Valley of Floods. Little happened during their trudge. It seemed that all life had vacated the territory.

"We are almost there. The camp should be at the base of the valley near the road," said Ackdominel, trying to penetrate the darkness with his gaze.

The bushes at the lip of the valley rustled.

"Who's that?" demanded Melanie, sword in hand.

"It's Orlor. Are you and your people well?" replied a dark figure emerging from the foliage.

"As well as can be expected. What has happened?" asked Ackdominel.

"I can't say for everyone. Not all the groups have made it here yet. I've sent out scouts to guide those they can find to the valley. So far we've had a good two-thirds of the civilians arrive and some companies of soldiers. I've done what I could, but we need you."

"You have done well with them, Orlor. Can you lead us to your camp? We are weary as death."

"This way. I'll dare say you'll be able to rest easy. I had Erum set Solin to patrolling."

"Good," praised Ackdominel.

Soon they were at the base of the valley under a canopy of trees. Some of the trees were dead from lack of sun, while others clung tenaciously to life. Refugees slept on all sides of the path.

"I'll let you rest now," said Orlor.

"Wait. Before you go, how is Elin?" asked Ackdominel.

"She is with the wounded now. When she awoke her head hurt tremendously, but it was quick to pass. She seems fine."

"Good! She is a precious resource I do not wish to waste. Sleep peacefully, my friend."

"You as well." Orlor walked away.

Ackdominel lay on the ground, wrapped in his cloak, and fell into an exhausted slumber.

\#

Garzug fumed impotently. The trail of the humans broke up as soon as they cleared the gap between the Twin Sisters escarpments. This meant that if she did overtake a group, they would be easy prey but overtaking any substantial number would be impossible.

"Curse you, wizard, with your tricky illusions!" she spat.

All around her was desolation. In her rage, she had outdistanced her troops and was now alone in the open. A wave of fear washed over her. She looked around but could see nothing.

\#

He was a small man of nondescript features, in ragged clothing. If he had kept count of the years of his life, he would have known he had seen sixty-three, but he gave up counting after the monsters had invaded his farm and killed. He tried not to think about her. He had loved her so! He and his middle son escaped to the mountains. Together they survived through the lean years. Then they left to reach the sea. His son had been one of the first to die. Now he felt nothing! Not angry, not sad, just tired. He had lain behind this boulder for hours. Resting or waiting to die, he couldn't say which. Then it came, a huge beast, part lion, part mule, part woman.

He lay hidden, but inside he knew it was time to rejoin his wife and sons. Drawing the knife he used for eating, he rubbed it with a herb. He'd been a healer. He knew his poisons. Soon the knife blade was coated with sap. Closing his eyes, he prayed.

#

Garzug scanned the horizon. Something clicked to her right, like a rock shifting. She turned. An old, scrawny human, armed with a small knife, leapt at her. She laughed at the creature's audacity and raised a forepaw to swat it away. The human buried the knife in her foreleg. She lashed out, separating him into two parts at the hips. Swearing, Garzug pulled the dagger from her leg. The wound was little more than a fly bite. Laughing she threw the knife away and moved towards the corpse. Upon the dead lips was a smile. She shook her head. The attack had been an insane gesture. A hot flash swept over her, and she had to force herself to inhale.

When Garzug's troops caught up to her, all they found was a corpse with blood-flecked lips.

#

When Ackdominel awoke, his body was an orchestra of aches and pains. He rose and looked over the camp. All about him lay the prostrate forms of his subjects. He took a step and almost cried out.

It is a good thing I didn't remove my boots last night. My feet are so swollen I doubt I could have pulled them on again, he thought. Making his way to Melanie, he shook her.

"Arrr! It wasn't a nightmare. Go away!" she said.

"It was no dream, but it is almost over. One more good day's march should get us to the human-held territories." Ackdominel helped Melanie to her aching feet.

"How in the names of the gods are we supposed to do that? The people are so exhausted they can barely move and what's left of my troops are scattered from here to doomsday, and if we are close to the front, there will be monster patrols." Melanie's gesture encompassed the human camp.

"Most of your fighters made their way here last night. So things on that score are not as grim as you think. As for the march itself... what choice do we have? We walk, or we die. I am going to walk."

Melanie stared at Ackdominel then said, "Something is hard in you. Something that wasn't there before. What's happened?"

"Why am I trying to save these people? I could have easily covered the distance from the mountains to the coast with my abilities, but I chose to fetter myself with refugees. Why? For the most part, I do not even know them. Why?"

Melanie stared at him. First anger crossed her face, followed quickly by confusion then understanding.

"Ackdominel, are you going to leave us, forget our people and walk away?"

"Of course not! I have an obligation. They are my people. My father taught me a king is like a father. His nation, his subjects are his children! I cannot desert them."

"Not for that reason, not really. There are lots of bad kings. The reason you can't leave them is that deep down inside you still see something in them worth saving. You've always seen it. It's why, back in the mountains, you never once considered a plan that didn't include them. I don't pretend to know why you do what you do, but if you're still doing something, it's for a reason."

Both fell silent. Ackdominel looked about sadly. He tried and failed to see the greatness he once believed lived in all men. Then he heard the sound of ripping cloth. Turning he saw a boy, of no more than twelve, tearing strips from his filthy shirt. The boy proceeded to wrap the strips around the feet of a young girl, who had literally walked her shoes off. The girl slept on, oblivious to his ministrations. When the child finished, he hugged himself for warmth and walked away. Ackdominel closed his eyes as a tear trickled down his cheek.

"Melanie, rouse our people. Today our trek will end!"

The humans left the valley nearly two hours after sunrise. As they shuffled forward, Ackdominel moved amongst the crowd urging them on. It was while he did this that he saw Trom, clad in a ragged surcoat.

With a feeling of dread, he called Trom's name. The warrior paused. As Ackdominel drew near, he noted the stump that was all that remained of Trom's arm.

"I am sorry."

"So am I," snapped Trom.

"Let me see it."

Trom held out the stump.

"Where is your armour?" Ackdominel inspected the wound.

"I gave it to a young fellow, said his father taught him how to use a blade. Wouldn't do me any good keeping it."

"This will hurt." Ackdominel took off his ring and pressed it into the stump.

Trom grimaced and grit his teeth. Ackdominel removed the belt that had staunched the flow of blood. Glancing at the stump Trom could see that new skin had sealed its end.

"Thank you, though it might have been better if you hadn't."

"How so?"

"What good's a one-armed warrior? I'll be a burden for the rest of my life."

"Nonsense! I have a task for you as soon as we are established on Haven, the island I mentioned."

"What?"

"I will need teachers for the next generation of warriors. You know we cannot spare able-bodied men from the front. You and others like you are perfect."

"Yes. Yes! We would be, wouldn't we?" agreed Trom.

"Think on it. I have to move on. There are others who need my aid."

The day passed in reasonable calm until evening drew in. As the gloom deepened, Ackdominel moved to the head of his people, hoping to see signs of human civilisation. Melanie walked beside him, occasionally stumbling from weariness. They trudged up a hill and saw a banner waving in the light of the setting sun. A group of human defenders surrounded the banner, as the beasts drove against them like waves upon a wind-tossed shore.

"That banner belongs to the Western Island King. Melanie, are you and your men up to one more battle?" said Ackdominel.

Melanie smiled wearily in reply and barked an order to be passed along the line. In fifteen minutes her troops were organised into square formations that advanced towards the monsters attacking the forces of the Western Island King.

Melanie's army fell upon the creatures of the Storm, slaughtering many of the beasts before they could organise to defend their back and flanks.

Seeing the tables turn, the Western Island King rallied his forces, pressing their advantage against the beasts that still outnumbered them two to one.

Ackdominel looked at the people crowded behind him. If the humans won the engagement, they would survive. It was now only a short walk to safety. If the beasts triumphed, all their efforts and sacrifice would be for nought. Leaving his followers, he walked towards the lines of fighting beings. He reached deep within himself, summoning the dregs of his power. Raising his hands in the air, he began to chant.

#

The Western Island King sat upon his mighty, grey stallion, clutching at a wound in his side, while the men of his guard fought and died around him. Even with the appearance of the mysterious new force the battle's outcome was in doubt. There was a sound like a whisper, not so much heard as sensed. The beasts clutched their heads in agony. His men made short work of their attackers in the moments they were debilitated.

#

Ackdominel's head throbbed. His reserves were exhausted, and he felt sick. He stumbled, leaning heavily on his staff, fighting back sleep as he did so.

As he plodded towards the man he assumed was the leader of the other human force, he noticed that the monsters were bolting through any hole in the human lines they could find. Approaching the mounted figure, he forced himself to stand erect. The man wore the insignia of the royal house on his tabard. This was a meeting of Kings. He would look the part. This brought another weary smile to his lips. His father would have been proud.

"Your Majesty, I am King Dominel of Bani, and Ackdominel, a wizard of the Secret Path. I bring my people to refuge in the human-held lands and a plan for the salvation of our kind. I ask your welcome."

"Granted many times over." The king grasped painfully at the wound in his side.

Ackdominel smiled and leaned against the horse.

Chapter 26
Alliance

Ackdominel had only vague recollections of the next few hours. He remembered being helped to a chariot and transported to one of the nearby keeps then a soft bed and sweet oblivion.

It was Melanie who saw that all the people found temporary accommodations in the keeps and deserted towns near the front.

When Ackdominel awoke, it took him a few moments of gazing at the tattered tapestries on the walls to realise where he was. He tried to move, and pain shot through him. He relaxed into a trance and took stock of himself. Practically every muscle was pulled, and he was bruised from head to foot. Turning his mind to his magical strengths, he gasped. *Demon spawn, it will be a full moon cycle before I'm recovered.* Deepening his trance, he started to work on easing the damage to his body.

Much later he moved to the edge of the bed and rose to his protesting feet. A white robe had been draped over a chair by the bed, along with a pair of fur-lined slippers several sizes too large for him.

"At least our host is a thoughtful and considerate man," mused Ackdominel. Donning the clothing, he opened the door and was pleased to see a page waiting in the hall beyond. The corridor was made of grey stone, lit by arrow slits at either end, with tattered tapestries hanging along its length.

The boy's eyes focussed on Ackdominel and he began speaking in the tongue of the Western Island.

Searching his memories from previous lives, Ackdominel found one four-hundred years earlier where he had spoken that tongue and drew the knowledge forward.

"Greetings. Prithee, lad, where be the glorious personage of thy most gracious king?"

The child stared at Ackdominel, trying to decipher the meaning of his words then replied, "He's in his chambers. I'll guide you there." The boy led the way down the corridor.

"Couldst thou inform me of my time spent in the realm of dreams?"

"Pardon? Oh! Oh yes! I think I see. You slept nearly a day and a half."

Ackdominel now understood the growling issuing from his stomach.

"Forsooth, I seem to be in need of nourishment. Couldst thou see fit to supply one such as I with subsistence?"

The child's eyes rolled towards the ceiling.

"You're hungry. Don't worry. The king has ordered you fed as soon as you enter his presence."

They had moved along several corridors and now stood before a heavy, wooden door with guards at either side.

"This is the Wizard Ackdominel, for audience with good King Darien," stated the lad.

The guards opened the door and moved aside. Ackdominel stepped through the doorway. The room was comfortably appointed. Along the far wall lay a canopy bed. A table and chairs occupied the room's centre. To his right, the wall was adorned with a hearth in which coals smouldered. After scanning the chamber, Ackdominel turned his attention to the king, who lay upon the bed. He was a big man, just past his prime, with grey hair and a neatly-trimmed, grey beard and moustache. His body was powerfully built, despite a thickening about his middle. As Ackdominel assessed the king a pair of intelligent, pale-blue eyes stared back at him from a handsome oval face.

"Come, have a seat," offered the king in Ackdominel's own language.

"Thank you, Your Majesty." Ackdominel accepted the offer.

King Darien rose from his bed, clutching at the side of his red robe, and took a seat at the table. "The food will be here in a few moments. I suspect you're hungry after your long sleep."

"Yes. I feel half starved, thank you."

"Let me get to the point. You said you were a wizard."

"Yes. One of the last of a vanishing breed."

"It is heartening to know you are only vanishing. I had thought you had vanished."

"Very nearly. There are now no more than twenty of us, and unless we act swiftly, there will be none."

"What can I do to aid you?" Darien leaned forward then grimaced. "I heard you could heal, would you mind?"

Ackdominel felt trapped, how could he explain his depletion to a person who hadn't studied the art magic.

"Unfortunately, I cannot. My reserves of magic were exhausted on the trek here. It will take time for me to rebuild them."

"Rotten shame that! This thing hurts like a demon's love bite."

"You do not doubt my claim?"

"Of course not. You have to remember, the persecution of magic folk wasn't as bad in my kingdom. Many of the lesser members of the orders managed to escape. They passed on what little they knew to their children. Sadly there were no true wizards among them. Since the trouble with the Storm started, I have put effort into gathering the old knowledge. Some survivors, a few books. It isn't enough, but I've had a taste of your world. I can understand your strengths and weaknesses, at least a little."

Ackdominel relaxed. Of all the kings he could have met in the human-held lands, this was undoubtedly the best. The door opened admitting a large man bearing a tray from which he set three places at the table.

"Three?" Ackdominel tore into the loaf before him.

"Your general will be joining us. By the way, where did you find her?"

"On my way to the mountains where I was trained. It is a long story."

"I've no doubt. Wish I had a general who looked like that. Morale would go through the roof."

"You should see her handle a sword." Ackdominel broke off a handful of cheese.

"Careful. You don't want to eat yourself sick. I have heard of her prowess with a blade, not to mention your abilities. I sent some of my men among your people to gather information. Some of the stories are incredible."

The door opened admitting Melanie, who after polite greetings moved to her place at the table.

Chapter 27
Some Explanations

Ackdominel and Melanie recounted the tale of their recent lives. When they were finished Darien told them of the progress the Storm had made. After this, all three fell silent. Finally, Darien spoke.

"We've finished with the past, so why don't you tell me of your plans for the future, wizard?"

"Gladly," replied Ackdominel. "To do that though, I will have to speak of the past once more."

"Then do so."

Ackdominel cleared his throat and began.

"First it is important to know that the persecution came as no surprise to the magic orders. Our seers had foreseen it. Knowing what would happen if the servants of the Covetous God annihilated us, we prepared against it. Many of our orders felt it necessary to create a permanent stronghold against the monsters, a haven in which we could muster our strength in peace. Thus setting to sea, wizards from many orders gathered over a section of ocean. This happened nearly three-hundred years ago. In the history of your island, it is known as the year of the waves. The wizards cast spells more powerful than any cast before or since. We reshaped the very earth, fracturing its surface and drawing the molten heart of our world upwards. Bubbling and hissing, the liquid rock formed an island of enormous proportions.

"Exhausted the wizards left the unstable land mass. There was nothing more they could do. The magics of the island's creation raged chaotically about it, making further magic impossible. Over a century later wizards returned to the land with workers sworn to secrecy. By then the persecutions were beginning. The magics around the island were still chaotic but much less so. These wizards built a village and a magical projector powered by the emblems of their orders. This projector, when adequately powered, will envelop the island in a shield impenetrable by any creature not of this plane of existence. These wizards also seeded the land with plants and animals before they left.

"Now it is time for the wizards to claim Haven and bring those who will come with us to its safety. By now the random magic of the island's creation will have dissipated. Thus the shield can be set without danger of damaging the power emblems."

"This is your solution? That we surrender our world to those beasts and escape to this island of yours?" Darien pounded his fist against the table.

"Of course not! That was never the intention of Haven. It is to be a refuge, a place to grow food, make weapons. A place for the non-combatants. A safe land from which we can fight, and most importantly, a place to train wizards. Our greatest danger is that the gates to this world are still open. The living wizards are too few to hold them shut, so when a beast of the Storm is killed, five more can enter to take its place. If we can close the gates, we can shift the odds in our favour."

"Hmm. A stronghold makes good military sense," mused Darien. "What can I do to aid you?"

"I will need ships and crews willing to sail into uncharted waters."

"They're yours and anything else I can aid you with."

"Thank you. If you are willing, I will leave in the morning."

"Ackdominel, the troops are exhausted. Maybe you should move the date back, so they have a chance to rest," suggested Melanie.

Ackdominel smiled at her before replying, "I said nothing about you or your army coming with me. I will be travelling with only a small group of our people. The army is to stay here under your command."

"Now wait just a moment. You'll need protection as you travel, let alone in Haven," objected Melanie.

"No, I will not. I never really did. A small armed force should be enough to keep any brigands away, and Haven is my land. Nothing will harm me there, unless we fall short of the power emblems necessary to operate the shield."

Melanie glared at him and snapped, "My troops are tired and have no real shelter. Where will we live? Have you considered that?"

Ackdominel was preparing to reply when Darien intervened. "I have more than enough room for your warriors. My troops have been horribly depleted since we engaged the Storm. I'm sure the other kings would gladly surrender a keep or two to take up any excess. As far as supplies go, take whatever you need."

Melanie sat sullenly as Ackdominel said, "Good. Since that is settled, I will leave tomorrow. Melanie, pick me out some travelling companions. Be sure that Trom is among them. One-armed or no, the troops will follow him second only to you."

"Yes, Your Majesty, King of Bani, High Wizard of the Secret Path," growled Melanie. She curtsied and strode from the room.

"I am too indulgent with her. But I couldn't ask for a better general for the kind of fighting we just went through. I wonder how she will handle dealing with allies?"

"If she can hold a section of the line, personality won't matter. Especially if she wears something frilly to strategy conferences, no one will care what she says," remarked Darien.

"That, my friend, would be a mistake. Never underestimate her. She is a remarkable person first, a beautiful woman second."

"Yes, well, it is easy to overlook that. Although, she does remind me of my late wife, so I should expect intelligence and fire. On to other matters. What are these power emblems you spoke of?"

"I should have explained that earlier. The energy projector is designed to protect the island, but to do so, it requires the power emblems of at least thirteen orders. Each has its nature determined by the order's beliefs. Mine are crystals representing what can, inaccurately, be called good and evil. Some groups have plants representing birth and decay. Others vials of water representing storm and calm. All the symbols represent polarities along some continuum. When Haven was prepared, there were forty orders involved. The danger we face is that too few of the mages will force their way through to Haven to fully activate the shield, leaving us open to attack."

"Is there anything we can do to help?" asked Darien.

"Once I am in Haven I can visit the other orders' strongholds and strengthen their shields. Unfortunately, power emblems cannot be transported magically. As for you, pray for us."

"You know I will."

"Good! If you will excuse me, I will go to my meditations. Tomorrow will be a tiring day."

"As you will, good Mage."

Ackdominel followed a guard to his sleeping chamber and was not surprised to find Melanie waiting at its door.

"My decision is made," he said.

"I know. I've picked forty able-bodied warriors to accompany you."

"Forty! I am not going to war."

"Few enough! And on this. My decision is made!"

"Very well, forty it is. I'm glad you came. I have a gift for you." Ackdominel slipped the healing ring from his finger and held it out to her.

"I… I can't! I… I don't know how to use it." stammered Melanie.

"You have watched me often enough. The ring will do the work. All you do is supply the energy. For me the ring simply makes healing easier, for you, it will grant the ability."

Melanie took the ring and slipped it on her finger. Immediately she felt as if something had sucked the vitality from her.

"Good. It should be fully charged by morning then you can heal King Darien. I am going to prepare myself for tomorrow's journey. I suggest you get some sleep. You look exhausted."

Melanie nodded and shuffled towards her quarters.

Ackdominel yawned, stretched, and entered his bedchamber.

The next morning he and his retinue of warriors gathered outside the gates of the keep where Darien held court. They were once more an impressive company with their armour gleaming. Ackdominel wore the white robes and cloak that marked him as the High Wizard of the Secret Path and was mounted on a light-grey gelding from Darien's stables.

Looking across the courtyard, he saw Darien striding towards him, completely healed.

"Take this scroll with you and show it to my harbour master. He will see to your needs. He's in the city of Qual," explained Darien.

Ackdominel began to laugh. "I am a fool. Here I was ready to set out, no idea of where I am going or who to talk to when I get there. I guess I am too used to running in a straight line. Thank you."

"Anytime. Let me save you once more. Wait and say farewell to Melanie. She was wearied after healing me. She should be down in a second."

Ackdominel swung down from his horse to wait. He and Darien chatted for a time before Melanie appeared in the castle's gate. She was clad in armour but wore no helm, allowing her hair to fall down her back in two braids. She ran from the gate, crashing into Ackdominel's arms with a force that almost toppled him.

"You weren't going to leave without saying goodbye?" she demanded.

"Would I do that?" asked Ackdominel.

"Are you sure you don't want me along?"

"You know you must stay."

"Yes. It's really what I want anyway. To fight the creatures of the Storm, to avenge my family, and you know the rest."

"Yes." Ackdominel hugged her. "Survive. Life is too sweet to leave it early."

"I will obey my King's orders." Melanie broke the embrace with tears in her eyes.

Ackdominel smiled at her, and mounting his horse, signalled for the march to begin.

Chapter 28
To the Sea

The first day of Ackdominel's journey passed with little event. He seldom spoke, preferring to stay in a light trance as he rode, rebuilding his depleted reserves.

Despite his somnolent condition, he did notice the landscape change. Where the monster-held territories were a wasteland of scrub bush, stunted trees and brambles, he now rode through a land of swaying crops, orchards and farm holds.

That night they camped in an apple orchard. So the next five days passed until midmorning of the sixth day they came to the port city of Qual.

The city gates were impressive affairs of heavy beams, bound with iron, set in a stone wall twice the height of a man, and they were shut.

"Halt. Who goes there?" demanded a gangly lad who stood on the rampart to the left of the gate.

"I am King Dominel of Bani. I come on urgent business with the Harbour Master of the Western Isle," announced Ackdominel.

"Bani was overrun years ago, you can't be its king!" challenged the youth, shifting uncomfortably in the oversized chainmail he wore.

"Nevertheless, I am who I claim to be. Open the gate and allow us to pass."

"I have to ask the sheriff's permission. I'm not supposed to let any soldiers in." The boy disappeared from view.

About thirty minutes later he returned with a man dressed in a garish combination of colours. The man was so fat his face was lost to pudginess, and his skin had an unhealthy jaundice tint. He opened a mouth far too small for his face and spoke in a mincing voice.

"Go away! We do not allow soldiers in our city. You are nothing but hoodlums and thugs."

"I have business with the Harbour Master of the Western Isle. Good King Darien tells me he is here," stated Ackdominel.

"He's here, and I've never met a ruder man. You can't come in. Now go away!" snapped the sheriff.

"Listen to me, you overgrown barrel of lard. Let us in, or I swear. I'll use my remaining arm to choke the life out of you," bellowed Trom, who was standing by Ackdominel.

"My my, aren't we violent! You see. Soldiers are nothing but a bunch of ruffians. I won't let you in," returned the sheriff from his protected perch atop the wall.

I could will dominate this bucket of lard, but I would rather save my strength for something worthwhile, thought Ackdominel. He then called "Archers HO."

Too fast for the eye to follow, ten battle hardened archers set arrow to string and drew, taking aim on the sheriff.

"Now, sir. Order the gate opened," commanded Ackdominel.

"This is dreadful! Just dreadful! You're nothing but ruffians," remarked the sweating mass of blubber upon the wall.

"Archers," began Ackdominel.

"NO! Wait. Go, boy, open the gate. Let them in. This is dreadful, just dreadful! Never in all my years. You're a horrid, horrid man," blubbered the sheriff.

The great doors of the city slowly swung open. Ackdominel and Trom entered, then the swordsmen. Finally, the archers released the tension on their bows and followed.

"I'll send word to the King! I will! You're an awful, awful man," threatened the sheriff, as he clambered down the stair from the battlement and waddled away.

"Your Majesty," said the young guard.

Ackdominel turned to look at him. The boy was grinning from ear to ear.

"Yes, lad?" asked Ackdominel.

"May I join your troop? I'm almost fourteen, and I haven't sworn allegiance. I'm good with a short bow, my da' taught me before, well before."

"What of your mother?"

The boy looked sullen as he replied. "The spotted fever, Your Majesty. Half a year ago. Please, I'm the sheriff's ward, and if I have to obey that coward another day, I don't know what I'll do."

"Your armour, is it yours or the city's?"

"It was my da's, I fixed the broken links myself," stated the boy, pride entering his voice.

"Gather your things, boy, I accept your service. You will be under my training master, Trom." Ackdominel indicated the one-armed warrior.

"Thank you, Your Majesty. I won't disappoint you. I'll only be a second. I don't have much, sold most for food. Thank you!" bubbled the lad. Bowing he ran into a sentry hut by the gate, emerging seconds later with a small pack on his shoulders.

"Good lad. Now guide us to the harbour," ordered Ackdominel.

"Yes, Your Majesty," replied the boy, leading the way down the wide, main road of the city.

As the troop moved forward, Trom fell in beside Ackdominel.

"How did a worm like that become sheriff?" asked Trom.

"Probably everyone better went to the front. I am more concerned by the crowding in this city than its administration."

"The place is a sty."

"It is flooded with refugees. Look at the number of shacks built on the street. Those two story stone houses used to be at the curb."

"Look out." Trom pulled Ackdominel to a halt in time to avoid the contents of a chamber pot that were thrown from an upper story window.

"Cities. Filthy places. Look at this street. It's nothing but litter and muck. A sure invitation to disease," grumbled Ackdominel.

"Stench is none too pleasant either." Trom nodded in agreement. His eyes focussed on some dirty-faced children standing in a doorway. As he watched their rail-thin mother appeared and pulled them back into their house.

It took half an hour for the troop to reach the harbour, where they were directed by a one-legged shipping clerk to Darien's harbour master.

The harbour master was a burly man of middle years, with a bushy, black beard and a barrel-like body. As Ackdominel approached, he could see harbour master was busy supervising the loading of several ships.

"Excuse me, are you King Darien's harbour master?" began Ackdominel.

"What? Oh yes. Watch that crate, you louts, and be sure and stow it low," bellowed the harbour master as a pair of seamen nearly dropped a large, wooden crate on the dock.

"I have orders from your king to show you."

"You do," began the man, who started screaming and waving at a pair of men who were loading a trunk onto a ship. "No! No, you barnacle brained idiots. That's to go on the Sea Queen. This is the Wave Mistress."

The harbour master turned back to Ackdominel. "Have to watch the thick-skulled sea urchins every second. Now you were saying something about orders from the king."

Seizing his opportunity, Ackdominel pushed the scroll of orders into the Harbour Master's hands. The Harbour Master paused to inspect the seal on the scroll then bellowed at a ship where a large crate was being tied amidships. "Not like that, you fools! Cross hitch the accursed thing, or it'll fall off the first bit of rough sea they hit."

Still muttering he opened the scroll and read. His face changed from consternation to scepticism to joy in a matter of moments.

"You're a wizard. I'll be the son of a sea witch!" Grabbing Ackdominel's hand, he shook it vigorously. "I thought all of your kind had been killed. Well, it's a pleasure to be wrong. By the way, my name is Annon, but let's not talk here. I've a shack over on the next pier and a drop of something to warm the blood. Come along. Then we can see about getting you your ships."

Soon Ackdominel, Trom and Annon were sitting about a table. Annon produced a large bottle and poured a dollop of its contents into three wooden tankards.

"Here's to hope," toasted Annon.

Ackdominel sipped at the liquid then started to cough and sputter as it made a flaming path from mouth to stomach.

The other two men laughed as Ackdominel gasped trying to regain his composure.

"What is that stuff, demon blood?" he exclaimed when he was able.

"It's a mixture of fermented grains thrice distilled. Like it?" commented Annon.

Ackdominel gasped more air over his burning throat, smiled and moved on to business.

"I need ships to transport myself and the first inhabitants to Haven. Can you spare them?"

"Ships won't be a problem. There have been enough lads who sailed over who won't be returning, we've plenty to spare. It's equipment that worries me. Food, tools, tents, these are in short supply."

"What can we do?" Ackdominel braced himself and took another sip of the liquor.

"Don't worry. I'll get you what you need, at least to make a start."

"How long will you need?" asked Trom.

"A week. Maybe a day or two more for a small group. Maybe one hundred people to get things started."

"If a week it is, a week it is, but please hurry. The sooner Haven is colonised the better," said Ackdominel.

It was nearly two weeks before Ackdominel departed with the first group of five ships bound for Haven. As Annon had predicted finding people willing to risk an ocean crossing to an unknown land had been the easy part. People leapt at the chance to escape the overcrowding of the city. Equipment had proven difficult and cost King Darien's treasury dearly.

When the journey started nature seemed to favour them, granting a fine day and a following wind blowing to the southeast. Ackdominel used this peaceful time to finishing recouping his energies. Each day he could be seen seated upon the forecastle, lost in meditation. During the second week of the journey, he started to sense something clawing at the edge of his awareness. At first, he put it down to his inactivity, but then the night watch on one of the ships vanished.

Arranging with the captain to be left alone on deck Ackdominel prepared for a ceremony. The stars shone brightly as he stood on the forecastle, a charcoal brazier smouldering in front of him. Relaxing his body, he scanned his surroundings with his mind. He felt a dark force become aware of his probing. It surrounded the ships like a cloud of putrescence. Ackdominel tried to push it away, but it resisted him.

He became so intent on studying the cloud he didn't notice the sound of wet feet on the ship's deck, or the stench of decay until it was almost too late. He leapt away at the last moment as a creature resembling a hideous old woman with gills on her neck clutched at him.

"Come to me, young wizard," whispered the apparition, in a voice surprisingly sweet and soft. The image before Ackdominel wavered and shifted until the hag was gone, replaced by a beautiful woman no more than thirty. Her luxuriant, red hair fell to her waist, embracing a generous bosom. Long, slender legs descended from her perfect hips and all her charms were clearly displayed by the flimsy gauze she wore. Ackdominel blinked. She was perfect! Even the delicate gills upon her neck served to enhance her beauty. He swallowed hard against a lump in his throat.

"Come to me," she repeated, in a tone that turned Ackdominel's blood to fire.

He felt his chest heave, and his knees shake. He desperately wanted to hold this young beauty. His body moved forward of its own accord. Wisdom told him this was an illusion. Knowledge told him he faced a beast that would drain his life force to prolong its own existence. Neither could counter the spell. He continued to move towards the beautiful apparition then paused, remembering. *Woodreana, I swore fidelity to her. My word. My honour.*

Ackdominel vacillated. The sea siren beckoned, but he had given his oath, and only the one he had sworn it to could release him from it.

"No," he whispered to himself.

"Come," coaxed the siren.

"No!" stated Ackdominel, with steel in his voice. The beauteous illusion faded, revealing the hideous sea hag.

"I am promised to another. You have no power over that. I command you back to your icy realm and trouble me and mine no more."

The beast before him released a screech that split the night.

"You may not come to my bed, but you'll go to your grave all the same. Come, my lovers, come and take my foe to his death," hissed the beast.

The sea about the ship seemed to boil as decaying corpses rose from the waters, clutched at the ship's sides and clambered aboard.

"You cannot escape. My loves will drag you down to the sea's floor, where you shall die. There is nowhere to run on a ship."

"Run? I can assure you, demon's daughter, I have no intention of running." Ackdominel drew his sword and quickly traced a circle about himself, muttering as he did so. Standing within the circle, he lifted his blade over his head and screaming brought it down with a slashing motion.

"Your spell is weak, wizard. It does nothing," chuckled the siren.

"Does it?" remarked Ackdominel, a smile on his face, as he watched the corpses collapse upon the deck.

"No," hissed the siren.

"Yes! I have broken your control over them."

"I do not need them to destroy one weak human." The siren lunged then slammed to a stop at the circle's edge.

Stepping back the siren lunged again, but as she did so, Ackdominel caught her with a spell of levitation and lifted her into the air. Sweat broke out on his brow as he struggled to hold his spell against the will of his adversary. Slowly he forced her closer to his smouldering brazier until she hung upside down over its heat.

The siren shrieked and threatened then pleaded and cajoled, but Ackdominel held fast. Steam gushed from her nostrils, and her struggles grew feeble.

The sun crested the horizon. The siren screamed and fell silent. In seconds all that remained of her was a shrivelled piece of seaweed. Ackdominel dropped the seaweed onto the dying coals of his brazier.

Chapter 29
Land Ho

It was seven days after Ackdominel's battle with the sea hag that the ship's lookout cried, "Land ho."

"What's it like?" Trom pushed his way past the sailors to Ackdominel's side at the ship's railing.

"Like. It is like, well... Except for the wizards' stronghold and the road we made to it, the land is untouched. Most of it is forested, pine, some hardwoods in the south. As for size, the coastline's irregular, but I would guess it would take five days to ride its width and fifteen to travel its length."

Trom hummed in reply.

"Set a course to the north, follow the coast," called Ackdominel.

"Move it, you louts," ordered the captain.

As if the captain's voice had broken a spell, the crew returned to their work. Slowly the ships shifted direction until they were running across the wind.

"I never would have believed it. I've sailed the sea all me life, and never did I guess there was land out here," remarked the captain, joining Ackdominel and Trom on the forecastle. The captain was a heavyset man, with hard chiselled features and skin beaten by sun and sea to the texture of leather.

"It was raised in a rarely travelled part of the sea. There was no choice in that."

"Well, Your Majesty, I owe you an apology. I never believed you until I saw it with my own eyes. What now, scout the coast and find a harbour?"

"There should be a bay not too far north. When the Wizards were last here, it was deep and had a good river access to the interior. Once there, we can offload the colonists and their gear. Then I want this ship to proceed up river. I must go to the Wizards' stronghold, and it's the quickest way."

They reached the bay about two hours before sunset. That night they set anchor and slept on the ships. Early the next morn every skiff was shuttling colonists and tools ashore. By noon Ackdominel's ship was offloaded.

"Captain, are we ready to move upriver?" asked Ackdominel.

"Yes and no, Your Majesty. Rivers are dangerous. We could bottom out, get stuck, or worse, strike a rock and spring our timbers."

"I am sure the river is deep enough. The wizards who supervised the building of the stronghold sailed their ships up it."

"Nonetheless. I feel we must be cautious. We can sail up the flow, but we'll do it the slow, safe way. If you're in a rush, you'd better walk, or take a skiff."

Ackdominel pondered his options before replying. "I see your point. Sail the ship your way. We'll have to prove it's safe or every other wizard who arrives will face the same difficulties."

The ship began its slow progress. Eagle-eyed sailors lay on the foremast, gauging the water's safety. Ahead of the ship, a skiff sounded the depth. Mid-morning of the third day a road made from slabs of rock appeared on the southern bank.

"This is as far as I can go by ship. Soon the river grows shallower," explained Ackdominel, looking over the midship's railing at the rugged terrain that surrounded them.

"That is something I can agree with. That's a blooming mountain ahead of us," remarked the captain

"Yes. We're at the foothills of Haven's central range. Up that road lies the wizards' stronghold."

"I'll prepare a landing party to escort you."

"No thank you. I will go alone. You get back down river. If the colony is ready to be left without the ships, go back to port and collect another group of colonists."

"Are you sure, Your Majesty?"

"Yes. I am not anticipating problems, but there is one thing that concerns me. If it comes to pass, I do not want any bystanders I must protect."

"Aye, Your Majesty," said the captain, with a shudder at the thought of something that could worry a mage.

Ackdominel picked up a pack he had prepared and called for the skiff to take him ashore.

The captain stood at the railing watching until Ackdominel disappeared from view down the road.

"I started this alone. It is only right that I finish it alone. Even if…" murmured Ackdominel, stopping his thought before he voiced it.

The road climbed at an ever steepening angle, and he spent that night with only a meagre fire for comfort. Early the next day he'd followed the road up to where the air started to grow thin and by late afternoon his lungs burned as he continued along the climbing path. Topping a rise, he saw his destination. Stretched out below him was a valley. The road descended into the valley by making two loops around its perimeter ending in a collection of stone houses. Ackdominel quickened his pace, but it was still late evening before he reached the village. Following its lone, dusty street, he came to a house with the symbol of his order carved into the stone by its weathered door.

Lifting the rusted latch, he opened the door on protesting hinges and stepped through. The air was thick and musty. Fumbling beside the doorway, he found a lantern with wax seals over both fill and wick holes. Breaking the seals he focussed his will and the wick burst into flame, shedding a golden light about the room. Simple, durable furnishings of ironwork or hardwood could be seen under a blanket of dust. Holding his breath, he threw open the shuttered windows.

Once the air was clear, he moved across the room to a set of shelves. These were filled with hides and bladders, all sticky with long dried oils. Using his eating dagger he opened one of these, revealing blankets and a pillow. Spreading them upon the floor, he settled to sleep.

"First thing, after setting my emblems, I string the rope bed," he muttered, as he drifted off.

When he awoke sunlight blazed through the windows.

Standing he stretched and breathed in the cool mountain air.

"Time to get moving." He walked across the room and opened the door opposite the entrance. This revealed a kitchen identical to the ones he had had in the lodges.

"They always did like this design."

After a simple breakfast, he opened the door to the right of the entrance. Within was a circle scribed upon a marble floor. A brazier marked each cardinal point, while a triangle was cut into the floor to the circle's east. Ackdominel moved to the circle's centre, knelt and removed the tiny throne from his pouch. Placing it on the floor, he pushed with his will. The throne began to grow, stopping when it had reached its previous size.

Leaving the ceremony room, he stepped through the final door into a comfortably appointed bedchamber. An iron rope-bed frame stood in the room's centre, but it lacked ropes. Ackdominel looked at it longingly, pulled the ropes from his pack and dropped them on the floor.

Leaving the house, he followed the main street to its end at a sheer cliff face. Grasping a protruding stone he pulled it and stepped away. There was the sound of something turning. Rocks shook free of the cliff. A section of the cliff face burst outwards as a large, round boulder smashed through a stone facade concealing a cave. The rock followed along the road until it crashed into the lake at the far side of the Wizards' village.

"Show offs," commented Ackdominel to the air, where he felt a presence. He started into the passage, which sloped steeply upwards and ended in a spiral staircase. Climbing the stair, he emerged upon a flattened mountaintop. Wind whipped around him and snow crunched under his boots. He could see miles in all directions. Turning he faced a huge circle of standing stones. Through the gaps between the stones, he could see another smaller, stone circle.

Removing his pack, he withdrew two wrapped bundles and moved past the stone circles. Ackdominel stopped when he came to a table made from milky quartz that stood in the centre of the inner circle. Slots had been cut into the table's perimeter, and light shone from a pool of water in its centre.

Thunder boomed, and clouds flowed in, blotting out the sun.

"You have decided to show yourself then?" Ackdominel remarked into the air. A chill wind whipped his cloak back and made it flap like the wings of a crippled bird.

"Did you doubt I would stop you?" replied a voice so deep it shook the mountain.

Ackdominel looked skyward. Above him was the embodiment of nightmare. Black tentacles writhed from the back of an ogre-like body, with skin the sickly yellow of a troll's. A large, furry head surmounted the serpentine neck, with a mouth of sharks' teeth and beady, red eyes. Fear coiled in Ackdominel's belly, but he fought it down.

"I doubted you dared to face me. Your way has always been to use deluded fools to do your fighting. What should I call you? Ragla of the ogres, Sukut of the trolls, or maybe the Covetous God?"

"My names and forms are legion, and none know my true ones. Your paltry labels wield no power over me. Leap from this mountain and I will let your soul go free, resist me and I will enslave you in the pits of Veluk forever."

Ackdominel took a step towards the precipice before catching himself and forcing control over his body. Unwrapping one of the bundles he pulled forth the crystal of light and placed it in a slot on the altar.

"Now you will die," roared the Covetous God and lightning leapt from the sky.

"Gnomes of the earth," snapped Ackdominel, pointing to a section of ground. The lightning arced away to shatter and blacken the rock.

"By the sun in morning and the moon at night, I command thee, demon, take thee flight. Leave this world in its sorry plight. Be gone, thee foul one, to the realms of night," commanded Ackdominel, throwing his hand into the air. Light leapt from his fingers striking the hovering figure, which wavered then began to laugh.

"Puny wizard. My minions hold more of this world then your kind. You cannot banish me from a place that is my own."

Ackdominel hid his smile and slowly moved around the table. He placed the dark crystal in a slot opposite the light one. Before he could do, more his mind exploded. Darkness flooded all his senses and pain ripped through him. Gritting his teeth, he pulled his personal shields tight around him. The blackness seemed to seep through his pores. In the darkness, he saw a grey light. It beckoned, and he moved towards it. Images beauteous and horrific flitted in his mind. The two crystals called to their master. Drawing strength from the crystals, he pushed out against the enveloping evil. Slowly his vision cleared and he stopped his foot just before he stepped from the cliff. Retching he fell to his knees.

"All the better, wizard. Now you will be fully aware of your defeat. I will add yet another world to my rule," gloated the Covetous God.

The clouds thickened above the god. Ackdominel could feel blood pouring from his nose. His head throbbed and his vision blurred. Struggling to his feet, he pushed the remaining taint of his foe's energies from him and waited. Lightning flew from the sky and Ackdominel expected death, but at the last second, the Covetous God roared.

"What is this?"

"Run, little brother. We cannot resist the dark one's will long, but we too are of this world. We would have clean skies in which to sport," whispered the air elementals that crowded the sky.

Ackdominel sprinted for the inner circle, stopping before the altar. He lifted his hands to the sky and called, "By the power of the elements four, by the secrets behind the secrets, by the wisdom of the twin Orders of the Secret Paths, I call thee forth, oh powers of light and dark. To this land a shield be. I claim this island for the gods and spirits native to this world, now and forever!"

There was a moment of silence. Ackdominel's remaining energies joined with the projector. Focussing his will, he forced the energy to envelop Haven. In seconds it was done. The shield was only enough by itself to halt the weakest of monsters, but it was there.

Releasing his hold on the shield Ackdominel turned to the Covetous God.

"Do you think this matters, mortal? You are but an insect and your shield a spider's web to me."

Ackdominel fell to his knees too weary to fight.

"It matters, enemy of life," replied a soft, female voice, that was a balm to Ackdominel's pain.

"You weakling gods. As my minions conquer your world, so shall I defeat you," snarled the Covetous God.

Ackdominel looked up and saw a group of beings standing around him. Some wore human guise, some looked like animals, and some were a mixture of both. All of them were beautiful to his eyes, and he drew strength from them.

"This island is not yours, demon. It has been claimed as a place for the spirits and gods native to this world. You have no right to be here unless one of mortal kind stands upon this ground and invites you in. You are an intruder and may not touch this place with your power," spoke a handsome male figure dressed as a warrior.

Ackdominel smiled and wiped the blood from his face. Staggering to his feet, he raised his arms in a gesture of banishing and spoke.

"By the sun in morning and the moon at night, I command thee, demon, take thee flight. Leave this island in its sorry plight. Be gone, thee foul one, to the realms of night."

Screaming in frustration, the beast vanished, and the sky slowly grew clear. Ackdominel felt a gentle warmth envelop him then with a whisper of wind the other figures dissolved from view.

He crawled to the stair's shelter before sinking to the ground. How long he sat there, he could never say, but it was full night when he returned to his house and fell asleep on the floor.

The sun slanting through the open windows woke him. After a hasty breakfast, he entered the ceremony room. Energies flowed about him, and he knew the throne of the Secret Path had established itself. Taking his seat, he closed his eyes and in seconds was in the Wizards' council room.

"Only nineteen doors left. At least four of them have been opened. Four more mages is a good thing." Taking his seat at the table, he called, "Come, my brothers, come my sisters."

After a time Woodreana stepped into the room.

"Where have you been?" she demanded, taking her seat beside him.

"I have reached Haven, and my emblems are in place. As well, I faced our true foe. He remains, but Haven is now beyond his direct reach." Ackdominel took Woodreana's hands in his and kissed her.

Woodreana pulled her hands free then clutched Ackdominel tight against her. "Gods of the wood! You stood against Driliss, goddess of the Lamia, and survived! I have been worried about you. Now I see should have been terrified for you."

Another door opened, revealing a woman in her mid-twenties, wearing a black, floor-length robe, girthed by a golden belt. The outfit was calculated to enhance her supple figure.

Woodreana and Ackdominel broke their embrace but sat holding hands.

"Who summoned me?" demanded the newcomer, stroking her long, black hair.

"I called to ask if you required aid," replied Ackdominel.

"My soldiers and I can reach Haven quite well thank you," she replied. Her attractive, angular features softened and a fire kindled in her green eyes as they examined Ackdominel.

"What of your civilians?" asked Woodreana.

"What of them?" she replied as she moved with catlike grace to her seat. "Woodreana, you are remiss. Who is our handsome comrade?"

Woodreana bared her teeth in a predatory smile and squeezed Ackdominel's hand. "He is my mate of long standing! How many lives has it been, beloved? Five? Six?, Ackdominel, High Wizard of the Secret Path. A white order. Ackdominel, Serinau, of the Dark Night."

"Greetings," said Serinau, her voice dripping come hither.

"Greetings." Ackdominel turned towards Woodreana and asked. "How stand the other strongholds?"

"Searun and I strengthened several shields before he left for Haven a week ago, but they are failing fast. Worse still, some of our comrades are only in their first lodge."

"Demon spit! We must keep our fellows alive and obtain their emblems at all costs. Serinau, have you time to spare now?"

The dark temptress smiled seductively. "What do you have in mind?"

Ackdominel looked at the ceiling for a long moment. "The three of us should be able to strengthen shields considerably, with the aid of the apprentice of the area. Mayhap we can delay their breakdown long enough for our brethren to complete their training."

Serinau shrugged and made a dismissive gesture with her hand. "Why should I? I like being exclusive! The more wizards there are, the fewer others there will be to serve each of us."

"Suppose we do not obtain enough emblems to fully energise Haven's shield. Would you like to be an ogre's exclusive plaything?" demanded Ackdominel.

The dark sorceress scowled. "I take your point!"

The mystics rose and passed through a door to one of the remaining shielded zones. That evening Ackdominel returned to his cottage exhausted, and with a profound sense of relief, strung his rope bed.

Chapter 30
Epilogue

Ackdominel sat in his favourite chair, a large affair with heavily stuffed cushions and carved, wooden, hand rests. It had been five years since he reached Haven. In that time towns had sprung up and much of what had been forest was now cultivated land. He glanced about the main room of his house. It was in its normal jumble.

I have to do something about this mess. Between strengthening shields and healing the wounded it is a wonder I ever clean the place. Oh, for an apprentice to help with the routine tasks. Sometimes I wonder why I let Elin get away from me, but they needed a healer at the front more than I needed her here. Curse it all. I'll get started as soon as I finish the letter, thought Ackdominel.

He picked up a scroll that lay on the table by his chair and broke its seal, revealing Melanie's spidery script.

\#

Dearest Ackdominel,

First name basis with a wizard-king. My father would have approved. I was glad to hear about your marriage. I'm sorry I couldn't attend. One day I would like to meet Woodreana. It was a novel idea to use the matching elfin bracers as a wedding gift.

Ackdominel paused; he could feel eyes watching him.

Not again. If the brat triggers it, it is his own fault for spying on me, he thought.

There was a yelp from the window as Ackdominel's anti-intruder spell took hold, lifting a grubby-faced child to the ceiling and leaving him dangling upside down.

"Do be quiet. I will be with you in a moment. Honestly, ever since Woodreana brought you villagers, we wizards have not had a moment's privacy! Always snooping, it's disgusting!" lectured Ackdominel.

"Please, sir, let me down," pleaded the young boy in the tongue of the Western Isle.

"In a while, I am reading at the moment." Ackdominel smiled at how quickly he'd managed to modernise his use of that language. *Now, where was I? Oh yes.*

Elfin bracers as a wedding gift.

Our battle goes well, although we've lost too many good men! We hold the eastern coast and have no intention of giving it up.

Interestingly enough, a few days back we had a victory. We were in the middle of a battle when the wizard Rumin appeared with his refugees. We caught the monsters in a pincer action and massacred them. That reminds me, congratulate Trom. The troops he's trained are surviving almost as well as the old-timers.

I have some surprising news. A few days ago a group of refugees arrived from our mountains. They told me that the shield had shrunk several times since we left and that the elves and dwarves were engaged in open combat against the monsters. Apparently, they're holding their own. Talion has offered those humans who remain in the mountains the protection of his sceptre.

Solin and Erum both say hello. They seem to be enjoying their life in the army, although Erum misses his father. He went to Haven last year.

Now for the real reason I'm writing. Believe it or not, I'm getting married. One of Darien's sons. I hope you can make it to the ceremony, but I know how heavily the war rests on your shoulders. Brallik, my fiancé, is wonderful and I'm as happy as the war allows.

That's all I have to report, so until next time, Gods willing, farewell.

Yours with warmest affections.

Melanie of the bloody field.

Ackdominel lowered the letter and smiled before his reverie was broken by a small voice.

"Please, sir, all the blood's rushing to my head. Could you please let me down?"

"Oh yes. Of course." Ackdominel turned to inspect the child.

He was no more than eight years of age, dressed in ragged leggings and coat. There was a lean, wary look about him and he seemed strangely familiar.

"Now young man, what were you doing peeping in my window?" demanded Ackdominel. Taking the boy under the arms, he set him feet first on the floor.

"Nothing! Well, I mean, I just wanted to get a look at the wizard of the Secret Path. After hearing the stories, I had to see you with my own eyes."

"Now you have seen me. What do you think?"

"Well, if it won't be displeasing you, your wizardship. You don't seem that different from any other man. Please don't turn me into a frog or anything for saying it."

Ackdominel smiled and repressed a chuckle. "Of course not. The robe's white. Now if Serinau had caught you, things might be different." At this, he let the chuckle out. "You are not from around here, are you?"

"No, sir. I'm from the Western Isle."

"Where are your parents?"

"My father died in the army years ago. Last year my mother died of a fever. I've been alone ever since. I hid on one of the ships. Please don't send me back. There's nothing for me back home."

Ackdominel nodded. "What is your name?"

"Lor."

"Lor," repeated Ackdominel, realisation dawning. "Well, Franlor, how would you like to learn the ways of wizardry?"

"Really?" breathed the boy.

A broad smile filled Ackdominel's face. "Yes. Can you read and write?"

"A little. My mother taught me."

"Good. Do you wish to be my student?"

"Yes," answered the child, his face alive with hope.

"Good! I want you to start your duties. Have you eaten today?"

"Yes, your wizardship. I begged half a loaf before I came to look at you."

"Good. You can begin by tidying up this place. When you are finished, clean yourself up and start reading this book," ordered Ackdominel. Taking a leather-bound volume from a shelf by the door, he passed it to the boy.

"I will be back later to answer your questions. Oh and, Franlor, make sure the place is clean."

"Of course, sir, but my name isn't Franlor."

"Of course it is. You simply do not remember it yet, but you will, old friend, you will."

THE END